NATURAL DISASTER

Spirit Seeker Book 5

Janna Ruth

SPIRIT SEEKER BOOK 5

NATURAL DISASTER

JANNA RUTH

First published in New Zealand in 2022

2nd edition 2025

www.janna-ruth.com

ISBN: 978-0-473-60403-5 (Paperback)

ISBN: 978-0-473-60404-2 (Ebook)

For all Story Seekers,

young and old.

1

When the five of us arrive back in Berlin, it's quite warm. Much warmer than I expected. I have to remind myself that it's mid-June and a heatwave is nothing out of the ordinary. Problem is, it's still May in my head. It was May when I was forced to leave Berlin, and spending an unknown amount of time in a dark little cell and a strange country with a completely different climate messed me up majorly.

Our trip to Berlin was soothingly uneventful. We spent most of the time in a small compartment on the train, where I listened to Bijan and Inga making plans. I would've much rather been alone with Wulf, but at least he never left my side, always available to give my hand a quick squeeze. Meanwhile, Henny was deeply lost in their own thoughts for most of the time, only occasionally asking a question or two.

Now, we've made our way back to the citadel. In front of us, the dark stone rises above the treetops, and the bridge over the moat is already in sight. There's the roadside kerb where the grey car stood. Where I was forced into the vehicle at gunpoint.

What am I even doing here?

I'm on the run. This will be the first place the SSA will look for me. They broke in once. Who says they can't do it again? *Won't* do it again?

The fingers around my hand tighten as if they're aware I'm this short of bolting. I glance at Wulf and find him studying me with concern.

One look in my eyes, and he turns to tell the others to go ahead. "We'll be in soon."

Together, we watch Bijan, Inga, and Henny cross the bridge and enter the citadel. After they've vanished from sight, Wulf turns to me. He lets go of my hand and puts both of his on my arms, once again peering deep into my eyes, as if I carry all my thoughts on my sleeve. "You okay?"

No. No, I'm not.

And that sucks! I was doing well here. Really well for someone with my background. How dare they take that away from me?

I only notice the tears when Wulf wipes them away with his thumbs. Then, he pulls me into a firm hug.

I could get used to these. The way he holds me as if he'll never let go gives me a sense of safety. I wish I could stay in his arms forever, because there's no other place like it. Certainly not the citadel.

"What if they come after me?" I whisper at long last.

It takes Wulf some time to answer. *They* are his family. *My family*, I amend, and almost tear up. How messed up is this?

"I wish I could tell you that you're safe here," he admits. "We did improve our security system. Miriam's sent me a couple of further ideas, and of course, they'll take you over my dead body."

Too bad the SSA doesn't have any qualms about killing their most promising seekers. Not even Wulf.

In a ragged voice, he continues, "I can't promise that you'll be a hundred per cent safe, but you have everyone in that citadel—person or spirit—looking out for you. We're not letting them steal you from us ever again."

In response, a warm breeze wraps itself around my shoulders. "I'll do better," Aeola whispers.

I cock my head into her silky body and sigh. "You did well. It's nobody's fault." And that's the scary part about it.

"Ready to go in?" Wulf takes my hand again, breaking our embrace.

"Well, I'm not any safer out here. Let's do it."

We don't even make it across the bridge. There's a loud cry, and then Camille comes storming out of the citadel. She throws herself around my neck, forcing me to let go of Wulf as I stumble backwards. "You're here!"

If I thought Wulf's hugs were firm, Camille teaches me better. Bone-crushing comes to my mind, and I'm loving every second of it.

At last, she lets go of me, but only to run her hands over my face, looking for injuries. Fortunately, those are all on the inside. "Wulf wouldn't let me come with him to Rome." She glares at him for good measure.

"You know why," he says, surprisingly stern.

She does, but I have no idea. Not that I'm mad at her for missing out on the gigantic shit-fest that was my time in Rome. "It's alright," I tell her. "I'm back now."

"And that's all that matters." Camille holds onto my arm as she steers my feet back into the citadel.

My hand longs for Wulf's, but I appreciate the cuddle from my friend. It tells me so much more than her words could. "How are things here?" I ask, in an effort to distract myself.

"Oh, rather quiet, in spirit terms at least, but there have been some changes," she admits.

Oh dear, more changes. I don't know whether I can handle much more. Why can't this all just be a bad dream, and I wake up on an early morning in May?

Camille picks up on my distress and checks with Wulf. He reluctantly explains, "She means Inga and Bijan. They've been visiting a lot, practically every day. Unless there was something else, Camille?"

I look back and forth between the two. Something's going on, even if Camille is shaking her head with a smile. "No, that's pretty much it. You'll see the rest in time."

Oookay. Sounds like the perfect mystery to drag me out of my self-pity.

We cross into the yard, and instantly, my gaze falls on Grune. His little trees have all grown so much since I last saw them. I can't go to him now, but I give him a wave from afar. In response, his branches sway in the wind.

"I'll see you later," Aeola whispers, just as we enter the main building.

I watch her fly to Grune and nestle herself in his crown. I'd much rather sit outside with them than enter yet another dark, closed-off space. "This one's alright," I mutter to myself. The citadel isn't meant to keep me in. It's here to protect me.

And it isn't really that dark. The hall is flooded with light, fresh flowers on the table. I notice a row of potted plants near the window. It's an unusual touch for this place, and I find myself looking at Camille for an explanation. "Whose idea was that?"

She chuckles. "Lukas'. To help him feel more connected to nature without having to face actual spirits."

I'd better not tell him that a small bush dryad has taken up residence in one of his pots, then. She's well-camouflaged, hair and dress made of the same luscious leaves as her plant.

"I'm facing Grune alright," my favourite grumpy spirit seeker says, rising from the table where he's been sitting with Leon, who's kissing his girlfriend. I notice his leg is out of the cast, and he's now wearing a simple brace. His eyes meet mine, and his confidence melts away. Looks like he's changed as well. *Oh, boy.* "I just never know whether I offend or please him," he explains, practically begging me to understand. "It's a chicken and egg thing. I won't know until my NAV has improved. But my NAV can't improve if I don't try it."

So, that much has stayed the same. It's still about the NAV, not the spirits. "It's a process," I tell him, not quite ready to jump into an argument.

Lukas doesn't press it either. "I'm well aware. Good to have you back, in any case."

Aww. Even he missed me. "It's good to be back." Even though all these changes are exhausting.

Camille lets go of me so Leon can give me a warm hug. "We missed you."

I missed them all as well. More than I would've thought possible less than half a year ago. They're home to me in a way little else ever was. "I missed you, too."

"Welcome back," Miriam greets. She holds an arm open for Camille, who leans into her, putting her head on Miriam's shoulder. At least, these two are still going strong. I would've been very cross with the passage of time if it had ruined that, too.

Then I feel Wulf's hand on my back. He gives me a soft push. "Come on, take a seat. I'll put some coffee on."

"There's cake in the fridge," Miriam announces, momentarily releasing Camille. "Bienenstich. Got it this morning when you called."

Minutes later, we're all sitting around the table with coffee and cake. Inga is cuddling up to Leon, while Henny and Bijan have found places at the far end.

I can't remember if I've ever had a piece of Bienenstich. It's a flat, square-shaped cake filled with vanilla pudding and topped with sliced almonds and a honey glaze. The first bite practically explodes with sugar in my mouth, but the nuts give it a tart taste that fits perfectly. For the rest of the afternoon tea, everyone keeps their chats SSA-free, for which I'm grateful.

It's still on their minds, though, if Wulf's frequent gaze and Miriam's forced cheeriness are anything to go by. I keep my head down, asking for a second smaller piece, and sip from my coffee. Let life be normal for just one minute.

That minute passes, of course, and far too soon, I find myself tucked in between Camille and Leon on the couch, recounting what's happened to me. Miriam has set up a laptop, inviting Rory and Brigid via video chat, which is fair, I guess, since Rory and his half-brother Eoghan helped organise my rescue. This way, I won't have to tell the story twice.

Early on, Wulf receives a call and leaves the room with a darkening face. I can only imagine who'd be desperate to talk to him. It's no one I ever want to meet again.

"So, when all their attempts failed, I was sent into the Colosseum," I say. "That's where they kept Vesuvius. It was a pretty neat way to get rid of me and use my death as a cautionary tale."

"One they actually told to us," Henny affirms eagerly, "without proof. When I found out they'd lied, that was it for me."

I nod, still thankful that Henny chose to leave the academy for my sake. I wouldn't have wanted to leave them behind. "Well, it almost worked. Vesuvius was furious, understandably so. But I managed to get through to him before he burnt me to a cinder, and we devised a plan. I'd help him get his eggs back, and he'd let me live."

"So, the ancient spirit is free now?" Lukas asks. I still hear reservations in his voice. It must be tough for him not to fall back into old patterns.

"He is. Wulf made the decision." Hopefully, knowing his idol did it and not me opens Lukas up to the idea. "But first, we broke into the research facility where the eggs were stored. There, we found pretty much every spirit that's ever been caught. No such thing as releasing them into the wild."

"Did you guys find evidence of the modified spirits?" Brigid asks. "You know, the ones they sent here?"

"We did." The proof was in Piero Vallesco's research notes, but I won't tell her that. Bijan and Inga are more than capable of filling in the details. "It's definitely the SSA that made the modifications." I still see pollution being pumped into the salamander eggs and shudder. Just imagine the outcry if it were done to humans, not spirits.

"Anyway," I continue, "we escaped thanks to Eoghan." I look at Rory, who's smiling encouragingly at me. "Is he back in Ireland yet?"

Rory shakes his head. "Not that I've heard of."

I wish that didn't worry me. But Eoghan left for the airport before we got on the train. He should've landed by now.

Rattled, I continue, "Well, to cut my story short: we went back to Vesuvius, and just as we were about to hand the eggs to him, Dante found us. He tried to stop Wulf..." *and threatened to kill me*. My breath catches in my throat, but I force myself to continue, "but Wulf returned the eggs to Vesuvius, and Vesuvius broke us out of the Colosseum."

Lukas' fingers are digging into the armrests of his chair, but once again, he doesn't mock me when he opens his mouth. "With Vesuvius free, will there be a new eruption?"

"No. Vesuvius promised to go to sleep for a while."

"He promised?" It's almost as if I can smell the sweat on his forehead. "That's... remarkable."

I feel a bit sorry for Lukas. He's obviously trying, but his instincts aren't placated that easily. And he's not wrong to worry about potential retribution from the volcano spirit. "I wish there was a guarantee, but we came to an understanding. The SSA needs to be stopped before we can establish better relationships."

"Count me in," Brigid says, eliciting a nervous chuckle from everyone around the table.

Despite their support, I believe going against a powerful, world-spanning organisation wasn't on anyone's bucket list. It scares me, too, but I'm ready to put my money where my mouth is. The spirits deserve better. And for that matter, so do humans.

"Well, we can certainly get Dante for all the crimes he committed against Rika," Inga announces. Just the mention of the academy's director makes my skin crawl. "Kidnapping, abuse, attempted murder. He's going down. We might even take down a couple of Vallescos."

"Not all spirit seekers are bad!" Lukas exclaims, shoulders drawn up to his chin. "If we abolish the SSA, people will suffer." With a glance at me, he hastily adds, "I'm not saying Dante shouldn't be held accountable, and what they did to you is reproachable, but..."

I wave him off. "I know what you mean." I certainly don't need to dive deeper into my recent trauma.

"It's not just him!" Bijan shouts passionately. "They're watching us all. There's a system behind it."

"Yes," Brigid says. "The entire board needs to be replaced, and an investigation launched. You need to press charges, Rika, so we can get the ball rolling."

Fortunately, I don't have to answer, because Camille objects. "Let Rika relax first. Why don't you press charges? Didn't they do something similar to you?"

As the discussion gets more and more heated, I find Rory watching me. When I return his gaze, he asks quietly, "Are you okay?"

I love that he's more worried about me than how to bring the agency down. "I will be," I tell him, willing myself to make it true. But right now, it's all a bit much, and I excuse myself to get a drink, only to leave the room without it. Once the door closes behind me, I sink against it.

The SSA needs to be held responsible, and I want to do it, but a legal battle? I can't even tell my friends who Dante truly is.

My father.

And the moment Dante realised, he let me go. That's not a good thing about him, but it is something. An extra layer of messed-up secrets.

Steps come down the stairs. Shortly after, Wulf appears. He notices me immediately. "Everything alright?"

"I just needed a break," I admit. Then I remember why he was in his room for so long. "You got a call?" I push myself off the door and walk over.

If I didn't know who it was beforehand, his guilty expression gives it away. "My father called, yes."

"Hmm." Humberto Vallesco, board member and the one who told Dante to hand me over to Vesuvius. "What did he want?"

"He wants to make sure you won't press any charges," he explains in a guarded voice.

I can't say it surprises me. "I see. Did he give you a good reason? Like, are they going to make it up to me? Was it all just a misunderstanding? Or do I get a lot of money?" I could use it to launch my pro-spirit campaign. I'm happy to pause the investigation for that purpose.

But Wulf shakes his head. "If you press charges, they'll press charges back."

"Press charges against me? What have I done?"

He can't even face me, his jaw labouring with suppressed anger. "Destruction of the Castel, breaking and entering a research lab, theft, and acts against humanity by freeing a powerful, violent spirit, and others."

My breath catches in my throat. I wish I could take a seat, but there's just space behind me. Crossing my arms, I manage to say, "Wow."

"Yeah, wow." I get why Wulf looks so disgruntled now.

"They're not even sugarcoating this."

He shakes his head, then sighs. "Rika." His hands find mine, pulling them from my guarded stance. "I'm so sorry for my family. They're the absolute worst, and I can't believe I didn't see that before now."

I sink into his chest, finding solace there. "I'm sure they were always great to you." Though a part of me wants to, I can't blame Wulf for what happened to me. He stood up against them at last. "So, they're gonna get away with it."

There's no point in believing anything else. Yes, what the SSA did to me was horrible, and by all rights, I should be the victim, but I've seen enough of the world to know how this works. The Vallescos, and with them the SSA, have money. I don't. They'll have the best legal team money can buy—plus they'll probably corrupt the judge. I'd happy if I had a competent duty solicitor.

"They will *not* get away with it," Wulf stresses, looking deep into my eyes.

He's too naïve for this. "Yes, they will. You can tell your dad I'm not going to press anything." If I do, they'll steamroll over me and hang me out dry. Worst-case scenario, I'll go to prison. And I can absolutely not be stuck in a cell ever again. "He wins."

"He does *not* win," Wulf stresses. "We just need to make sure we're not rushing into this. We'll find a way."

I love him for his enthusiasm. He wants to make this right, atone for his foster family's sins. But I know it's to no avail. The Vallescos have all the power. I'll just have to be glad they won't press charges just to get me out of the way once and for all. If that happens, I'll refuse to stay quiet. Even a judge's verdict won't erase the doubt I'd sow in my defence. If only I was strong enough to risk prison for my cause.

"Where are you going to sleep tonight?" Wulf asks after a while.

The question feels so out of place, it drags me out of my gloom. "I haven't thought about it." But now I do. Every fibre of my being yearns to be outside, to sleep under the stars in Grune's embrace. "Agnes got me when I crossed the courtyard." It's not safe out there.

"The outside doors will be locked, both of them. There's a security system with an alarm and cameras," Wulf explains. "And I can bring you to Grune."

"Like a bodyguard?"

His lips curl into a slight smile. "Something like that."

"Sounds like a plan to me. I'll be safe with Grune." The dryad won't let anyone near me.

Wulf keeps his promise, delivering me to Grune after dinner. The others were disappointed by the news of Humberto Vallesco's threat, but I'm secretly glad I don't have to dissect my trauma in front of a court. It's bad enough as it is. Being outside helps ease the pressure of it all. I sink into Grune's embrace and appreciate the firm touch as he moulds his bark around my back. Aeola is there as well, folding herself into my lap like a cat.

"It's good to have you back, spirit seeker." He calls me that, even though I couldn't be further away from those trained at the academy. To him, I'm a better spirit seeker than they'll ever be. "And you brought a new friend."

I watch Glut, skirting the perimeter, scratching at the ground. He reminds me a bit of Lukas when he steals glances at Grune, but doesn't come any closer.

"Don't be afraid. Grune doesn't bite," I call out, beckoning him closer.

"I trust he will not try to set a fire," Grune growls, but he sounds like a grumpy grandfather, more bark than bite.

"Never, ever, ever," Glut says, pressing himself flat to the ground.

Chuckling, I stretch my hand out to him. "I may just be speaking for myself, but I could use a little warmth." As warm as the day was, the nights are still a bit cold.

Delighted, Glut scrambles towards me, making himself a nest on top of my outstretched legs. Aeola looks at him and purrs, enjoying the gentle heat as much as I do. I wish this moment would last forever.

"So much pain." Grune's voice vibrates through my muscles, making me shudder.

For a moment, I consider holding it all in, but then I show him. I'm not sure he understands the bond I had with my mother or what it means to never have had a father, only for him to show up as your worst nightmare. I never needed a father, never wanted one. I would've been happy to never know his name. But now it's been forced on me, and everything's gone from bad to worse.

Even if the dryad can't grasp the details, he senses my inner turmoil, breathes in the pain the weeks have caused me, and soothes my wounds. I know they'll eventually scab over. I'll heal and be stronger for it. Not by running this time. But by standing up and fighting.

"I'll do everything in my power to make them see. The time to close our eyes to a dying world is over. We need to step up. And I will," I promise. At the very least, using my voice for those that don't have one—at least not one most people can hear—will give me something to focus on. I'll turn this into a good thing.

"Don't be scared. It's only Wulf," Grune informs me, long before I notice Wulf's heavy steps echoing through the courtyard.

He steps into the soft orange glow of Glut, standing well within Grune's reach. The fact he's carrying a sleeping bag gives me a flashback to that cold April night.

"Still got some space for me?" he asks, nodding towards Glut and Aeola.

"You want to give it another try?" I ask, trying to not get my hopes up. The last time ended with me throwing a punch at him.

I've been around Wulf long enough to know he's blushing, even though it's too dark to see. He scratches his neck and moves a little closer. "I'm not here for Grune. Sorry, Grune," he says with a quick look at the crown.

"Then why are you here?"

Another step, and now I see his features clearly. "Let's just say, you're not the only one who's scared tonight."

I chuckle softly. "You're really taking this bodyguard business seriously, aren't you?"

He flashes me a quick smile. "If you'll let me."

Instead of an answer, I pat the ground next to me, trying not to grin at him too much. He's here to protect me. Because he cares. Something has shifted between us, and while I'm not ready to jump into it right now, I'm glad he'll be by my side. I feel safer around him, however illusionary the impression might be.

"But no waking at night," I warn as he sets his sleeping bag next to me.

I try not to watch as he undresses down to a pair of shorts—rather tight shorts—and into the sleeping bag. "If you don't punch me."

"It might be a reflex," I say, trying not to pay too much attention to the fact he's almost naked.

"I'm not trying anything," Wulf says in that severe voice of his, "but can I hold you?" He raises the shoulder near me, indicating his intentions.

Do I want him to hold me? "Yes."

Tentatively, he puts an arm around my shoulders. His touch is so gentle. Every nerve end feels on fire. I pat Glut to remind myself what real fire is, and ever so slowly sink into Wulf. It should be awkward, but it feels so right to sleep like this, surrounded by those who love me.

My true family.

2

I feel warm. Warmer than I've ever felt in the morning, and it's not the sun, which hasn't yet climbed over the stone walls. A bundle of warmth is nestled in my lower back, but the biggest source of heat is that under my head. That very naked, bulky chest, rising and sinking with a steady rhythm. Wulf.

Oh, shit!

What do I do now? I must've slept on him last night, using him as a pillow, as if I've ever needed one before. His arm is laying across my back, and his fingers are moving ever so slightly. There's still a layer of sleeping bag and my clothes between his arm and my back, yet I feel his touch as if he's running his fingers over my naked skin. I wish he would.

Gosh, Rika! Get a grip. This is literally the last thing you need right now. Then why is it impossible for me to move my head and let him know I'm awake?

Time passes, stretching out indefinitely. My world is reduced to Wulf's heartbeat under my ear, my arms around his chest, and his fingers trailing along my side. He's totally awake, and probably waiting for me to get off him. Wouldn't it be wonderful to just lie here and never move again? To keep this moment frozen in time?

I sigh, at long last, giving myself away.

"You okay?" he asks softly, instant worry in his voice.

I don't want him to worry about me, not constantly at least. "Sorry about this new assault." Sleeping outside is clearly not our strong suit.

Wulf laughs. "I like this one a lot more."

My face burns. I have to move. The longer I lie here, the more awkward it'll become. With a deep breath, I slowly extricate myself from his embrace, careful not to rock the little salamander rolled up on my other side. Wulf lets go of me, shuffling himself up to a sitting position. I watch him roll his shoulders, releasing the tension in his muscles.

"Are *you* okay?" He's not used to sleeping on the ground like this, and on top of that, I've used him as a pillow.

Wulf grimaces. "Yeah, I'm alright. Not sure if I could do this long-term, but it's not as bad as I expected."

"You sacrificed your comfort for me," I tease. Joking makes it much easier to deal with the sight of his bare chest. I already miss the steady rhythm of his heartbeat.

"I'd say I woke up pretty comfortable." For a moment, Wulf looks almost cheeky, but the illusion vanishes quickly when he glances towards the main building. "We should probably head inside before someone sees us."

I'd love to say they should mind their own business, but I definitely don't need another complicated issue in my life. I've got feelings for Wulf, and according to the spirits, he loves me. But so much has happened. We've learnt things about ourselves and each other that we can't ignore. It'll be some time before we can consider such trivial things like hugs and kisses.

"Rika?" Once again, his face is creased with concern.

How can I think about a romantic relationship when worry is at the forefront of his mind? Yeah, we have other issues, and now's not the time to want more from him. I'm already getting so much. "I'm good. You want to head in first? Sneak up to your room?"

"But how will you get to the hall?"

"Using my own two feet?" I know what he means, but in the daylight, the courtyard seems only half as scary. Surely, the SSA won't waltz in under clear blue skies. "I can't be scared of my own shadow. The gates are still locked, right?"

Wulf nods. "They are. It's just..." He sighs. "You don't need to push yourself."

"What do you mean?"

"To get over it. These things take time. And you're allowed to take it."

Now it's my turn to sigh. On the street, you either get over your trauma or you get buried with it. "I'll survive."

He leans forward to cup my face in his hand. Once again, his fingertips send little sparks of electricity through my skin. "Surviving isn't enough. I want you to live."

Can I kiss him now?

Before I completely melt into his gaze, I clear my throat and pretend to look for my clothes. I'm dressed. He's the one sitting there half-naked, spouting sweet, caring words at me.

Wulf's hand falls away, and I hear him getting out of his sleeping bag and into his clothes. I don't look until I hear him exhale loudly. "Is something wrong?"

"My clothes are wet." He's put them on, but judging by the way he's standing there, shuddering, it's not a great experience.

"That's the dew," I explain. "You left them outside. They'll dry soon in the sun."

He politely declines the notion. "I'd better get changed." I guess he's not an outdoor convert just yet.

Despite his words, he's still standing there, staring down at me.

"Go!" I tell him. "I'll see you at breakfast."

"Anything in particular you'd like?" he asks, a little playful at last.

"Surprise me!" And the rest of the crew.

Wulf laughs and finally gets a move on. I watch as he goes, sighing contentedly as I sink back into Grune's bark.

The surprise is a plate of mozzarella, tomato, and basil, plus some dark rye bread and lots of fruit. But the best part of it is the table's been brought outside, and we're eating our breakfast in the warm breeze. Leaves are rustling—my favourite background noise. I don't know about everyone else, but this is the best meal I've ever had. There's laughter and little inside jokes, and nobody talks about the SSA or their horrible agenda for the entirety of breakfast.

Once finished, I let the sun shine on my face while I enjoy one last cup of coffee. Or rather, Aeola enjoys it, soaking up the smell of roasted beans.

"So, when do we start training?" Lukas asks. He's still in a brace, so I'm confused. Surely he's not planning on interrupting his healing process for the sake of keeping in top form.

"Training?"

He glances over his shoulder at Grune. "This whole nature-loving stuff. I want to improve. Remember?"

"Oh." How do you train your natural attunement? "I'm not sure, you can train it."

"There must be something I can do. I can't just wait around, hoping it'll happen one day."

Of course he can't. Lukas is an achiever. And everything in life has to be achieved. And he's probably bored to hell at being incapacitated for so long. "Look, I've never done this on purpose."

"You taught Leon!" he counters.

"Luke," Wulf says warningly. "This is not the time."

"No, no, it is time," I say, sitting up straight. This isn't only about raising Lukas' NAV, so he can become a better soldier. It requires a shift in his attitude. A shift towards a pro-spirit lifestyle. "We need more people capable of seeing spirits for what they really are. As for Leon," I glance at him on the other side of the table, "all I did was introduce him to spirits and tell him about them. What they want. How they live."

Leon nods sagely. "It's in your mind, Lukas. You need to open yourself up, will yourself to listen. It's nothing you can do on a schedule."

Sulking, Lukas leans back. "So, what do I do then? I tried being closer to that... to Grune. But it's a tree. I mean, do you want me to hug trees and collect stones? I like nature well enough," he protests. "But...".

"You're just constantly aware of how it could kill someone," I say, taking a sip from my cup.

"You promised you'd teach me," he complains. "So, introduce me. If it worked for Leon, it'll work for me."

He doesn't get it. Yes, I helped Leon, but he did most of the work. It was his willingness to embrace spirits which made his NAV soar. I sigh. "Sure. Well, Lukas, this is Aeola. She's sitting on my head, getting high on coffee steam."

"I'm not high!" Aeola pouts. Every wisp I catch of her is stained brown.

Lukas blanches. His fingers dig into his chair as he stares at the top of my head. "Is that so?" His voice is so strained I fear his jaw will cramp up. This won't work. This won't work at all.

"Relax," I tell him. "First thing you need to learn is to stop seeing every spirit as a potential danger. Sure, Aeola can call the wind, but she's pretty happy with her coffee right now."

"Very happy," she purrs.

Wulf is smiling at me. For once, no concern mars his features. Aeola's presence doesn't frighten him in the slightest. He knows her and everything she's done for this team.

He's not the only one watching me. Henny's been fascinated by the sylph on my head since the start of breakfast. "This is so different," they say at last. "I'd never considered how sylphs would react to smells, but it makes so much sense."

I'm glad at least one of those new to this is ready to open up. Then again, it might be easier for those who can actually see spirits with their natural abilities.

Lukas is pouting now. "This'll never work."

"When have you ever given up on something?" Leon teases gently. His arm is conspicuously wrapped around Inga's lower back. "Just give it time." He looks so happy and relaxed.

"Can *you* see the sylph?" Lukas asks, slipping back into his claws-out defence.

"No, not quite," Leon admits. "I sense when she's there, though. She always brings such warmth with her."

On my head, Aeola swells with pride. "Don't flatter yourself, Little Miss Sunshine," I say, only to find everyone staring at me. "What?"

Wulf chuckles. "They're probably not used to you talking with her or with thin air, for that matter."

"I wish there was a way to make spirits visible," Inga says, leaning forward. "The problem with most people is they're completely unaware of spirits. I don't mean other spirit seekers, but normal people. They've been fed all this bullshit for generations and have to take it at face value. It'll be hard to challenge their misconceptions without tangible proof."

Getting spirit seekers on my side is hard enough as it is. Asking an unattuned person to accept that the invisible thing they're afraid of just wants to play? Who'd believe us?

"Not necessarily," Miriam says. "I agree with you on the proof. But to be honest, convincing others we need to change our ways might be easier than we assume. There are so many sceptics. People no longer believe blindly. I mean, most of them don't. And there are already groups calling for an end to spirit seeking, however misguided they might be."

"Climate change is a big topic," Camille agrees. "The SSA's been trying to blame it on spirits for decades, but most people realise it's our fault. Rika's narrative would work well with them."

My narrative. I don't know whether it's the fact she's putting it all on me instead of saying "our narrative" or that "narrative" sounds like a tool for manipulation, but it rubs me the wrong way. "I'm just speaking the truth."

"Your truth," Lukas interjects, before catching himself. "Which I guess is a lot truer than what we learnt in school."

"In any case," Miriam continues, eager to make a point, "I can't see spirits, can't even sense them, so I *am* one of these people. And because I hate not knowing, I've been working on ways to detect spirit activity. We can use our scanners, for example. I might not be able to create a beautiful drawing of Aeola, but I can make the spirit energy she leaves behind visible."

"You might be onto something," Inga says. "It wouldn't be live, but it *is* proof. We can show people how many times spirits pass by unknown without ever disturbing anything." Her eyes widen. "Now that's an idea." She leans back and grins at Leon, who reciprocates the smile.

Miriam almost jumps off her chair in excitement. "Oh, I have so many ideas. You should come to the lab with me. We'll figure something out." She checks with Camille. "If that's okay with you?"

Even I can see Camille forcing a smile. "Why wouldn't it be?"

Miriam isn't fooled either. "I could leave this to Inga and Bijan, if you'd rather…"

Camille tenses up immediately, shaking her head. "I'm good. You enjoy yourself. Solve puzzles."

I'd thought they'd left all their problems behind when we left Ireland, but something's wrong. I wonder if it's the same thing standing between Camille and Wulf. It seems like I have a lot to catch up on.

"What's going on with you and Miri?" I ask Camille when we're tidying up. "You don't believe she'd exchange you for research in a heartbeat, do you?" Direct questions demand direct answers. At least, I hope so.

"Oh no. She loves me. It's all good." She walks off again to collect more plates.

I hurry after her. "Then what is it?"

"Nothing."

I've never experienced Camille being this evasive. "Something's bothering you."

Camille stops and turns to me, sighing deeply. "I'm okay, Rika. Seriously. You have so much on your plate. We should focus on that, not me."

"I thought we'd been through that. Just because I struggle, doesn't mean I can't be there for you." I want to be there for her. On the streets I would've shrugged and walked away. But Camille is my friend.

She smiles warmly. "Sure, but Miri and I are all good. You don't need to worry about us."

With that, she picks up the last two plates and vanishes inside, leaving me alone. So, what do I do now? Join Miriam, Leon, and Inga in the lab? No, I had my fill of research in Rome. Wulf is nowhere to be seen, and Camille just made it clear she doesn't want to spend time with me. I notice Henny standing in the courtyard under Grune's branches, looking up at the dryad.

"He's so powerful," Henny says when I stroll over to them. "It should alarm me, but he doesn't feel dangerous."

"You should ask Lukas about that." I smile at Grune. "He can be dangerous, but he chooses not to be."

"Only when I must," Grune says.

I check with Henny, but they didn't hear him. As brilliant as they are, their NAV isn't quite high enough at this point. "So, what do you think?"

"That you're amazing," Henny admits and laughs. "I've never met anybody like you." They look into the distance, seemingly lost in thought. "It was all wrong. But how? How did they get it so wrong?"

"If people have an agenda, it colours their whole perception. They only see the attacks that do happen, never the ones that don't. A peaceful spirit is only a danger lying in wait."

"Men fight what they can't understand," Grune adds. "You need to bring understanding."

I snort. "It's not that easy. I need to find people to listen first." And then what? Am I supposed to give talks, interviews, workshops?

"Is he talking to you?" Henny asks, awe in their voice. When I nod, their face lights up a little. "This changes so much, Rika. You know, communication is the key."

"I hope so."

"Wow." Henny gazes at Grune, momentarily lost in admiration. After a while, they turn to me with a sigh. "Wulf will probably kill me for telling you, but the SSA's reached out to me."

My body reacts immediately, all muscles ready for flight. "Why doesn't he want me to know?"

"Says you've got enough on your plate."

"Oh, please!" I groan. "They have to stop doing that. First Camille's keeping secrets, now Wulf. If I can't handle it, I'll let everyone know."

Henny smiles. "You're the woman who took on a volcano. And brought him peace. I trust you."

Warmth spreads through my limbs, easing the muscles. "So, what do they want from you?"

I'm glad Henny decides to walk a bit. It's easier to talk when your muscles are moving. "They want to know where I am, and when I'm coming back to complete my studies."

"So what? They're pretending you're on a holiday?" Carina knows about Henny's involvement. She would've told on them.

"Pretending is the right word. The texts are getting stronger, though, reminding me I can't graduate if I don't attend a minimum of classes. Or how much I owe them." Henny rolls their eyes but becomes serious quickly. "After what happened to you, I'm scared. What if they force me to come back, and... and what will they do to me if I do? Or what if they go after my family?"

"I'm sorry." It's my fault they're in this situation.

Henny shakes their head. "No, you've got nothing to be sorry for. It's just... I haven't heard from Eoghan. Have you?"

"No." Does that mean he's been missing for twenty-four hours?

"I tried to call him, but nothing. His number has been cancelled." If there wasn't a red flag before, then a giant one is flying now. "I texted Wiola, but she told me he's dead to her."

"What?"

Henny sighs. "It looks like they're not pretending with him. Carina might have said something to her. Gosh. This is all such a mess. I wish he'd come with us. I can't bear the thought of that wool-headed idiot being hurt somewhere."

I haven't known Eoghan for long, and most of that time he played the ass to perfection, but I find myself worrying about him as well. My thoughts fly to Rory, imagining how this must affect him. I'm not sure how close the half-brothers truly are, but Eoghan had a way of contacting him. And I don't.

"I need a phone," I say, barging into Miriam's lab. "I should have some money, but I have no idea which one to buy or how to set up a contract. Maybe prepaid would be safer." With the SSA controlling phone lines now, probably.

Miriam laughs, raising her hands. "Slow down! I'm already a step ahead of you. Or rather, Camille was. She picked out a phone for you the moment you went missing."

"How was that supposed to help me?"

"It wouldn't have, but she wanted you to have one once you returned. Which is now. You should go and ask her. I bet it's in her room."

With my enthusiasm curbed a little, I shift my weight. Should I ask Miriam the question I asked Camille? Will Miriam be more truthful or has she also been briefed to avoid burdening me?

I find myself annoyed at Wulf. I'm aware he's only worried, but after Rome, I don't want anyone to control what information I'm given and what's kept from me.

"Anything else I can do for you?" Miriam asks. She's been working on her computer, looking at spirit energy images.

"Actually, there is." The idea came to me during breakfast when I thought about reaching out beyond the spirit seekers. "I need you to find someone for me."

"Who?"

"My family."

3

When I'd asked Miriam to help me find the Travellers involved in the Spring Cleaning, I hadn't expected her to get me results the same day. Tracking someone without a place of residence should be hard, but apparently some of them had settled in Neukölln after they were released from prison.

It's taken me three days to build up the courage to seek them out. Now I'm on my way, my new phone won't stop ringing. I'm almost ready to throw it over the highway bridge I'm crossing in Neukölln. Convincing Wulf to let me go alone after several days of being cooped up might have been the toughest bit of this little adventure. Besides, I'm not alone. Aeola is floating next to me, trying her best to avoid the exhaust fumes rising from below.

The phone rings again. "Yes. I'm still alive and in Berlin," I tell Wulf, barely checking if it's even him calling. "If you continue like this, I'll run out of battery before I meet them."

"Why do you have to do this alone?" he asks, sounding worried.

"Because," I step off the overhead bridge and seek solace under a nearby tree, "we don't want strangers in our business. I don't even know whether they want me." Maybe it would've been good to have him with me. Then I would be more annoyed than scared. "I'm fine."

"Okay. I'm sorry I'm getting on your nerves."

I wish I could see his expression, but I'll just have to do with imagining his warm brown eyes. "I've got you on speed-dial if anything happens."

"Good."

"You need to trust me."

"It's not you I don't trust," Wulf protests.

"I know. But remember, you want me to live. I can't do that hiding from the world." I refuse to live my life in fear of the SSA.

Through the phone, I hear a gigantic sigh. "Well played, Rika. Well played."

"Bye now." I turn him off before he can protest any more, and turn the phone on silent for good measure. Then I face Aeola. "I should've never gotten a phone."

Aeola laughs. "But you love it when he calls you."

"I don't. It's annoying."

"Then why are you always smiling when you talk to him?"

"I'm not!" We bicker until we reach the big block that's been turned into a Romany village. Not a slum lacking real infrastructure, as I've seen so often, but comfortable, warm flats. According to Miriam's internet research, it was built around ten years ago as a government initiative. That one was much better than the Spring Cleaning two years later.

As expected, Miriam couldn't find a trail for my mother or the others who'd been staying with us then. But some of the Travellers arrested that day were released only a few days later and offered a place in the still-new village. Only a few took the government up on it, though, with most choosing to leave the city.

"Hi, uhm... I'm looking for Mihaela Petrescu or Dragos Novac," I tell the lanky youth who's hanging outside the entrance.

"What's your name?" he asks, his chin raised in challenge, even though his eyes seem stuck on my blue hair.

"Marika Csorba. Magdaléna's daughter." I'm done hiding my mother. I understand why she did it, but apart from causing me all this pain for years, it did little to save me from the SSA.

The teenager shrugs and heads inside. I take it as a sign I should follow him.

It really is some sort of village in between the high-rise buildings of Berlin's southern district. There's even a garden with a playground on the inside that reminds me of the newly forested citadel. I wouldn't necessarily expect to find Travellers here, but it looks like a safe space, and sometimes that's all that matters.

The boy takes me down corridors and past playing children to a corner in the courtyard, where the washing is being hung by a group of women chatting loudly. "Miha," he calls. "There's someone for you."

A woman turns around and looks at me in confusion. The youth hangs around, curious about what I might want. The looks I'm getting hurt. There was a time I was no stranger to the Traveller community. Now I stick out like a sore thumb with the muted colour scheme on my body and my bright blue hair.

Eight years ago, I hardly knew Mihaela Petrescu. I wouldn't even have remembered her name if it weren't for the Spring Cleaning police report. But as she looks at me, I find myself remembering her easy smile. Back then, her eyes had been framed by starry lines. There are even more now. This is a woman who loves to laugh.

The whole lot of them, women of every age and colouring, strain their necks to see what's going on. Mihaela stands in front of me, still not recognising me. "You were looking for me?" There's a slight wariness in her voice. We don't like people looking for us. My mother even less than the rest.

"It's me, Rika. Magda's daughter."

Almost immediately, the sun rises on her face. All the wariness slips away and the wrinkles around her eyes come into full effect. "Rika, darling!" Her arms open, and before I can even process the warm welcome, she's wrapped them around me to hug me tight.

Then it's all just one big blur of faces as Mihaela introduces me to the other women, often adding their partners and children and even parents. "I love your hair. So blue," she coos in between.

Self-consciously, I touch the tips of my hair, grown to just below my shoulders. After Rome, my roots are in bitter need of a new dye job. "Thanks, uhm..."

Yeah, I'm totally overwhelmed. I came here on a mission to reconnect with my people and ask them about the spirits. I never expected to be greeted like their long-lost daughter. But I guess that's what I am. We're all family. Even someone as secluded as my mother had ties all around the different groups. It's as if no time at all has passed, and I'm a Traveller child once more.

Suddenly I have tears in my eyes, thinking of my mother and the distance she put between us when I needed her most. The SSA took her from me. But they also took me and her family from her, isolating her completely.

"Oh, darling, don't cry," Mihaela says, wiping my tears away with her big hands. "It's alright. You're home here."

That only brings new tears to my eyes. It takes me a couple of minutes to calm down, to sort all the conflicting feelings vying for my attention. The loss of my mother has risen back to the top, the disappointment from finding her in my worst nightmare, the truth about my father, and this incredible feeling of belonging I suddenly feel.

"I know," I say at last. "I... Were you here all this time?" Stupid question. The police record said as much. It's just that I barely stepped foot into Neukölln, the very district where the Spring Cleaning took place. It's not Berlin's nicest area, either.

"I was." Mihaela guides me to a little bench under an apple tree. The flowers have long been replaced by small, bright-green apples that won't ripen for a few months yet. She puts an arm around my shoulders. "How have you been?"

Instantly, the Colosseum flashes before my eyes. Dante's grip on my arms. "I'm okay." The last thing I want to tell her is my whole sob story. "What about the others? I heard Dragos was here? What about Pavel or Elvira?"

"Dragos left years ago, hasn't been to Germany in ages. Pavel, too. Oh, he would love to see you. Do you want me to ask around?"

I say, "Yes, please," faster than I can think of the phrase.

Mihaela laughs. "He always had a sweet spot for you, his little spirit." My heart flows over at the memory. "What about your mother? How is she?"

Truth or lie? "She is... I haven't seen her since then."

"Oh, darling!" Mihaela's eyes widen, and she hugs me again, patting my back. "Do you know anything about her? They didn't find her, did they?"

"Who?" I ask, curious how much Mihaela already knows.

"The people she was running from. Always changed routes, that one. Spent too much time on her own, never keeping her feet still."

A chill settles around me. All my life, my mother has been running. Running from retribution. Still, it came for her in the end. And now I'm at the same point. The SSA wants me. Dead if possible. Will I follow in her footsteps and run? I don't want that. I don't want to be alone all my life.

"She ran from the SSA," I whisper. "Because of her spirit connection. That's why they wanted her."

Mihaela doesn't take the news well, blanching as I mention the SSA. She fusses with my hands. "Oh, dear…"

That's not the whole story, but it's time to get back to why I came here. "I need you to know something."

"We don't talk about them," she hushes, throwing nervous glances at the others.

"But we have to." I totally understand her fear. We Travellers have always been discriminated against because of our belief in positive spirit relations. We've been ridiculed, blamed, and threatened. I realise now the SSA must've always had an eye on us. How else did they even approach my mother in the first place?

"We need to talk about it because the world needs to change," I say, my tears all dry. "I know it sounds scary. The SSA is powerful and—"

"You have no idea how—"

"I do."

One look in my eyes, and Mihaela shuts up. There's no laughter on her face now. Instead, she takes my hands and holds them tight, allowing me to take a deep breath. "They will come for me again, sooner or later. But I'm done running. I want people to learn, to see, to understand. We Travellers respect the spirits and their territories. We've always treated them right and pursued good relationships, haven't we?"

Mihaela's eyes are still locked on mine. She nods.

"I talk to spirits. There's a sylph in this courtyard who I trust more than any human soul." A gentle breeze carries that trust right back to me. "And I've met other spirits. They want an end to the war the SSA is waging. This world needs an end. It needs people to stop treating nature like a trusty old dog that'll come back no matter how much we kick it. I want to spread awareness. Spread the message."

"Darling." Mihaela raises one hand to cup my cheek. "We've done that. Our voice isn't strong enough."

"It has to be." There's not much time before the entire world goes south, spirit intervention or not. "People are changing. I... I work with the local spirit seekers."

As expected, Mihaela draws a sharp breath. Her hands pull away, but I grab the one in my lap.

"Listen! They're on my side. They agree."

"You can't trust them. The SSA feeds and clothes them, teaches them all their horrible lies." Her hand returns the grip, but now the pressure feels desperate. "They'll never learn."

"They already have," I assure her. "When I first met them half a year ago, they thought I was crazy, but they've become my friends, and they believe me. Not the Eastern ones. The ones in the Citadel of Spandau."

"Wulf Bachmann?"

There it is again. The name that induces terror into so many hearts, and awe into even more. He probably wishes he could burn that name now. "Yes, Wulf. His NAV is high enough to hear the spirits. And when I taught him, he listened. He's one of the good guys, and he's ready to go up against the SSA and add his voice to ours. The citadel is a safe space."

From the corner of my eye, I notice Aeola flying further up all of a sudden, and for a moment, my heart skips a beat. Has she seen something?

Mihaela shakes her head. "No, no. It's too dangerous. They'll hunt us, make up laws. They'll conscript our children, take them away from us."

My heart grows heavy as I realise how long this has been going on. The Spring Cleaning wasn't an isolated event. I want nothing more than to tell her it'll never happen again. But it will if things don't change. "It'll be different this time. People are more accepting, more willing to learn." I have to believe that. As terrible as Mihaela's future vision is, the possibilities I see have the potential to be wonderful. "It'll be different this time."

"No! It'll never be different enough. Not with all the attacks. They'll blame us for them. Blame those who'll listen to us." Mihaela nods to herself. "We need to take care of our own, take care of the spirits, and hope they'll spare us."

Well, this is disappointing. I glance up at Aeola. With a start, I recognise two other sylphs next to her. Are they bullying Aeola? I can't see from here.

I want to let go of Mihaela's hands, but she clasps mine tightly. "Don't do it, Rika. Let it go. Let the pain pass. You're so young. Live and enjoy your life."

"I can't. Not when spirits and humans suffer for it," I tell her, distracted by my worry for Aeola.

At last, Mihaela loosens her grip. "I'll ask around for the others," she tells me, but her heart's no longer in it. "You take care of yourself."

"I will," I say, already rising from the bench, my face turned upwards. No wind's picked up, which has to be a good sign. It just has to.

Half a minute later, Aeola turns back around and flies towards me, leaving the other sylph behind.

"What was that about?" I ask, not caring about Mihaela sitting on the bench next to me.

"There's trouble at the ball tower. My sisters have rounded up some air spirits," she says, worry hitting my face like a blast.

Quickly, I pull out my shiny new cell phone. Eight missed calls and a bunch of texts. "The TV Tower is under attack."

We waste no time. Mihaela calls after me, but I hardly hear her, retracing my steps as fast as I can, turning away from all this love and care to face battle once more.

4

I arrive at Alexanderplatz half an hour later. A strong wind's blowing newspapers, cardboard bowls, and leaves all over the pavement. The Berlin Television Tower is next to the metro station on the other side of the square. Its massive grey concrete base stands in stark contrast to the spindly metal tower rising above it. The sphere of glass and steel is surrounded by thick clouds. Lightning hits the red rod on top of it repeatedly.

The stairs are blocked by several police cars. Policemen and women are wearing helmets and shields to protect themselves against the debris slung at them. They're not letting anybody through, not even me.

"I'm with them," I say repeatedly, pointing towards the spirit seekers battling wayward sylphs. To my chagrin, I see Robert with his two lackeys there. After he was struck with lightning, I'd hoped he would retire. Though he's suffered more than me, there are no dendritic scars on his arms.

"Where's your staff?" the policewoman asks, pointing out that I brought neither weapon nor armour to this battle.

"I... Lukas!" The blond spirit seeker has just come closer, tracking a sylph by the looks of it. With his brace, he shouldn't even be out here, much less engaging in battle. When his head jerks up in my direction, I tell him, "She already took to the air again."

Lukas groans, but then he grasps my situation and hobbles over. "Let her through. She's one of ours." As soon as I'm past the barricade, he complains, "Where were you?"

"I'm sorry. Next time I'll fly here."

"Good luck in this storm." Then his face goes lax with insecurity. "Is this something where we have to stand back and watch you talk to them?"

Judging by his position on the outskirts, Wulf has already relegated him to watching the action. Perhaps that's why he seems almost eager to have others join him in his suffering. Well, if there's a way to resolve this peacefully, I'm all for it, but even I know that sometimes fighting is all we can do. And talking to sylphs while they fling metal rods and garbage at you can be a tad difficult. "I don't even know the situation."

Lukas rolls his eyes. "It's not that hard. Sylphs attacked the TV tower. A gnome's blocking the door, locking everyone in." He nods over his shoulders. "Wulf is at the entrance."

I want to ask why the gnome is blocking the door, but Lukas wouldn't know, which means I'd better get my ass over there. As I take the stairs, I check with Aeola, "What's this about?"

"The spirits they're hunting are hiding in the tower." Her body is wrapped around my arm to avoid being blown away.

"What about the gnome?"

"Must be Alexander." She lets go and shoots off into the sky. "I'll deal with them," she howls, barely audible in the storm.

"Alex—? Wait!"

The last time Aeola faced her sisters, I had to drive them away or they would've ripped her apart. This time, there's nothing I can do. As Lukas just learnt, I can't fly, and there's nowhere to hide in the tower.

"Rika!" Wulf has noticed me and drags me under one of the giant concrete legs at the base, just seconds before something big slams on the ground where I was just standing. A sign of some sort. "Camille..."

"Already on it!" Camille answers, slicing her staff through the sylph that ambushed me.

It's a good hit. In fact, it's a great hit, with not even a hint of direction from me or Wulf.

Before I can wonder how Camille's improved this much, Wulf brings me up to speed. "Listen. There are people trapped inside. The doors have been slammed shut by a gnome, which would be the least of our problems if there weren't sylphs trapped in the tower as well. Robert wants to break through the stone, but that might bring the whole structure down. Can you talk to the gnome?"

The information rushes to my head. I'm still trying to make sense of it when Robert strides up to us. "Talk to the gnome?" He only notices me then. "What's she doing here? Shouldn't she be in Rome?"

How does he know about Rome? *No! Focus! One problem at a time.*

I leave Robert to Wulf and hurry to the door, where Leon is already trying to talk to the glass. "We don't want to hurt you, and we don't want to hurt the sylphs either. We just want to get the people trapped inside out." As I step up next to him, he lets out a deep breath. "Oh, thank god, you're here. I tried talking, but..."

I put a hand on Leon's back and face the door myself, then the frame on top of it, where the rock has fused with the glass. "Alexander? Is that you?" Of course, the gnome would call himself after the square. Or was the square named after him?

The concrete wall shifts in an unsettling manner and two slightly darker eyes look down at me. "You know me?"

Not really, but I'm slowly piecing the different pieces of information together. "Aeola told me about you. You're... protecting some spirits?" I'm totally guessing here.

Alexander blinks. The concrete shifts some more, and now I can clearly see something like slabs of stone holding the door shut. "A tempest and their babies. Maybe two sylphs. Why?"

So, he really is helping the spirits. I can't wait to unravel this story. But right now, I need him to open the door. "There are people trapped in the tower. Can you let them out?"

"They're safe. The walls won't crack," Alexander tells me, his shape melting into the concrete again, but then he hesitates. "You're Grune's girl, aren't you? The true spirit seeker? Aeola's friend?"

I nod. "Yes, I am. Please, I know they'll be frightened."

"The tempests are frightened, too." He's still hesitating.

"I'll vouch for their safety. No spirit seeker will take their staff to them."

Next to me, Leon stiffens, but after a short moment, he backs me up. "I promise."

Alexander lets out a deep-seated groan. Once again, the rock shifts, but now it's drawing away from the glass. The automation mechanism doesn't work, but the small door next to the main entry gives way easily when Leon pushes the handle.

"Thank you," I whisper to Alexander, though he's already vanished from sight. Then I throw my head back over my shoulder. "Wulf! We're going in."

I see Wulf say something to Robert, whose face darkens in response. Then he walks over to me, activating his headset. "Robert will take over ground control. Camille, Lukas, you stay with him. I'm going up with Rika and Leon." He waves his hand, rushing me forward.

Just as he's about to close the door behind us, Bijan slips in. "I want to see this," the rogue seeker says.

Whether or not Wulf approves I'll never know, because in that moment, the door is bolted shut again.

A trickle of cold sweat runs down my spine. *I'm locked inside a concrete structure. Look up. There's a glass ceiling. Glass. I'm not trapped. I mean I am, but...*

A hand falls onto my shoulder, pulling me out of my panic attack before it really sets in. I turn to stare into Wulf's dark eyes, using his steady hold to even my breathing. He nods encouragingly. "We'll be out soon."

I return his nod, ready to look around. The foyer is milling with people, but no spirits. Many have taken cover. Others are standing in groups, chatting as if this is normal, like they're waiting for the elevator. A few are already accosting Leon, asking when they can leave the building.

"It's too dangerous outside. The police will handle the evacuation," he tells them. "We're here for the spirits."

"The elevator's stuck," someone cries, and I shudder once again. Worst nightmare material right there.

Wulf steps up next to Leon, raising his free hand. "Please, remain calm. You're absolutely safe down here. The storm will pass soon."

Let's hope he's right. The sylphs outside certainly won't negotiate with me.

A minute later, we begin our ascent up the stairs. I'm sure there are at least a thousand steps ahead of us winding around the tower. Safe to say, my legs are already cramping in anticipation.

"So, what's all this about?" Wulf asks, seemingly having enough breath to spare.

"Well..." I huff. "Aeola's sisters... are bullies. They were hunting a tempest... and babies... I mean, their babies. They've taken..." I stop, catching my breath. As distracting as talking might be, it makes it even harder to climb these stairs. "Alexander, the gnome, offered the spirits sanctuary. The sylphs are howling because they can't get to them. That's all I've gathered so far."

"They won't submit to the sylphs," a voice next to me says.

Out of the stairs, a gnome has appeared, somehow flowing up the stairs. He looks like he's taken his cue from the basement of the Television Tower. Where other gnomes are round, he's all edges, topped off with an oversized hat which looks like a slab of concrete. It takes me a moment and Wulf's suddenly tense face to realise that we're flowing up the stairs as well. It's a weird sensation. My feet are definitely stuck to a step, but the step itself is rippling through the others.

"This is marvellous," Bijan exclaims.

In contrast, Wulf's knuckles are white from the effort of not using his staff to stop the stairs from moving.

"Thanks for that," I tell Alexander, rather enjoying the lift. "What do you mean by 'won't submit'?"

"The sylph sisters want every air spirit to submit to their rule. But most of the others don't want to. They're happy the Erlking is gone and they can live their lives freely. The tempest up in the restaurant just had their babies. They don't want another battle. The sylphs neither."

"What about you?" Wulf asks. "Your name's Alexander?"

"You can call me Alex. That's what most Berliners do," the gnome replies, graciously.

I chuckle. "Like the square?"

"Oh, that. I would love to claim that for myself, but they insisted on naming it after that Russian tsar who came to visit. Lovely chap. We laughed about the coincidence. He told me he'd be happy for me to continue guarding the square, and so I did."

"You're..." Wulf stops himself, rubbing his face. "I'll never get used to this."

Bijan leans forward. "What's being said?"

"Not now." Wulf shakes his head. "You don't think you could do something about the stuck elevator?" he asks.

"I guess I could." Alexander faces me. "Be careful up there and remember your promise. Meet me for a coffee when it's all done."

The steps stop moving suddenly, causing us to lurch forward. We're almost at the top with less than fifty stairs ahead of us. Meanwhile, in the shaft next to us, I hear something moving again. The elevator.

"Gnomes drink coffee now?" Wulf asks, eyebrows raised.

"This one does, apparently." I'm as baffled as he is, and a little miffed that after eight years on the streets, I've never met Alexander. "We're almost at the sphere."

We walk past the lowest level with its AC and cooling equipment and head to the first of two visitor levels: the viewing platform. Normally, it's full of people, but they must've evacuated earlier. Clouds obscure the city beneath us, and I take a deep breath after the oppressive concrete walls of the staircase. The relief only lasts for a second before something hard hits the glass. It's gone too fast to see it clearly.

If the sylphs are dragging up heavy things, we're all in dire danger, not just the spirits. I don't know how sturdy the windows are. They might've been built to withstand hail and wind, but not construction debris.

"They're gonna break through." My sentiment's echoed by a small sylph hiding out on the ceiling. She looks so scared her threads have solidified.

"They won't," I tell her despite my own misgivings. "Are the others above?"

"The tempest went crazy," she says, then shudders when something else hits the windows.

I turn around, only to see a long metal pole aimed straight at us.

"To the shaft!" Wulf bellows, pushing us all back into the staircase. Just before the door closes, I see a sudden wind pushing the pole aside. Only the length of it clanks against the windows, leaving the viewing platform intact.

"Aeola." I recognised my friend the instant she appeared.

The little sylph from the platform has joined us in the shaft. "She's been fighting them for a while now. She's so brave."

There's so much adoration in the small spirit I find myself beaming. "Yes, she is." At the same time, I'm worried she'll get hurt. If only there was something I could do. "Where are the tempests?"

"In the restaurant, with all the others." All the others. That doesn't sound good.

Wulf has heard her answer and pushes up ahead to the restaurant platform. When I catch up to him, his face has turned white. "Holy shit."

"What is it?"

"Don't!"

A plate sails through the door, crashing against the wall behind us. At the same time, a wall of panic slams into me. "What's going on?"

"The tempest is on the rampage." Wulf holds the door closed, allowing only the slightest slit for us to peek through.

I'm not sure if the restaurant normally rotates, but the speed of tables swishing by is sickening. Chairs are sliding from one side to the other, while dishes, cups, and glasses are flying in the air. Countless shards are scattered on the ground or creating deadly little whirlwinds. On the ceiling, currents of lightning crackle.

A micro storm mimicking the one outside.

"What do we do?" Leon asks, his face almost as pale as Wulf's.

Wulf takes a moment to think. "We need to break the wind. I'll go first. Once it calms down a little, you follow. Rika—"

"I'm calming the tempest," I say, firmly. The storm they've caused needs to be broken, but I won't let him hurt the spirit, who's clearly already terrified enough.

Wulf regards me for a moment, obviously tempted to object, but then he nods. "Do your magic, but be careful."

That's easier said than done. Though I wait until Wulf's staff has slightly lessened the storm, the rotating restaurant still catches me unaware. I put one foot on the platform and I'm on my bum, gasping in pain as my legs are pulled away under me. A chair hits me in the back. I clasp its legs, using the seat to shield myself from an armada of knives whirling through the air. By then, I'm already past the entrance again, feeling sick.

"You need to get to the other side!" Wulf is suddenly beside me, one arm around my shoulders. He's grabbed a serving plate to guard my face, protecting me against oncoming missiles. "Come on!"

He half drags me across the floor to the windows. On our way, something even faster moving slams into us, leaving behind tingling marks. It's the tempest, running in circles in their panic. They haven't even noticed us.

We make it to the windows before we're hit a second time. On this side, a small strip doesn't move with the room. Because of that, it's cluttered with broken chairs and plates.

"This is the safest space," Wulf says, sounding out of breath. His eyes are wide. He blocks one missile with his makeshift shield and slices his staff through a whirlwind of shards. "I don't think we can stop this without our staffs."

"Well, they won't stop if you attack them!" I shout at him. The panic of the tempest is sinking into me, setting all my nerves on fire.

Wulf looks at me, utterly helpless. "Then what do you want me to do?"

I watch the tempest fly past us, its stormy mane all tangled up in shards. "Nothing," I say, forcing myself to calm down. This isn't my panic. It's theirs. But if I can calm down, maybe they can, too.

With determination, I jump back onto the platform, finding momentary shelter under one of the bolted tables. A cup hits my knees, causing me to cry out in pain. "You need to..." *stop,* I want to shout at the tempest, but they're past me so fast I can't even finish the sentence.

Taking cover under the table, I look for my next chance. All I see is flying debris that'll leave me bruised for weeks.

Calm, Rika. You need to calm down. The tempest is your priority, nothing else.

Closing my eyes, I ignore the slicing pain on my arm and bump against my side. The wind whistles in my ears, but I tell myself to listen.

"I won't let you take them. I'll die before I let you put a breezy hair on my babies," is what I hear when the noise starts to make sense.

"Your babies will be safe," I say into the void. "We're here to protect them. The sylphs won't harm them."

I repeat those sentences again and again, using the repetition to calm my nerves. Each word comes out stronger than before. I ooze calm and confidence into the storm, and slowly, I feel it slacken around me.

Something cold pushes into my face. Startled, I open my eyes.

The tempest is right in front of me, looking at me with their dark, horse-like eyes. Electricity runs through their veins, crackling in their mane, where all the debris has been caught. The storm around us has settled, and the platform has thankfully slowed to a near-stop—it's usual speed.

I reach out, putting my hand against the cold wind. Tiny sparks fly to me, like the current that runs through the fence of a paddock. "You okay?" I ask.

"You're the girl who stood up against the Erlking," they say, breathing on the scars on my arm.

Nodding, I repeat, "I won't let those sylphs harm your babies."

In fact, the clouds outside have lifted enough to let sunlight through the windows. I yearn to find out what's happened to Aeola, but I need to focus on the tempest. They're far from calm, lightning still coursing through their body. My hand strokes the wind while I keep our gazes locked. "Let me help you with these."

I stand up so I can reach their mane, slowly pulling shards out of it. "What's your name?" I ask, to further calm the spirit.

"Flitzer," the tempest answers.

"How fitting. You're very fast."

"The fastest," Flitzer boasts. "The Erlking's fastest steed."

I remember them now. They were the tempest the Erlking fled Central Station with after his original one was destroyed. "You served the Erlking?"

"Never had a choice. He forced himself onto us. Never cared if any of us got hurt."

"He was a tyrant," I agree. Some shards fall to the ground through the tempest's body as they slowly release the tension.

"When you got rid of him, I thought I'd be at peace at last, but then his daughters started demanding my babies as soon as they were born." The tempest lets their head hang. "I don't want them to suffer the same fate."

I look around, trying to find the babies, but I can't see them. "Where are they?"

The moment I ask, the tempest bristles, a wind rising again. It's only then I see Wulf has made it across to where the kitchen is located, its door shut. The tempest raises their head, lightning crackling once more.

"Wulf, don't!" I shout. "Drop the staff!"

Startled, he turns around, letting the staff clatter to the ground. A gust of wind slams into his face, pushing him backwards. Quickly, he rolls for cover behind the bar.

I put my hand on the tempest's flank, trying not to shirk away from the current inside of them. "He wasn't going to hurt them."

"He's one of them!" the spirit whinnies.

"No, he's one of mine. A true spirit seeker." At least, he's on the way to becoming one. "Shall we go to your babies together?"

The tempest calms again, and slowly, we make our way over. Wulf looks at me, the question on his mind clear for me to see. I mouth a "later" and open the door.

Several frightened eyes are looking up at me. About twelve humans, staff and patrons, have sought cover in the kitchen. There must have been some sort of wind in the kitchen as well because it looks like a mess, sauce splattered all over the floor and walls.

"Is it over?" an old lady asks, cowering next to the fridge.

"Yes, you can take the stairs down, just... move slowly." I motion the tempest with me to the side so the people can pass. Their panic makes the tempest shirk a little, but I keep my hand on their flank, and soon, the kitchen is empty.

Just then, a sylph flies down to meet us, dragging two tiny tempests tangled in her hair. "Never, ever again, Flitzer! These two are whirlwinds of the wildest sort!"

"Thanks for taking care of them, Briesa," the tempest says, love oozing out of them as they envelop the two foals.

They come to their parent and tell them all about the fun they had in the kitchen and ask if they can go home now.

"I want you to meet Rika," the tempest says. "She's the human Aeola talked about, the one who'll help spirits where she can. Say hello."

Promptly, the two tempests storm at me, their wind picking up my hair and swishing it into my face. Tiny sparks jump from their manes onto my skin, tickling me. "Are you a nice human? Why are you so solid? Do you like flying? I love the wind. Once, I hit a tree, and it was not happy. Do you want to see my scar?" Their questions and stories are as fast as their parent's run, making me dizzy. But their joy is so infectious I'm laughing, all the tension flowing out of me.

"I would love to fly one day, but I'd prefer not to hit a tree. That's a very impressive scar." The scar is tiny and will probably vanish within days. "I bet the tree looked worse."

One of them bops my nose with his and exclaims loudly, "So warm! Are you a salamander?"

The other lands on my shoulder and snuggles into my cheek. "I like it."

"I like you, too." I catch the second one in my arms and stroke his prickly fur. Sure enough, he purrs.

"This is amazing," a voice says, dripping with awe.

Confused, I turn around. There's Bijan, and he's got his phone out; in front of it, an unfamiliar contraption, which screams Miriam.

"You've been filming me?" The words barely making sense even as I speak them.

"You and the spirit energy. Get ready for fame, Rika. You're going viral."

5

"What do you mean, 'I'm going viral'?" I return the two tempests to their parent and try to catch a glimpse of Bijan's phone.

There I am, talking to thin air. Slowly, the energy reader adds the spirit energy to the video. The resulting red cloud looks nothing close to a tempest, but it becomes very clear that I'm not even an arm's-length away from a spirit, and happy about it.

"You filmed the whole thing?" This could've gone terribly wrong. The tempest could've chosen to ignore or kill me instead.

But Bijan looks excited, his eyes so wide, they're more white than brown. "I did. I expected you to succeed, of course. I mean, I would've loved to film Vesuvius, but this was perfect."

"Perfect for what?" Are they going to study spirits from this recording? They can't even hear what their answers are.

"For our new line of attack," Bijan explains. "We can't sue the SSA, but we can prove to everyone there's a different way. You calming down a wild spirit in full attack mode will turn a lot of heads and kickstart the conversation."

My head is reeling with information. They're going to put this online, making me the figurehead of an anti-SSA movement.

"Don't worry," Bijan grins at me. "We don't need you to be in mortal danger every time. Now that we know Miriam's camera system works, we can try to capture your air spirit or that dryad at the citadel." He turns his gaze back to the recording. "I won't post it directly. We want to process this a bit better, and you need to provide subtitles for the spirit. I can't wait to find out what they said."

Feeling a little helpless, I search for Wulf. His face has darkened throughout the conversation. Now, he steps in. "Perhaps we can put that aside for a moment and concentrate on the active mission."

Right. We've calmed the tempest and evacuated the people trapped in the kitchen. That leaves a bunch of angry sylphs attacking the Television Tower. Only, they aren't.

Sunlight floods the restaurant, making the shards glisten. Outside, several sylphs and other air spirits have assembled, but they're not directing the wind against us. On the contrary, it looks like they're guarding the sphere.

"What's happening out there?" I walk past the debris to the windows, ignoring how they slant outwards so you can see the ground far below.

I search for Aeola and find her flying past the sylphs, nodding to each of them. When she approaches my spot, I knock on the window. I can't hear her through the glass, but she grins almost as wide as Bijan. The message is clear. We've won.

"Robert says the battle's over," Wulf says, stepping up behind me. He keeps a notable distance from the windows, as most sane people probably would. "Let's go meet up with them."

Bijan and Leon have already left the restaurant. Wulf puts a hand on my back and gently leads me to the door. The tempests follow our lead, but once we're on the staircase, they gallop down. I'm glad Wulf and I are taking it more slowly, though I wouldn't complain if we could use the moving step again.

"Are you hurt?" Wulf asks. "You're favouring your left leg."

"My knee was hit." Among many other parts of my body. It'll look lovely tomorrow. "It's just a bruise. How about you?" I throw a glance at him, looking for obvious gashes or similar wounds. Thankfully, there are none.

"I'm good. Great work. Once again." He chuckles lowly. "This'll be one hell of a debrief."

"Are you gonna send a report back to Rome?" I ask, trying not to sound too interested.

Wulf sighs heavily. "I forgot about that."

"You forgot?"

"That I can't just do a normal debrief, write a report, and send it back with the traps. I'm not sure how long they'll even keep me on as a commander." The realisation of all these repercussions seems to dawn on his face only now. And to be fair, I haven't truly considered how this would affect his life and career either.

"Do you think they'll sanction you?" I wish Wulf would just quit, but I guess that's not as easy as it sounds.

He shrugs. "If I were anyone else, I'd probably already been fired, blacklisted, and sued. I mean, I'm the one who released Vesuvius."

"I thought they were going to blame that on me."

"Yeah. And that's exactly it. You're the one they're trying to get rid of, while I..." He shrugs again. "I have no idea what'll happen next. That nothing has happened so far is driving me crazy."

"Understandable." I rub his arm for a split second. Just as with my family, I don't really know where I stand with him at the moment. To gloss over my awkward attempt at comforting him, I return to topic. "I think you should send the report. Exactly as it happened. You can even name me."

Wulf frowns. "You want me to rub it in their noses?"

The longer I think about it the more sense it makes. "Yeah. They chose to turn a blind eye. Let's see how long they can keep it up if my way produces results."

"It hasn't," he says, not sounding that serious. "By SSA standards, a successful mission would result in a package of filled traps. We may have captured one sylph, but that's about it. They'll probably say we got lucky."

"Well, we'll get lucky again. And again. And maybe one day, they won't be able to ignore it."

Wulf's gaze lingers on me for such a long time the dull concrete walls around us become interesting. At last, he sighs. "I guess that's better than this social media campaign Bijan and Miriam have come up with. You're not going to give them permission, right?"

"Why wouldn't I?" To be honest, going public is scary as hell, but what other options do I have? We're almost at ground level, so I stop. "I made a decision in Rome. I'm done running. I want to fight."

Pained, Wulf pulls a face. "It's too dangerous. They're already after you. My father warned us. Do you think he'll stand back and watch you become the face of the pro-spirit movement? As soon as they get wind of this, they'll come for you."

"They're coming for me, anyway. We just don't know how."

"This will force them to act immediately!" He gets more and more agitated. "We just got you back, and you want to put a siren on your head and shout it from the rooftops?" With some effort, he calms himself. "Look." He takes my hand and runs his fingers over my knuckles. "If you lie low for a while, we can make them think they've successfully cowed you. We'll spread the word but quietly."

I listen to his objections patiently, though I wonder whether all this concern is for me or his own hesitation to continue going against his family and the organisation he's dedicated so much of his life to. Either way, it's hard to say no to his pleading eyes. "You're right." Wulf exhales in relief. "I want to shout it from the rooftops. And I will."

A look of dismay passes over his face again. He wants to draw his hand away, but I clasp it in both of mine. It's my turn to plead. Like with the tempest, I try to exude calmness.

"I'm not going to rush into this. Once we're home, I'll sit down with Miriam and Bijan and everyone else ready to make a stand." Whether that includes Wulf is up to him. "The way I see it, the SSA's actively looking for a way to shut me up before I go public. Which means I'll have to go public before they succeed. Once it's out there, doubt will grow. If I suddenly vanish, it'll get noticed. The more people are involved, the harder it'll be for them to stop us."

Wulf winces. "Okay, okay, let's say you get out a few videos and gain some followers. They've got public opinion on their side. You'll be the object of a smear campaign of some sort."

"In that case, I'll tell my *followers*,"—it's such a strange word, as if people are interested in following my lead—"about the SSA. I know it's a 'they-said-she-said' situation and most people won't believe me, but it'll still be worth it. Ideally, we get the SSA investigated. At the very least, my ideas are out there. They'll grow, whether I'm there to see it or not." I'd much rather see it than not.

"You're willing to die or go to prison for this?" It's clear Wulf doesn't agree with either risk.

Weirdly enough, prison scares me more than death. "I'm willing to use my voice. This is bigger than me. Much bigger, and if that's the price for changing the world, so be it."

A hundred emotions are battling on Wulf's face. Then he crushes me against his chest. "Even if you make this job as hard as possible, I'll do everything in my power to protect and support you."

Downstairs, the police are evacuating the people from the foyer. Alexander has left the tower's premises, no longer blocking the door. The spirit seekers have gathered to the side. As far as I can see, only three traps have been filled. As we walk up to them, Robert is berating Camille.

"...let it escape!" He turns to Wulf, pointing at Camille. "I get that your team can't tell a sylph from a smoke ringlet, but she refused to follow my lead. Let a sylph escape right under her nose."

Wulf manages to keep a straight face. "That's unfortunate."

"Unfortunate? It's incompetent. Ever since *she* turned up, your team's been running amok." He glares at me. "I thought the SSA took care of her. Why is she back again?"

It's as if the temperature has dropped a couple of degrees. Wulf takes a step forward, ignoring Robert's personal space. "What do you mean, 'took care of her'?" he asks, sounding awfully chill.

"Didn't you know? Camille picked her up from the streets. She never graduated from the academy. After that fiasco on Teufelsberg, I reported—"

Wulf's staff hits Robert above the ear, sending him flying to the ground. A collective gasp can be heard from all around.

"What the—" Robert turns around to jump at Wulf, but whatever he sees in Wulf's face makes him hesitate. He wets his lips twice. "What was that for?"

Wulf doesn't answer immediately. I can see the muscles in his back bunch up and release again. Then he offers Robert a hand. "For being such an asshole."

Robert must be extremely confused because he takes Wulf's hand and lets himself be pulled up. Wulf draws him close to tell him in a low but no less malicious voice, "You go after my team again, I'll get you transferred to Siberia." He must be really upset to pull his privilege.

He might no longer have that kind of leverage with the SSA board, but Robert isn't aware of that. The East Berlin commander blanches. His eyes find me. "But she can't be part of your team."

"She must be if the SSA received your report and decided to leave her here with us," Wulf explains, sounding more and more strained as he continues. "And since her NAV is higher than yours, you'll listen to her should we ever have to fight together again." His tone makes it clear that Robert better not think about ever leaving his base again.

Slowly, the group dissolves. As Camille walks past me, she says, "I'd keep him if I were you."

Contrary to her, Wulf looks disgruntled. He rubs his neck ruefully. "I shouldn't have lost my temper like that."

"Probably not," I admit. "But if you hadn't, I would've." I should've known that Robert wouldn't keep quiet after I made my stand on Teufelsberg. Getting hit by lightning sadly didn't make him forget everything I'd said and done. Somehow, I'm almost glad Robert's the one who ratted me out. It beats any of the Budapester seekers or Lukas, for sure.

Wulf glances at a point above me. "I'll leave you two alone and wrap up the mission with the police."

While he walks away, I turn to find Aeola hovering above me. Worried, I check her for injuries, but apart from a few tiny shimmers of thinned fabric, there's nothing. "What happened out here?" I ask.

Aeola settles on my shoulder, running her wind through my hair. "I called in a few favours, and together we sent my sisters flying."

"A few favours?"

"When you were gone, I asked around. You know how my father never cared for any of us, and thus, we didn't care for each other. But being with you taught me how important it is to stick together, so I began to search out spirits, talk to them, and find out what they need. That's how I met Alexander and so many more."

I turn to face Aeola, who floats effortlessly from my shoulder to hover in front of me. Her beautiful hair and dress are in constant motion. She looks like she's gotten taller somehow, more confident. There's a strength inside her that wasn't there before.

"I see."

"We don't like bullies," Aeola says. "Human or spirits."

Beneath us, the ground shifts, and for a split-second, it feels like we're in an earthquake. Then, Alexander breaks through the ground, carrying two chipped cups of coffee in his currently giant hands. "I always said we needed to adapt. Live with the humans, not against them." He offers me a cup. "I would've brought you one, too, glimmer, but you don't appreciate the liquidity of coffee enough."

"Did you just call me glimmer?" Aeola asks, trying her best not to sneak a sniff of hot coffee.

"And what's wrong with that?" Alexander prompts. When Aeola doesn't answer, he turns to me. "You did a good job with the tempests. Guess Aeola and Grune have it right. You are a true spirit seeker. Just like that other Alexander."

"The tsar?" It might not even be the wildest thing I've heard today.

There's a crunching sound from Alexander that makes my hairs stand up. "No, that one was okay. Didn't really have much time for spirits. I meant the one they named the university after. The nature guy."

"Alexander von Humboldt?" I ask. That makes a lot more sense.

"That's the one. Lovely chap. Wanted to know all about the different rock types but was more of a dryad guy. Like you, I guess."

"Rika is a sylph girl," Aeola announces, unusually stiff.

Alexander regards her with a measured glance and grumbles, "Alright, alright. Sylph it is."

"I'm an honorary sylph now?" I have no idea how we got here.

Aeola sways as she thinks through the question. "I guess we could call you that."

"Well, glimmers. It was lovely to chat to you," Alexander announces. "I might swing by the citadel later, see if I can catch Grune to discuss the issue with Unter den Linden."

"What's the issue?" Unter den Linden is the grand boulevard running from the Brandenburg Gate to the museum island. It's named after the linden trees planted there.

"The usual. Roots breaking through stone. I just want him to rein in his dryads a bit. Crush you later!" And with that, the ground swallows Alexander again.

"He's a peculiar one, isn't he?" I ask Aeola.

The sylph rolls her eyes. "If you talk to him too long, he'll claim he built Berlin and Coelln with his own bare stones." She shifts a little, looking thoughtful. "Camille's improved quite a bit, hasn't she?"

"How so?" I remember how Camille didn't need a single direction to attack the sylph earlier.

"She saw me. Which was fortunate because she almost got me with her staff. Not that she hit anything today. I think she was actively avoiding catching any spirits. Which means she knew exactly where not to hit."

"So, you were the sylph that got away." I stretch my neck to find Camille.

She's standing with Leon, laughing at a joke. Could it be that her NAV's also improved while I was gone? If I consider everyone, she would be the most likely to improve. But then I remember the little hints Wulf and even Miriam dropped, and I get the sinking feeling that her sudden expertise stems from a different source.

I accost Camille after dinner before she can vanish with Miriam, dragging her away under the guise of girl talk. We walk our usual route around the citadel, enjoying the late-night music of the crickets. The days are so long, it's still light at nine in the evening.

"So, is this about someone starting with the letter W?" Camille asks, her eyes glowing with glee. "He was quite swoon-worthy when he knocked Robert off his feet, wasn't he?"

"He was okay."

Camille raises an eyebrow. "Only okay?"

"I appreciate the gesture, but there are currently other things on my mind." Before Rome, I was ready to throw myself at Wulf, but since then, a million other things have been vying for my attention.

"What other things?" Camille sounds a little disappointed. "You're aware he's head over heels for you, aren't you? If today didn't prove it, going up against his family does."

"Yeah, I wish that had more to do with the spirits than me." I'm almost sure it does.

Camille rolls her eyes. "I'm sure he's in it for the spirits as well, but that's not what gets him out of bed in the morning. Or should I say, off the ground? You two spend the nights together, don't you?"

"We spend the nights sleeping. He's just there to make sure no crazy woman abducts me in the middle of the night." This isn't the time to tell Camille about how I woke up on his chest one day. Since then, I've kept the snuggling to a minimum, which is getting harder each day. "But speaking of spirits..."

"We were?"

"Your NAV has improved," I say bluntly. "What is it now? Close to 400?"

The instant shift in Camille's demeanour tells me everything I need to know. She looks ahead, sucking in her cheeks while straightening her back. "I haven't got around to testing it yet."

I guess I can play along for a while. "Really? I thought Miriam would be all over you, running her tests."

"Miriam has a lot on her hands. She's finally submitted the paper. Now she's finishing up her other thesis chapters. She wants to hand in by the end of August, but I bet she'll be done in July." As Camille leads the conversation astray, her shoulders relax again. "After that comes the defence and everything. She'll have her PhD by the end of the year. Isn't that cool?"

"That's great." Why can't we just have a lovely chat about potential boyfriends and actual girlfriends? "Can you tell me what you did to improve your NAV?"

Camille stops. She still looks ahead, taking a couple of deep breaths. When she turns to me, the smile is gone, replaced by a tense grimace. "What do you mean? Leon's improved much more than me without doing something special. Why aren't you asking him?"

Wow. Someone's getting defensive. "Well, I was just thinking with Lukas wanting to learn and others in the future, it would be good to have a few alternatives. Leon's path doesn't seem to be easily replicable. So..." *Oh gosh, cut it out, Rika. You're just torturing both of you.* "How's your rehab going?"

"How..." Camille's face goes slack. She starts walking again, slowly. "Good. I... Okay, fine." She turns back to face me and leans forward in a whisper. "Listen, Rika. You don't need to worry. I've got it under control."

"Got what under control?"

"You know what." She sighs heavily. "If you have to know, the drugs help me see the spirits. They improve my NAV. I pop one before battle and I don't need an idiot like Robert to tell me what to do. Now, don't tell Wulf!"

"You can't take drugs, Camille!" I step towards her in dismay, but Camille falls back.

"I'm not taking them for fun! The drugs help me do my job. A job I wouldn't have if I hadn't been gaslit into taking it." She huffs, relieved she's finally got it off her chest.

Meanwhile, I try to keep up with her and wrap my head around the whole issue. "What do you mean?"

Camille's calmed a little. "Shouldn't you know? We've all been gaslighted by the SSA. All this training, the indoctrination. I had spirit friendships, like you! And then I assaulted them for years." She throws her hands in the air, blinking tears away.

"So, now you're taking drugs so you can assault them better?" This makes no sense.

Camille stares at me slack-jawed, and I almost feel sorry for her. At last, she catches herself. "You're right. I shouldn't have gone into battle today." She swallows. "I told Wulf I quit, but he won't accept my resignation."

Her revelation pulls the floor out from under my feet. "You did what?"

"That's why he's so grumpy," Camille explains. "I no longer want to be a spirit seeker. After you got kidnapped, I handed in my resignation, but he and Miriam talked me out of it. They're so blind. They think they can advocate for change while still collecting their SSA pay checks. I can't do that. It makes me feel icky." She looks to the side. "So, I started taking them again."

My heart goes out to her. I can see how she could slip back into destructive behaviour after such trauma. To be honest, if I wasn't sure it would make everything worse, I'd turn to drugs or alcohol to forget everything that's happened to me. "And do they know about that?"

Camille shakes her head. "No. And I would appreciate it if you didn't tell them."

"What?" She can't possibly expect me to keep this quiet.

"Rika." Her dark eyes bore into me as she puts her hands on my shoulders. "The last thing Wulf or Miriam need right now is to worry about my well-being. I'm fine. I have it under control. I only take them once in a while in an emergency."

Utterly helpless, I wince. "There'll always be an emergency."

Camille snorts, weirdly amused. "With you around, I agree." She sobers up quickly enough. "I'll stop. As you said, it's highly hypocritical of me to keep fighting spirits. So, without a battle, there's no need for drugs, right?"

For some reason, I don't believe her. What if an Erlking-like spirit attacks us? Can she truly sit back and twiddle her thumbs? "You promise you'll throw them away?"

"Together with the whole SSA," Camille says, and there's a mean edge around her mouth.

She lets go of me while I'm still working through my response and strides away. I follow her through the gate and run into Wulf, carrying his sleeping bag. He looks after her in confusion. "Are you two okay?"

I stare at him, unable to reply. How can he not see what's going on with Camille? Unfortunately, I've just promised her to keep quiet. "Why aren't you accepting her resignation?"

Wulf sighs. "Because I don't think she should be on her own while she's still in rehab."

So, he's really oblivious. The truth hammers against my chest, begging to be released, but I swallow it down. "Even if she quit, you wouldn't throw her out, right?" I mean, I'm still here.

"Of course not. But she'd leave." His forehead creases as he glances over his shoulder towards the door Camille has vanished through. "Her issues won't resolve because she leaves this job... this environment." He scratches the back of his neck. "Call me stupid, but I still believe I can help her. If she sticks around."

Slowly, I'm processing the scope of the problem. Help Camille. I can't tackle her drug problem, but maybe I can help her in a different way. "I might have a plan."

6

Over the next week, I develop a series of training approaches with Miriam, making use of the citadel's virtual reality lab and the frequent spirit guests we now have, thanks to Aeola. Together, we want to find a sure-fire way of improving people's natural attunement. Since it worked so well with Leon, my favoured approach is exposure therapy. And none of the spirits are more happy to oblige than Alexander. There aren't many gnomes in Berlin, which has led to an over-inflated ego that makes him believe he rules the city. Now, he regales us, his loyal subjects, pretty much every day.

One good thing is his inclination to bring food from the various eateries around Alexanderplatz, which has sparked an idea in me. To-day's food of choice is a currywurst. The sausage is lathered in hot sauce, covered by a layer of yellow powder. The smell is so intoxicating Aeola won't part a millimetre from Alexander's arm.

"You want us to share food with... a piece of rock?" Lukas asks, a bowl of leftover rice in hand. His brace is off, and he's eager to get back into shape. Instead, I have him join us.

"Sit!" I wave him down impatiently.

Everyone else—that is Camille, Leon, Henny, and Inga—is already seated, carrying various items from lunch in their laps. Bijan and Miriam are standing nearby, eagerly trying out their new camera gear for the newest YouTube video.

Alexander is cool with it, so cool in fact that he's donned a fashionable black slab hat. All my attempts to explain how the camera will only capture his spirit energy have fallen on deaf ears. Probably because he doesn't have any.

Lukas grumbles to himself as he folds his legs under himself, still tender with the healing one. Louder, he complains, "Do we have to film this?"

"We're only filming Rika's interaction. Ready when you are, Rika," Miriam says, hardly containing her excitement. As with every new project, she's launched herself whole-heartedly into it. So much for being busy with her PhD.

I take a deep breath, trying not to think about how much of this is a performance. If I'd wanted to be an actor, I would've gone for that. *Focus on Alexander! Just treat him as the guest he is.*

"Uhm... Welcome to the Citadel of Spandau." So far, so good. "It's an honour to welcome you... I mean... Can I do it again?" Maybe I should've taken the script Miriam offered to write for me. But then again, that would hardly be natural.

Neither is my stilted approach.

I start again, this time talking freely. "It's nice to see you again, Alexander. How was the trip?" He hates crossing the rivers, especially the Havel.

Unfortunately, Alexander is a much better actor than me. Or at least, he's more passionate. "It was horrendous! An ordeal of immeasurable difficulty." His voice soars dramatically. "I almost drowned crossing that feeble string of metal you call a bridge. Who would've thought of me then? Submerged in water, subjected to the screeching voices of prepubescent nymphs for all of eternity. No one, I tell you! No one! It's with the purest of luck that I've made it here in one piece."

"I am so not going to transcribe that," is all I've got to say to his monologue.

"You'd dare censor me? Hide my true self from the world? Cover it in lichen until all my crystals are dull?" To show his dismay, he crumbles inwardly, his slab-hat drooping.

Massaging the bridge of my nose, I can't even think of a proper answer.

"What's going on?" Lukas asks. "Is he insulting us?"

Cue another dramatic gesture. "Insulting you? I should be the one who's insulted. Why do you bring me such amateurs to work with? He wouldn't see a rock if it hit him in the face."

Suddenly, the ground shifts. Lukas jumps up, howls in pain, and drops his bowl, rice spewing over the ground. Camille and Inga gasp sharply. Only Henny, who can see what's going on, and Leon stay calm. The ground settles again.

"That... that was an attack," Lukas complains, eyes wide open and panting. He must've hurt his leg with his sudden movement.

I glare at Alexander. "Not helpful." Training Lukas is hard enough without spirits playing pranks on him. "Sit, Lukas. He was just messing with you."

Lukas stares at me. "Just... I'll show him what it means to mess with me. Let me get my staff and we'll see who's laughing then."

Annoyed, I get up. "That would probably be Alexander and me, giggling at you trying to beat up thin air. What happened to welcoming spirits with open arms?"

"He attacked us!" Lukas shouts.

"Could you please be quiet?" Camille asks. "You're ruining the video."

She points to where Alexander is lording on his little rock over Leon, who has his head bent while preparing something in his bowl. Curiously, I step closer to watch him foaming a green liquid with some sort of wooden brush. Each movement is so meticulous, so calm, that even Alexander has quieted down. Everyone's watching Leon.

At last, Leon presents his bowl, which is really more a fancy cup, to Alexander, the painted front facing the gnome. Afterwards, he cuts what looks like a gooey white blob with powdered sugar and offers a piece to our guest as well.

"Please accept our offering, kami," Leon says in a velvety voice.

Alexander looks impressed. He has completely forgotten his antics and makes a gravel river to send over his cardboard bowl of currywurst. "I accept your offering if you accept mine, seeker."

Leon looks askance at me, and I translate in a hushed voice, "He wants you to eat some of his."

Once again, Leon bows his head. "Thank you, kami." He picks up the food almost as delicately, using the little wooden fork to pop a piece of sausage into his mouth.

Meanwhile, the green tea gets soaked into the rock while the gooey white thing vanishes as if it's fallen into a crevice. A crunching sound is all I can hear, though that's more Alexander's nature than the consistency of the offered sweet. Slowly, he finds his voice again. "Odd taste, I have to say, but not too bad. Could be a little sweeter. Like a lot."

Chuckling, I decide to paraphrase his answer to Leon. "He likes it a lot."

Leon beams. "I'm glad you do."

"And cut!" Bijan shouts. I completely forgot about the filming. "That was awesome. Way to go, Leon."

The whole group seems to relax at once.

"What was that?" I ask Leon.

"My mother would probably be deeply embarrassed because I made a dozen mistakes, but I thought a tea ceremony would be fitting for today. I'm glad Alexander liked the mochi."

"Oh. Is that what it is?" I ask, looking curiously at the white ball. A dark red paste is visible in the open cut.

Leon cuts off another piece. "You want to try?"

"Yes, please." As I thought, the consistency is nowhere near crunchy, but it's not as sticky as I thought it would be. Just soft with a faint but distinct sweetness, much like a ball of dough but with far less sugar. I like it a lot, but I get how one would only eat it piece by piece instead of stuffing their face with it.

"Did you see him?" I ask Leon once I've finished.

Leon shakes his head but keeps on smiling. "No, but I could feel his presence. Old, steady."

"Who are you calling old here?" Alexander protests. "Just because you're a barely crystallised baby doesn't mean I'm old. I haven't even lived a hundred million years yet."

I can't stay serious. Bursting into laughter, I tell Leon the short version. "You might want to rephrase that old part a bit."

Instantly, Leon flushes. "Oh, no, I didn't mean... Gosh, Alexander, I'm deeply sorry. I didn't mean to insinuate you were old. You're hardly weathered, though I'm sure you've weathered a lot of storms."

"Oh, yes, little nucleus, the stories I could tell you. Have you ever heard of the Great Storm of 1345?" He takes a deep breath, or whatever the equivalent for a rocky gnome is. "The houses were still small then." He stops himself from looking around. "When will I get the rest of my food?"

"Sorry." I check with the others. "Who else wants to share their food with Alexander?"

Lukas snorts. "Mine's already on the ground. Can't he eat it from there?"

Camille groans. "Very polite, Lukas. Why don't you eat from the ground?" She moves forward with her own bowl to where Alexander's rock is. "Where exactly is he?" she asks, but it sounds stilted, and her body position betrays that she already knows the answer.

So much for throwing her drugs away. I cross my arms. "Really, Camille? You took one for training purposes?"

"Shut your mouth, Rika."

I check with Miriam, who frowns at me. We're both distracted by Wulf who's waving me over. I guess now that we've got a video, the group will be fine without me. Henny might not understand what Alexander is saying, but they see enough of him to catch his drift. Some bonding time alone with the spirit might even do them good.

"What's the matter?" I ask Wulf when I catch up with him on his way to the gate. "Is it Eoghan? Have you heard something?"

Wulf shakes his head. "Not yet. But we've got a visitor," he says, pointing to the gate.

My mouth feels dry, while my heart is nearly jumping out of my chest. "Is it... is it them?"

"I don't think so." He opens the first gate, and we step into the darkness of the gatehouse. As promised, the gate is now kept locked all day long. "I might be wrong, but I think this one's for you. In a good way."

Well, now I'm confused. But Wulf doesn't elaborate and opens the door. Three people stand in front of the citadel, all wearing huge backpacks that I know contain their whole life.

They're Travellers.

"Rika Csorba?" The man in front asks. He must be about fifty, tan face, weathered lines. The face of someone who's spent all his life outside. "We saw the video and heard your call."

Over the next few days, more Travellers arrive. Some of them come alone, some bring their entire family. Wulf lets them camp out in the courtyard amongst Grune's trees. Grune accommodates the newcomers by making sure the grass grows soft and green. I don't know any of them, but apparently some are related to me, distant cousins who share some obscure great-grandfather, and others are related to them. Some have seen my videos online, which are being watched by more and more people each day, but all received Mihaela's message. She didn't want to join me, but she passed on my vision, and others have come, some from as far as Romania.

"They're not gonna stay forever, are they?" Lukas asks, barely containing his disgust as he looks around the tent city that's popped up between the young trees. The smoke of half a dozen cooking fires rises in the air.

The Travellers aren't our only guests. Sylphs are hanging out in the air, soaking up every smell as they chat to Aeola, and young dryads play hide and seek with Glut between the trees. And of course, there's Alexander, entertaining the crowd with his wild stories. None of the others can hear him, but a few are able to see his antics, and the gnome doesn't truly mind whether or not they listen.

"They can stay as long as they like," Wulf says, looking almost as grim as Lukas. "We've got enough space."

As usual, a word from Wulf shuts Lukas up immediately. "Sure. Well, if you need me, I'll be in the training room." He must be so glad to finally have the green light again. His gaze flickers to me. "Unless you've got some exposure training planned for this afternoon."

I point towards the Travellers. "Go and expose yourself to the spirits over there. Should I ask one of the sylphs to hang around you?"

Lukas' eyes flit about nervously. "Maybe after I'm done with the physical." With that, he flees towards the safety of the training room. Knowing him, he'll be in there until dinner.

"Have you had any success with his NAV yet?" Wulf asks, mildly interested.

"Miriam retested him two days ago, but nothing substantial." I hesitated when Miriam brought up the NAV tests. I'd much prefer they get used to benevolent spirits without worrying about their numbers, but I've been informed that's not the scientific method. "You're all expecting results too quickly."

Wulf shrugs. "It took Leon less than three weeks to jump from 112 to 250. Now, he's scratching 300."

"Well, it's not a guaranteed process. Look at the Travellers. Many of them are familiar with spirits and respect and value them, but most never cross the 300 barrier. I bet most people who don't notice spirits now will never notice them. No matter the training."

Thoughtfully, Wulf rubs his chin. "So, there is a limit to the potential. Spirit seekers are already scoring high. We can improve their NAV, but we can't raise a troupe of 400-plus people."

"Now, why would you do that?" This sounds suspiciously like the old Wulf.

He leans against the sun-baked wall and looks around. "Well, as much as I appreciate your efforts, the world is still faced with disasters.

Hopefully, we can mitigate most of them, but I still believe spirit seekers are needed. True spirit seekers."

Part of me wants to strangle him, but I force myself to keep my voice calm. "You want to continue to fight."

"We don't have a choice. And before you have a go at me, Grune said the same thing." Wulf pushes himself off the wall. "Remember? A true spirit seeker works together with the spirits in their area, but they also protect that area from spirits who can't be reasoned with. Like Aeola's sisters. If the Erlking reappeared tomorrow, do you think you could get on his good side?"

I guess he has a point there. "He'd kill me before I could try."

"So, yeah. I think the SSA is still needed. Just not how they operate today." Wulf sighs, probably because I'm rolling my eyes. "If we can make them see—"

"I made them see!" Annoyed, I take a step away from him. I just can't with him sometimes. "They know what I'm capable of, and their response was to kill me. I don't know what you think will change that."

Wulf groans now, shaking his head. "Well, giving interviews to regional newspapers won't make them like you any better."

"So, it's my fault now?" The interview request came yesterday after the press got wind of our new spirit hotspot.

He realises his mistake immediately, wringing his hands. "That's not what I said. It's just all this publicity. We're forcing them into a corner. There might be more interviews after this one, and someone will ask the SSA to comment. Ask me to comment. What am I supposed to say if it comes to that? Do you want me to publicly denounce the SSA?"

As he keeps talking, I find myself staring at him. "Yes." It should be a no-brainer. "Why would you defend an organisation run by murderers?"

Wulf swallows heavily. I half expect him to come back with the old "they're my family" but thankfully he leaves out that bit. "Because if I don't, we'll have the Ireland situation everywhere. Politicians will lobby for the SSA presence to be removed, the funds cut, and thousands of spirit seekers will lose their jobs. And then what? We get a flood and thousands of people drown because there's nobody reining in the spirits."

"Except there is!" I shout back. "People like me might be able to calm those waters or ask befriended spirits to help out."

"People like you are damn rare," Wulf replies, and this time, he sounds more desperate than mad. Rubbing his face, he tries a different tune. "I want nothing more than for you to succeed, but there's a mountain ahead of you, and you've only taken a picture of it. Getting rid of the SSA is not a good thing. Look how many of us are on your side once we realised what you could do."

He might have a point. It could be decades until we've rectified our mistakes and established a harmonious relationship between all spirits and humans. We might never get there. "Is getting rid of the SSA board a good thing?" I might sound a little petulant here.

Pain flickers over Wulf's face. "Yes. That would seem necessary."

"Well, they're not gonna do so on their own accord." I decide to cut him some slack and step closer again, running my fingers over his arm. "You said it yourself. The SSA has been steeped in corruption since it formed. You left Rome because you didn't want to get dragged into it. Even if we put enough pressure on your parents to step down, they'll just be replaced with their strawmen. If you want the SSA to survive, it needs to change from the ground up."

He closes his arms around me, pulling me close again. "I know. I'm just worried it'll all go up in flames, and you'll be the first to pay the price. And then everyone else I know," he adds in a low voice.

"New beginnings are always scary," I tell him, trying my best to avoid thinking about the very real danger to myself. "They take some time to straighten out, but it'll be worth it. You'll see."

Wulf says nothing to that, just holds me close and breathes in my hair.

Someone clears their throat. Miriam. "I don't want to interrupt, but a new group has arrived, and they want to meet you, Rika. Also, that interviewer called. They want to come by tomorrow."

Reluctantly, Wulf lets me go. "I'll let you get back to work." As he walks away, he looks somehow lost.

I tear my gaze from his forlorn back to face Miriam. "What do they need me for?" To be honest, everything's been moving so fast it's beginning to scare me. Everyone needs me. Travellers and spirits want to talk to me, Bijan wants me to make a video each day, and I need to train my fellow seekers. I feel like I'm doing all of it and nothing sufficiently.

"One of the men wants to speak with you. Over there." Miriam points to the group of newcomers who are being welcomed by the others.

Every time someone wants to speak to me, I get my hopes up that it's Eoghan. Rory hasn't heard from him all this while, and Henny and I are worried sick. But once again, my hope is dashed. That isn't Eoghan. It's an old man with a beard: a Traveller. Our eyes meet, and I'm running, running until he opens his arms wide, and I fall into his embrace.

"Pavel!" I cry out, tears streaming down my face as I hug the old man close.

His laughter rings in my ear while he closes his arms tight around me. "My little spirit."

It's been over eight years since I last saw him, but he still feels exactly the same. So warm and loving. This is what it should've been like with my mother. That I get from Pavel what I couldn't get from her makes this moment all the sweeter.

He lets go of me only to run his hands over my tear-stained cheeks. I never noticed how short he is, the same size as me. In my memory, he was always taller. "Look at you. What a beautiful young woman you've become."

"I missed you so much!" No matter how much I try, I can't stop crying.

Pavel hugs me once more, stroking my hair. "I thought I'd never see you again. Never stopped looking, always asked about you first."

See? This is what I mean. My mum should've done that. "I was here..." I almost choke on my words. "I was in Berlin all this time."

"But not with family," Pavel says, his thick brows bunching together. "They took you away from us. You and your mother."

I shake my head and step back in an effort to dry my tears. "They tried, but I left the youth home after four months. I've been on the streets until... until I came here. And my mum..." So much for stopping the crying. "The SSA got to her. They've brainwashed her. She works for them. She... she threw everything away. Including me."

Pavel stretches out his hand. "Come, let's talk about it while we walk. I have to pay my respects to Grune."

"You know him?" My fingers grab his as if I were a little child.

"You know I can't grasp spirits like you do," Pavel reminds me, "but his story is well known, and I've always paid my respects to him whenever we came to Berlin."

Hand in hand, we approach the big dryad. As if Grune has sensed us, the leaves are rustling. Moments later, his gentle face appears in the bark. He has the same energy as Pavel, wise and patient.

Pavel's fingers squeeze mine for support as he lowers himself to one knee. "It's an honour to sleep under your branches once more, Grune.

My travels took me far and wide, but I return to you. Here is a gift from the shores of the Volga." He places a handful of seeds at Grune's roots.

Curious as ever, Glut comes close, flames igniting on his back. Before he can interfere, I bend and pick him up. Curled in my arm, his fire is doused.

For a moment, nothing happens, then half of the seeds vanish into the ground. The rest remains untouched. "Those have no place in my forest," Grune says. "I welcome you back, Traveller. May you find shelter and peace under my trees."

It's been years since I've heard those words, so often spoken to my mum. The old greetings make my skin tingle. This, right here, feels right. This is how the world should be. Respect, even if we don't understand each other. Even if we make mistakes, such as bringing a potentially invasive species to a forest.

Pavel collects the remaining seeds and puts them back into his satchel. With my help, he hoists himself up again. "Let's talk about your mother."

"There's nothing to say, really. She made her choice. Voluntarily or not." I stroke Glut's back to keep myself calm.

"Oh, but there's a lot of difference in that." Pavel frowns at me. "You're not cross with her when it's the SSA you should be mad at, are you?"

"I'm plenty mad at the SSA. But she... she almost got me killed." I won't forget it was her who led Dante to me when I first managed to flee his clutches.

Dante. Just thinking about him makes my skin crawl.

Glut picks up on my feelings and turns a little too hot. I use the excuse to avoid Pavel's gaze and put Glut back on the ground. He mewls a little but then finds something new to focus on.

Pavel watches me thoughtfully. "You know, I met your mother around the time she gave birth to you. We didn't always travel together, but she became family that day. You became family."

As long as I can remember, Pavel has always been around in my life.

"I watched you take your first step, and I was there when you fell through the ice in winter and reappeared almost immediately because the nymphs you'd played with in summer brought you back to us."

Whenever that accident happened, it's been wiped from my memory. "That sounds terrible."

"You should've seen Magda. She was beside herself, begging and pleading. That woman loves you more than her own life." Pavel clasps his other hand over our two. "You're the reason she ran, even from her own people. She knew they would come for you as they came for her."

"At the Spring Cleaning?"

Pavel shakes his head. "No, before that. She told me her story one night. She was barely eighteen when she caught the attention of the SSA. Back then, they charmed her with all that knowledge they had. Your mother always wanted to learn all she could about spirits, loved nothing more than to observe them in the wild."

I know that part about her. Some of my fondest memories are of the two of us in some remote area, watching the spirits go about their lives.

"She fell for the recruitment speech. She even loved the lessons, but she had her own ideas, and as she always did, she gathered a little following. People liked her ideas. They listened to her."

"They planned to overhaul the SSA," I finish for him. I've heard the story before. "The SSA stopped them, and my mother ran away. Pregnant." It still baffles me how she could've ever fallen for Dante, even back then.

Pavel nods sadly. "And she's been on the run ever since. Until they caught up to her in Berlin. But your mother didn't just run. As I said, people listened to her, and she told them stories. Much like you're doing now."

"What?" I know so many of my mother's stories, but this is new to me.

The old man smiles. "Yes. The both of you are two peas in a pod, aren't you? The ideas your mother had during her training never left her. She couldn't rail against the SSA, but she could share her vision. She built a network, finding naturally attuned Travellers in all of Europe. That's why they're here, Rika. If Magdaléna Csorba's daughter calls, we come. We're ready to fulfil her vision. Your vision. And our vision."

With tears streaming down my face once again, I hug Pavel as tight as I can.

7

"I've grown up with spirits. It's hard to believe this narrative of dangerous beasts that need to be put down when you watch them living together peacefully in the wild," I find myself telling yet another journalist.

With my spirit infomercials blowing up over the last weeks, the traditional media wants in on the excitement. It's taken a while to convince some of the other Travellers to agree to be photographed, but it's safe to say the conversation has started. People want to hear about how to work with the spirits instead of against them.

Of course, there's a lot of scepticism, but I'm no stranger to that. I leave all direct communication to Bijan and his network while concentrating on the people around me.

"But you do more than that," the journalist asks, checking her notes frequently. "I've heard you've befriended spirits. Is that really true?"

Most of the criticism stems from the lack of natural attunement. A live video will show up as blank to all viewers, and the processing that Miriam does has been accused of being fake. I've been called a madwoman and a conspiracy theorist. Plus, some racial slurs once the news of my background broke. But those are only a few loud voices, and after what I've been through with the SSA, I couldn't care less about them. There are far more who are starting to reconsider what they've been taught.

"Yes. I guess I've always had an advantage because my NAV is so high I can not only see and hear them, but feel their intentions. There's nothing to be scared of when you know the little spirit in front of you just wants to play. And then when I grew up, I made hundreds of acquaintances. Without spirits, I would've died countless times. And yes, some of them are very dear friends to me." They're even family, but that would make me sound even crazier than I already do.

The journalist looks around curiously. "Is there a spirit with us right now?"

"No." Though I can see Aeola playing catch with some of her friends. "They don't really get why we have to talk about it so much. But if you want, I can introduce you to Grune later. He's the dryad who watches over the Grunewald, and sometimes, he blesses us with his presence here at the citadel." He's also the most cooperative spirit to demonstrate that which can't be seen. No one can argue about real and fake when his branches curl gently around my body.

"I would love that."

"Another busy day?" Wulf asks me when we sit down on top of the little tower where I first mingled with Aeola. With so many Travellers camping outside, he no longer sleeps at my side. Instead, we have these long talks away from everyone else.

I lean into his side and sigh. "It'll all be worth it, won't it?"

"I had another call."

Shocked, I sit up again. "From your father?"

Wulf nods, not looking happy. "You've reached them. He saw the videos, saw the coverage. Told me to shut it all down or he can't promise anything."

"How charming." I feel sick to the stomach. I knew this would happen eventually, and it's a good thing that my message has now reached beyond Germany. But Wulf is right; the SSA won't sit around and let me continue. "So, what will he do? You said no, didn't you?"

"I said it's out of my hands. And then he rightfully called me out on it, because it's happening in my SSA base and it's my team who appear in the videos," he adds ruefully.

I would be more impressed if he actually stood up for us. "So?"

Wulf deflates a little. "He said if I can't put a stop to it, he will. And yes, that means firing me and everyone else, throwing everyone out of the citadel and replacing us with a proper team. And then he'll sue me for selling SSA secrets and accuse me of treason. Right after he has you put into prison. Called you a couple of names I will never repeat, and me a traitor to the family I owe my life to."

"But you still said no?" Don't get me wrong. I feel terribly sorry for Wulf. No one should be put between two stools or threatened by their dad like that, but if he caves, this will all be for nothing.

Wulf holds my gaze a little too long before speaking again. "I have until Friday to delete the YouTube channel."

I can't believe it. "Really? After what they've done to me? To you?" I jump up and stride towards the stairs.

"Rika, wait!" He runs after me. "I'm not gonna do it."

"But you didn't tell him that."

"I needed time!" Wulf grabs my arm, finally having caught up to me. "It's not just my decision. Leon's, Lukas', Camille's, and Miriam's lives are also on the line. Plus, all the Traveller people. Henny, Inga, Bijan."

Shaking off his arm, I plunge on ahead. "Yes, yes, you've got responsibilities. So sensible all the time."

"Well, one of us has to be."

I finally stop my descent. In fact, we both stop. Even our breath seems to be caught up in a trance. "You think I'm not being sensible?"

When Wulf averts his eyes, I snort, breaking the spell. I turn away from him and hurry down the rest of the stairs, ignoring his, "Wait! Rika!" shouts.

I storm out of the building, shutting the door in his face—poor bats. They don't deserve my anger. But I can't with Wulf. A sensible person would've known that making deals with murderers is a big fat no-go. Foster parents or not, you don't sell out your beliefs like that.

"Rika!" Wulf calls after me. "Could you please stop running from me? I just want to—"

"Hello, Wulf."

In my anger, I've run past the woman addressing Wulf in a soft but firm voice. She's standing on the path, Lukas behind her, and smiles at Wulf, who's stopped short. "Mamma?"

Oh dear. This isn't good. This isn't good at all.

The woman turns her head and gives me a brilliant white smile. She's beautiful like her daughter, though her features are softer and her hair curlier. "And you must be Marika Csorba, I believe?"

She knows my full name, the one that can't be found on any official document. The anger has evaporated. I feel hot and cold at the same time, but mostly terrified as I walk back to Wulf. "You said they couldn't come here."

His face is full of confusion and a streak of panic, which lets me know she's not here at his invitation. Lukas takes the hint and quietly slips away, getting as much distance between us and him as he can.

Signora Vallesco is still smiling as if she were at some grand gala. She raises both of her hands. "Don't worry. I'm not here to drag anyone back to Rome. Though a visit was sorely missed last time you were in the city," she adds sternly for Wulf, then proceeds to kiss him on the cheeks.

He is still staring at his mother. Slowly, the muscles of his jaw begin working again. "Why are you here?"

"That's best discussed over some coffee, not standing around outside. Why don't we three sit down somewhere quiet?" She puts her arm through Wulf's, expecting him to lead her.

Wulf is so overwhelmed he doesn't even bend his arm for her. "Us three?"

Right. That's my cue to disappear. I know the citadel better than her. I can find a hiding spot. Perhaps Grune will hide me in his tree until she's gone. "You two catch up. I'm on dinner duty today."

"Oh, what are you cooking?" his mother asks, as if we're the best of friends.

I was thinking of opening up some frozen food and throwing it into the oven. If anyone complains, they can cook themselves. That doesn't sound like a good reason to vanish in the kitchen, though. "Uhm... rice. With mushrooms."

"A risotto? How lovely. I'll have to show you my grandmother's recipe." Signora Vallesco shoos me ahead. "Go on! We'll cook together. We can talk then."

Didn't that work splendidly?

"Maybe we should talk in private first?" Wulf says, finally getting over the surprise and trying to save me from this ordeal.

His mother doesn't give up so easily. "Don't be a macho, Wulf. We're going to help Marika cook. Yes, that includes you."

I want to say that Wulf is a much better chef than me, but I'm pretty sure she knows that. It looks like we don't get a choice here. One thing's for sure, though. I'm on chopping duty. No way will this woman get hold of a knife in my vicinity.

Thanks to the beautiful weather outside, the common room is completely deserted. This is as private as it gets in the citadel nowadays. As I'm herded behind the kitchen counter, I eye the possible escape routes. Signora Vallesco might only be a distraction, while the real terror is yet to come.

Either way, she assumes control. "Wulf, you know your kitchen best. I need garlic, broth, white wine, parmesan, arborio rice, and of course, our mushrooms."

Wulf doesn't move. "Mamma, why are you here?"

She shoos him away. "Move, boy. We can talk and work. For how many people are we cooking?" She tries to glance outside at the Travellers. "It's not gonna be all of them in this little kitchen, is it?"

"No, we just cook for ten."

"We'll need a big pan then." Signora Vallesco begins rummaging through the cupboard.

Meanwhile, Wulf and I share a glance. Helplessly, he shrugs, before starting to amass the ingredients.

"Oh, onions. Marika, dear, chop two big ones for me, please?"

"Sure." Is chopping onions part of the new torture program? Maybe instead of psychological terror, it'll be more physical now.

Signora Vallesco sets to rub the biggest pan she can find with garlic while keeping up a constant chatter about this recipe of hers. "It's been given from mother to daughter for countless generations. You can never have too much garlic. It cleanses the palate."

As I peel onions, I dig through her meaningless words for the subtext. They're a family of tradition, doing things always the same way, and now their family has to be cleansed of me. I'm so nervous my knife keeps slipping off the onions, missing my fingers by bare millimetres.

"Oh, darling, you need to hold it like this." Signora Vallesco takes the knife out of my hand—so much for that plan—and curls her fingertips away from the blade. After a few cuts, she groans. "Wulf, this knife isn't properly sharpened. Do you have another?" Aka, this knife is not sharp enough to slit Rika's throat.

He crosses his arms, watching us darkly. "Why don't you tell us why you're really here? I spoke to Father just hours ago."

She hands me back the knife, giving up on the cutting herself. "I know. He told me about it."

"And then what? You hopped onto the next plane?"

"Pretty much." At least, she's honest about it. Without even looking properly, she tells me. "Cut them smaller, please. People don't like big chunks of onions. They stand out too much."

Yep, definitely subtext. Never thought I'd be compared to a big chunk of onion, but apparently, I make people cry now.

Her attention is back on Wulf, her back turned to me and my knife. No, I'm not contemplating murder. I'm not like them. I'm just thinking how absolutely sure of that she must be not to fear me even a little bit.

"This has gone too far. He has gone too far," Signora Vallesco quickly amends. "Giving you an ultimatum? Threatening you like that? I told him he's lost his mind." The cheeriness has gone and so has her need for subtext. "I'm here because I can't stand by while my family is torn apart."

"Oh, yes, evil me, tearing innocent families apart."

Silence stretches in the room, and I notice both of them staring at me. Oh, shoot. Did I say that out loud? My ears are burning. Where's a gnome to swallow you when you need one?

Signora Vallesco clears her throat, now turning back to me. "If I understand correctly, you're a part of this family, are you not? You're my brother's daughter."

What perverted game is this? She can't be serious. "I don't have a father."

"Everyone does." She rolls her eyes. "I never liked mine much either, but that didn't make him go away. You're family, Marika. And I am here for you as much as for my son."

Great. We're playing *that* game. "I'm good, Signora Vallesco. I've got my own family, spirits included." Since I'm already on a path of bluntness, I might as well go all the way.

But Signora Vallesco only smiles. "I've heard that. And I'll be thrilled to see it in action. And please call me Alena, dear."

"What the hell is going on here?" Wulf looks as bewildered as I feel.

"Language, son!" Annoyed, she shakes her head at him. To me, she's much milder. "Are those onions ready? We'll put them in now."

I hand her the board without a word, still trying to make sense of the whole situation. Her husband wants me dead, gone, never existed, but she's already said she doesn't agree. So, what? Does that mean she's open to my ideas? Has she watched my videos and actually seen how peaceful the spirits and I are with each other? Completely without enhancement? I never asked Wulf how high his parents' NAV was, but with two children and Dante in the elite stream, they obviously have some talent.

"Fine." Wulf puts on a terribly fake smile. "Dear Mamma, would you please explain why after weeks of radio silence you decided to come here now and pretend to care for spirits, hours after Pappa threatened to cut me off and make my life a living hell?"

His mother takes a deep breath. "That is exactly why. Don't you think that this has been blown completely out of proportion? Your father threatening you. You being completely insubordinate from one day to the other, sneaking around Europe, going rogue? And a daughter of the Antonellis almost killed instead of welcomed?"

I give her props for that. At least, she's acknowledging the murder attempts instead of brushing them off as misunderstandings.

Alena shakes her head in dismay. "This family suffered a terrible loss less than four months ago. What would Piero say if he could see us like this? Is this what he died for?"

No. He died over the insane idea of capturing strong spirits so the SSA could make them even stronger and sow terror and chaos in the rest of Europe.

"He'd probably make some jokes and then look at us with his puppy dog eyes once he realised how real this is," Wulf says in such a dejected voice, I want to hug him.

Instead, I watch his mother do that. "Yes, he would," she whispers, tears glistening in her eyes.

So much for being part of this family. I feel like an intruder. If this were my family, I should be grieving with them. But Piero is the one behind the spirit-pollution programme. And no matter what Wulf or Carina say about his noble vision, it would've never got this far without him. Even if they weren't used against humans, it would've still torn spirit communities apart. So yeah, not that I wish the guy dead, but he certainly didn't make my list of people to mourn.

The two in front of me are hurting because of it, though. I keep forgetting that before I knew him, Wulf had just lost a brother. He succeeds so well in putting that pain on the backburner for my sake.

"The onions are cooking," I find myself saying, suddenly eager to cook this stupid risotto.

Alena comes over to take a look. "They're frying, dear. Let's put the rice in. Check on the broth for me, won't you? Wulf, you can grate the parmesan."

The broth is already on the stove. A giant pot of slowly simmering liquid. "It's not boiling yet."

"Well, hopefully it does soon." For a few minutes, the only talk is about the correct cooking of the risotto. When it's at the stage where every so often a ladle of broth is added until it evaporates, Alena looks at the both of us. "The biannual conference in Brussels is coming up," she says almost carefully.

"What conference?" I ask, checking with Wulf.

"It's like a spirit seeker convention," Wulf explains, his arms crossed. "Mostly research reports from the labs and a training camp."

His mother is a little more forthcoming. "It's the only time after our training at the academy many of us come together. It's a chance to compare notes, revive old friendships, make new connections. We also hold the general meeting, which decides the course of the agency for the next two years. And usually, some European Union delegates join us and gather input for their policies or advise on ours."

"I wasn't planning on going," Wulf says, which is a surprise to me. I thought he'd be all over this event. He could have mentioned it, at least.

"I noticed when I checked the participant list," Alena uses her scolding tone again. "Well, I thought we could use the conference to come together on neutral ground. You, us, Marika, the rest of your team if you want to include them. We need to straighten things out. I don't want to see this family fall apart." She takes a deep breath, using the time to add another ladle of broth to the rice. "Also, I'd like to have you as a speaker."

Next to me, Wulf sighs deeply. "To talk about what? Vesuvius?"

"About the challenges of spirit seeking in the 21st century," his mother answers. She's obviously put some thought into this. "You're our most decorated active spirit seeker. And yes, you've completed some spectacular missions, but I leave it up to you which ones you want to include as examples. People want to hear from you, Wulf. I'll lose my organiser position if I can't get a talk out of you."

Then she looks at me. "And I want to invite you as well."

"What? To the conference?" *No, Rika, to a pool party.*

"As a speaker. The programme is pretty full, but if I shift a few things around, I can fit you in."

I still don't get it. "Why would you invite me?"

"Because you offer a different perspective." Wulf's mother looks at me incredulously. "I've watched your videos. You've got a lot to say that should be of great interest to our active seekers. Some might even already know who you are. I want this programme to be as comprehensive and diverse as it can be. Don't you think your ideas are of international importance?"

I feel heady with the way she puts it. Yes, I wanted to spread the word, but "of international importance" sounds way too grand. And yet, it's exactly what I need. This is an enormous chance. Too big a chance to come from the centre of the rat's nest. Why would the SSA want to give me the stage? Is this what Wulf's mother meant when she said she wanted to bring the family together? Including me?

Wulf notices my rising panic and slips a calming hand on my back. "We'll think about it."

His mother doesn't stay the night. She leaves right after dinner, forcing Wulf to drive her to the airport. Despite the loads of risotto, only the team who's supposed to be here has eaten with us. Henny and the two rogue spirit seekers have stayed out of sight for the entire evening. The risotto itself is annoyingly divine. Oh well, I've got the recipe now. The SSA has stolen so much from me, I might as well steal their risotto recipe.

By the time Wulf comes back, I still haven't decided what to make of the offer. He sits next to me at Grune's tree and sighs. This afternoon and evening have been exhausting for both of us. Next to me, Glut is already asleep.

"This can't be a genuine request, can it?" I ask him, biting my thumbnail. After growing so nicely for a few weeks, I've nibbled my nails down again in the last hour.

"I think it is." He sounds even more surprised than me. "We talked in the car. She's not quite sure what to make of it, but believes I wouldn't follow your lead if there wasn't some merit to it. She's taking a chance on you."

"Against your father's will."

Wulf groans, tipping his head back. "According to my mum, he's calmed down. I've yet to hear from him, though. Not that he ever apologises. Usually, he sulks for a few days and then pretends it never happened."

I don't know what to say to that, so I keep quiet. Apparently, we're back to humanising his parents and defending their decisions.

"I think you should do it," he says.

"Why? Won't they all tear me apart?" We all know how this usually goes.

Wulf turns to me, looking tired. "This is a conference not a cage match." He grabs my hand and squeezes my fingers. "Think about the chance she's giving you. You can talk to thousands of spirit seekers, make them see spirits the way you do. We do," he adds belatedly. "This is where we can actually change things. The proper way."

I draw my hand away. "Oh, the proper way. I forgot. We have to be sensible."

"Rika, please. Don't throw this away. I'm not saying you should stop everything else, just consider adding it to your strategy. Contrary to your avid follower base, the spirit seekers will understand what you're telling them. A good lot of them will even see it with their own two eyes." He gets to his feet, hiding his rejected hand in his pocket. "Just think about what you could do."

I don't give him an answer, and he's too tired to wait for one. With a sigh, he bids me goodnight and leaves. I watch him go with a sour taste in my mouth. His words make too much sense to be ignored, but the prospect of entering a conference full of spirit seekers scares me. No security, no buffer, just me and the SSA. How on Earth is that supposed to work out well?

8

After the first panic-filled night and a few talks with the others, I'm convinced the conference is too good a chance to pass up. It's risky, but if I can reach even a few spirit seekers, it'll be worth it. The problem is, I've never made a speech in my entire life. Fortunately, I've got a few experts around to help. Miriam, Leon, Henny, and Camille have joined me in the lab to work on my presentation. While the others are jumping at the chance, Camille has crossed her arms and glowers at the huge whiteboard that has 'Rika's Pro-Spirit Talk' in bold letters at the top.

"Did Wulf's mum say anything about the content of your talk? I assume she doesn't want you to be too provocative?" Miriam asks, seemingly ignoring Camille's death glare.

Alena has enthusiastically added me to the programme. If she's playing a game, she's a better actor than Alexander. "No. She said she doesn't want to give me any kind of direction. I know best what I want to talk about. She just wants me to give her a title ASAP, so she can amend the programme."

Miriam scoffs. "Titles are the worst."

"I can brainstorm some," Camille offers. "'How the SSA gaslights everyone'. 'Why the SSA should be burnt to the ground'." She huffs. "Sorry, but I still think we should stay far away."

We have that in common. "I have to do it. It's our best chance."

Camille shakes her head but seems to accept it for now. "If you think so. Well, before we get to titles, we should consider the content first."

"Yes. Let's think this through." Miriam taps her chin for a moment, then turns to the whiteboard. "If we don't have any limitations, we should make this as powerful as we can. What's our main message?"

Before Camille can spew more vitriol, I say, "That we need to work with the spirits instead of fighting them."

Miriam puts down the notes. Working with spirits. No fighting. "Okay, so, we need an introduction, a few examples and proof of concept, and a rallying conclusion. How much time do you have?"

"Fifty minutes. But there's supposed to be time for discussion." Whatever that means.

Miriam nods sagely. "That's always the case. Let's try to keep our talk to thirty-five minutes. There's probably going to be a lot of discussion, but we need to get our ideas out first."

"You think people will argue with me?"

"A discussion is standard for every talk. People will have questions, allowing you to go into more detail. We'll prepare extra slides, just in case." Miriam looks more excited than she has in days. "This is going to be fun."

"Fun?" My life is on the line. The future of this planet is on the line. Nothing about that screams fun to me.

"Yes! Brand-new theories are the best. People will get their undies twisted trying to find faults in it, and there will be loads of discussion, leading to all these new theories. They'll probably ask you to write a paper on it."

Camille steps in at that point. "Miri, not everyone's a scientist. Let's get Rika through the talk first. Alive."

I appreciate the sentiment. This whole talk of presentations, slides, discussions, and scientific papers almost wants me to call Wulf's mother and cancel. But no. I'm not giving her that satisfaction. I may have no degree to my name, but I will give this talk, and it'll do the job.

"So, introduction, what does that mean? Remember, I've never given a presentation in my life." There's nothing that can be done about that, but I can talk. I just need to know the rules.

Miriam has a new idea. "Once we have your slides ready, you'll practise with Lukas and me. He's brilliant at giving talks."

Oh, dear, as if this couldn't get any worse. Now I'm getting our resident A-student on my case. "Okay. Whatever it takes."

Camille pats my arm and stares into my eyes. "We'll all be there to support you."

"That's right. And I can also practise with you," Henny says. "I'm quite good at this as well."

"Thank you!" I say, almost too quickly.

Everyone chuckles, and the tension eases. Then Miriam sits down for a moment, leaving her whiteboard behind. "Okay, so this is how I'm envisioning your presentation. In your introduction, you'll show some of the data that indicates how spirit activity has grown in the last hundred and fifty years. Don't worry, I'll take care of the graphs. There's a link between industrialisation and spirit activity, which supports your theory about why spirits are so angry. This angle is important because it's both scientifically supported and frames a major problem: spirit activity will continue to rise and what we're doing isn't working."

So far, so good. I know talking to the spirit seekers will be different from social media. Basically, I have to picture them as a bunch of Wulfs, all eager to protect humanity from further disasters. "Is there a way to put the concept of true spirit seekers in?"

"No." Miriam shakes her head. "I mean, I'd avoid the term. It's too confrontational. You're basically telling them they're all frauds. But we'll use what we learnt in Ireland, put a couple of historical examples and stories in that show there are alternative ways of dealing with spirits, and link it back to our theory that the damage we've been doing to nature has led to our current problems, so if we respect and protect nature, we might be able to revert the process."

"But that's bigger than the spirit seekers," I protest. "We need every human to take care of our planet if we want to curb the destruction."

Miriam nods. "Yes, I know, but you need something big to lead into the boring section of your talk. It's not really *boring*, but there's usually a lot of data representation that only becomes interesting again when you draw your conclusion. So, that part is where we put your personal examples in. Maybe let's start with the NAV barriers. This way, you can sneakily establish yourself as an expert. We have to be careful not to become too personal, otherwise we'll get the same feedback as online, that it's all made-up. Because we have one major problem: no one's able to back you up. In science, that's huge. Results need to be replicable, and because of the NAV barriers, we can't do that here. You're the only one above 500."

Leon raises his hand. "Do we need to, though? I mean, I'm happy to serve as an example for Rika. You've got my NAV tests. If there's one thing that'll bring spirit seekers around, it's the potential to improve our NAV. Take Lukas. He's only putting up with spirits, so he can be better at fighting them."

"Which is exactly why he doesn't improve," I point out.

"So, what's my problem, then?" Camille asks provocatively. "Because as nice as your progress is, Leon, if it's not replicable, it's useless. You might just be an anomaly."

"I think we're drifting off-course a little," Miriam says, looking at Camille worriedly. "Including Leon's success will be a major drawcard, he's right. The spirit seekers will want to sign up for your method, whether that includes talking to spirits or not."

Camille scoffs. "Only Rika has no method. My NAV is still the same. However, there's one thing that helps."

"Yeah, I'm not going to tell people to take drugs," I mutter, then bite my tongue.

Of course, everyone heard me. Camille is glaring at me, while Miriam frowns. She looks at me, then at Camille. "What does she mean?"

"Nothing," Camille says, a little too fast. "What Rika is referring to is Bealtaine, and how my misstep there resulted in a NAV elevation. As bad as it sounds, the drugs helped."

On the other side of the table, I see Henny squinting.

"Assuming you weren't hallucinating," I reply tartly. I'm furious she'd continue to lie even now, and my resolve to guard her secret is teetering.

Miriam is still irritated. "Right. Well, even if that worked, we have no data that it'd be replicable."

Flippantly, Camille replies, "We could try it out."

"Camille!" I'm aghast.

And so is Miriam. "You can't seriously be joking about this!"

"Well, I took some weed," Henny says, in an attempt to defuse the tension. "At home. But it never made a difference."

Unfortunately, that only fuels Camille. "How would you know? Your NAV's always been high, and you haven't exactly been tested under the influence. Or am I wrong?"

"Stop it!" Miriam cries. "This isn't funny! No drugs. And no talk of drugs." She's huffing while everyone looks down.

Camille and I share a look and keep our mouths shut. It's Henny who apologises. "Sorry. Let's get back to the talk."

"Yeah," Camille chimes in, easing up. "What's the conclusion?"

Miriam has lost her passion for the project, though. "That communicating with spirits will offer an alternative to fighting. It has a better track result, and it might mitigate future events."

Camille puts her hand on Miriam's, looking deep into her eyes. "Then how about this title? 'Ending the War Against Nature — how communicating with spirits can prevent future disasters'."

"That's perfect," Miriam whispers and smiles.

Crisis averted. For now, at least.

Henny, Leon, and I stroll out of the lab soon after to leave the other two alone. It's another warm day, and the Traveller camp is bustling. Camille's secret weighs heavily on me, so heavy that I consider confiding in Henny and Leon. But just as I've built up the courage to do so, Henny asks, "So, are we going to include anything about Piero Vallesco's project and the polluted spirits?"

I shake my head. "I'd love to stir that pot of shit, but I want to get the spirit seekers on my side, and I can't do that if I set the whole agency on fire." I sigh. It sucks that we have to play nice with the SSA to get results. I guess that's what Wulf calls being sensible.

"Eoghan is still missing," Henny points out.

"I know." The SSA obviously has something to do with it, and the thought frightens me more than it should. I grab their hand. "We'll get to the bottom of that in Brussels. Talk or no talk. You're coming, right?"

Henny nods. "Oh, I'm coming! I'm gonna make sure I'm seen out and proud. Good luck, getting rid of my voice. Besides, I worked on the polluted spirits problem. Should it come up, I can back you up." A shadow passes over their face. "I'm still mad they used me for it. And mad at myself that I didn't ask the right questions."

"You're asking them now." I can't fault Henny for being tricked into doing the groundwork for the SSA. They never knew better until I came along. "Will the others be there?"

"Probably. The conference is mandatory for year two and three. There's usually a poster exhibition for academy students only. I was actually working on mine before you came. Never finished it, though."

"What was it on?"

Henny pulls a face. "Combining spirit remnants. Purely theoretical, of course. Yeah, I want to burn it as well."

"The maths is still interesting," Leon says. "What if it could be the basis to restore spirits?"

"With other spirits' body parts?" I ask.

His eyes widen. "No. We'd have to find an alternative, of course. Something equivalent in energy. Maybe like a prosthetic wood for the holes in a dryad. It's just a quick idea."

"Would that be possible?" Healing spirits is probably even more provocative than talking to them. "If it works, we could reverse some of the damage caused."

Leon shrugs. "It's just an idea."

"A brilliant idea."

"Agreed," Henny says. "If my maths can be used for that, I'm all in. Is this just a quickfire idea, or do you *have* a plan?"

"It was actually Inga who came up with it." Leon scratches his head. "You know how nature will eventually regrow, just as spirits will, but there are things we can do to speed the process along. It might start with a prosthetic or... Hey, how about transplants? What if Grune gifted parts of his wood to other dryads? Instead of making staffs, he could be making lungs. Symbolically speaking. We'd just have to find a way to transplant them. With maths."

Henny grins. "With maths."

"Go!" I push both of them back to the lab. "Get working on those ideas. This could be huge when we talk to other spirits." I'm literally buzzing with excitement. This could change everything. "I'll even learn maths if this works."

Leon laughs. "You're on!"

I'm glad Henny's in a better mood. I wish there's something I could do to find out what happened to Eoghan, but our best shot lies in Brussels. Hopefully, he's not rotting in a cell in Rome.

As I stroll over to the Traveller camp, I allow myself to dream a little. What if we went to Brussels, and my presentation was actually well received? Yes, the SSA leadership wants me to shut up. Or at least a part of them do. But from the many spirit seekers I've met in the last half year, most of them came around. They're not bad people. They've just all been taught the same lies. Even Wulf's mother seemed open to what I had to say. And as promised, she got his father to stop the whole ultimatum idea.

I find Pavel sitting in Grune's shade, Glut warming his lap. There's no sign of Aeola. These last weeks, she's been out and about so much, we've barely had time to talk. That'll be another good thing about going to Brussels. Her and me, back on the road again, off to change some spirit seekers' minds.

"Hey," I say to Pavel as I sit beside him. I still can't believe he's back in my life.

"Hey, little spirit." He's been whittling again. Now he shows me the little figurine and turns it in the sun. "Does this look like Alexander?"

I can definitely see some resemblance. Considering Pavel is carving the spirits solely from my description, he's doing a pretty good job. But... "He wouldn't be caught dead in those clothes. The hat is far too small."

Pavel laughs. "Oh well, another try, then."

"Sorry."

"No, no, I wouldn't want to insult him. We all know he's quite vocal." Pavel nudges my side.

"He's aggravating," Grune chimes in, his thick branches aching. "Takes himself too seriously. Can you believe he tried to talk me out of Berlin? I would get the woods, but he claims the city. As if he built it with his own rocks. He didn't even move here until the fifteenth century."

It's hard to keep a straight face. If someone takes himself too seriously, it's Grune. Alexander is cocky, but he's also fun. "I like his flamboyant nature."

"A gnome should be more settled."

"I like you even more, if that helps." I snuggle into the wood and feel it give way behind me. Then I notice Pavel watching me. "What is it?"

He smiles. "You look happy. Content." I feel myself flush. "This is who you are. One with nature. My little spirit." But then a shadow passes over his face. "Are you sure going to Brussels is the right way?" He puts his whittling away and squeezes my hand.

"It's a huge chance to make things happen." I nudge Glut. "I hope you'll tell Vesuvius all about it." The salamander lights up with the responsibility.

Pavel sighs. "I'm frightened for you. We already lost you once, twice after what I've heard. If anything, the SSA is ruthless."

His words bring back the fear I've managed to stuff down deep inside. "Wulf says it's changing. Or that it can change." I'm not sure

I believe that as well, but I'll try to get as many spirit seekers out as I can. "When I was at the academy, I met some students, and there's potential for change." I think of Tiago and how he didn't even want to fight. Learning how to communicate with spirits might be a welcome alternative for him.

Pavel nods and squeezes my hand. "Your mother always believed that, too. But look at her. Trapped and lost to us."

"I'd rather die than end up like her." The words are out before I can stop them. They leave a slimy taste on my lips, but they're true.

Pain flashes in Pavel's eyes. "And that would be a huge tragedy. This world needs people like you. Alive."

I put my other hand on top of his. "And it needs me to speak up. There won't be a chance like this ever again."

He takes a deep breath and exhales softly. "You may be right about that. And whatever your decision will be, you won't go alone. I can't speak for all of us, but I'll travel to Brussels with you. Your family will always stand behind you."

Without a word, I put my arms around his neck and squeeze him tight. "I'll make you proud."

"You already have, little spirit. You already have."

9

Three weeks later, in the middle of July, we arrive in Brussels on a warm summer day. The city is bursting with tourists, all attracted by the quaint little houses, cobbled streets, and delicious food. Our bus takes us past the modern buildings housing the EU commission and parliament, the sprawling parks, an *actual* palace, and housefronts painted with bold-coloured comic strips.

The SSA has organised hotel rooms near the conference centre for us, courtesy of Wulf's family. I expected some run-down little hostel in a dark backstreet, but the bus parks in front of a spacious lobby with liveried footmen and a carpet on the street. They attend to our luggage before we've even stepped out of the bus.

"Bachmann, Wulf," Wulf tells the prim lady at the check-in. "Berlin delegation."

Delegation. That sounds fancy.

"Wulf?" a voice rings through the hall. A woman, half a head smaller than me, comes to our group, her eyes wide with joy. "Haven't seen you in a while."

"Louise." The two embrace. "How have you been?"

"Good, good. I can't wait for your presentation. Read the mission report about Vesuvius, of course, but I want to hear everything!"

Awkward. Looks like Vesuvius' escape at the beginning of June hasn't been made public yet.

Wulf doesn't even wince. He smiles and nods. "You'll hear all about it."

"Let's have a drink tonight." Then she sees another spirit seeker. "Hey, Hakan! Look who I found."

A man who was sitting in one of the red armchairs raises his head in confusion. Once he sees Wulf, though, he jumps out of it and strolls over. "If it isn't Wulf Bachmann, the volcano slayer." The two men clasp hands. "How are you?"

Oh boy, this is going to be a long week. Fortunately for the rest of us, the receptionist has found our keys, each with names attached. Most of us are sharing, but like Wulf's key, mine is for a single room, and I don't know how to feel about it. I don't like being singled out, especially if I don't know whether it's a gesture of goodwill, a bribe, or a way to get me alone.

"Here's your key, volcano slayer." I pass the chip card to Wulf in a rare moment he isn't shaking someone's hand.

The repeated title makes him wince at last. He grabs the card and somehow my fingers with it. "Sorry. And thanks. I'll... I'll see you later?"

"If you manage to leave your fan club behind."

"Have some respect," Hakan shouts after me with a wide grin. "The man's a legend."

Knowing how much Wulf hates being called that, I throw him a look of pity. "See you later, Wulf."

"Your team?" I hear Louise ask. Then I'm out of earshot and in the elevator with the others.

"This is going to be our reality for the next week, isn't it?" I'd almost forgotten how revered Wulf was in the SSA. Everybody adores him.

Lukas snorts. "He's the best spirit seeker of this generation. What did you expect?"

"Not you, too." With the whole town full of spirit seekers, he won't be able to set a foot in front of the house without being surrounded.

"I'm surprised you didn't stay with him, Luke," Leon teases. "I thought you'd soak it all up."

Lukas scrunches up his nose, and the rest of us laugh. It's just our core team now. Henny, Inga, and Bijan have taken up rooms of their own somewhere in town, while the Travellers are sorting their own accommodation. As for the spirits, they're doing their best to stay out of sight.

"Wow." There's no other way to describe the sight of the floor when the elevator doors open.

The corridor is wider than my room in the citadel. There are plants every few metres and seating opportunities, as if it's expected people will hang out outside of their rooms. The lights could've been stolen straight out of a baroque castle, full of playful detail. But none of that compares to the luxury that awaits me when I set foot in my room.

Room is the wrong word. This is a whole flat with a bedroom almost as big as our common room, and a round bathtub that could sit at least five people. The bed is big enough to sleep a whole family, an appropriate size for the massive TV on the opposite wall. Fresh flowers decorate every flat surface. A pitcher with lemon water and assorted snacks welcome me officially.

I dump my sorry little backpack on a chair near the massive wardrobe and turn around in wonder. After eight years on the streets, my room at the citadel was pure luxury, but this? This is a whole other world.

A low whistle brings me out of my dream-like state. I stride over to the floor-to-ceiling windows and open the door to the balcony, greeting Aeola. "There you are. Have you been seen?"

"I don't think so." A fresh breeze lifts the light curtains behind me.

Instead of bidding her in, I step out on the balcony. We're up high enough that I can see the beautiful spire of the old town hall. The Grand Place is probably less than five minutes from here. "It's beautiful up here."

"Tell me about it!" Aeola giggles. "Do you want to know how the food is?"

"I only have to sniff you to know you've already sampled some."

"The waffles are delicious," Aeola protests.

I breathe in the sweet smell of baked goods. "Seems like it."

"You should have some."

"Don't be greedy," I tease her. "I will. Can't go to Brussels without tasting a waffle, right? Or chocolate. Or beer." I'll probably skip the last one, but Lukas will be all over it if Dublin was any indication.

Aeola flies into my suite and explores the space. "Are you gonna sleep here tonight?"

I study the huge bed. "It would be impolite not to. And the balcony isn't really an option." While it looks perfectly safe, it's a little too high for my comfort. "If you can't find me tomorrow, I've got lost in the bed."

Before it comes to that, though, the others pick me up for registration.

"Why do you get such a big room?" Lukas complains.

"Come on," Leon interjects, "ours isn't bad."

"Yeah, but we've got to share, and it's not a suite like this." Lukas strolls into my room without asking. "Who's paying for all of this?"

His gaze finds mine and he pales a little. "Well, at least, you're getting some sort of reparation."

I roll my eyes at him. "Yeah, they've definitely upgraded the accommodation from last time." Just thinking about the stale and lightless room at the academy makes my stomach turn. This might still be a prison, but one I could actually bear spending time in. If I don't drown in the unnecessary luxury. "I bet Wulf's is bigger."

Of course, Wulf chooses that very moment to come out of his room, which is opposite mine. He looks through the open door into my suite. "Probably about the same." He smirks, picks up his staff, and closes the door behind him. "Ready to check out the conference space?"

"Should we take the service stairs?" I ask, trying to keep my face straight. Meanwhile, Lukas leaves my room and I close the door.

Wulf winces. "Don't tempt me."

Together, we get into the elevator. Miriam and Camille are standing in the back, whispering and giggling. The sound makes me happier than I thought it would. Camille might not have wanted to come, but now that we're here, she seems more relaxed than in all our time at the citadel. Maybe this trip will be good for them. Give both of them a break.

Luck is not on Wulf's side, and a few spirit seekers join us on the way down, each of them recognising Wulf. Not everyone embraces him, but the way their eyes light up, they probably can't believe their luck to see the legend in the flesh. Wulf smiles through it, but I can see how it's beginning to tire him. As soon as we leave the elevator, he grabs my arm and whispers, "Definitely service stairs next time."

I laugh out loud. "You can skip warm-up then."

It's the first time since his mother's visit that we're laughing together. Wulf puts an arm around my shoulders and points his staff down the street. "Have you ever been to Brussels? Or is this the first time I can show you around someplace?"

"It's not my fault you skipped Rome." I will most certainly not put another foot in that city. "But no, I haven't been. Aeola's already tasted the waffles for me, so I expect you to bring me to the best vendor."

Wulf bursts into laughter. "As you wish. We're skipping dinner for waffles."

"Who cares about waffles?" Lukas complains, calling out over his shoulder. "We're doing a craft beer tour."

"Without us," Camille says, her face a bit tense. "Miri and I will do our own tour. No beers."

Miriam slings her arms around Camille and kisses her on the cheek. "I've got a much better idea of how to seduce you. No alcohol needed."

Leon scoffs jokingly. "Oh, please. You just need to ask Camille, bat your eyelashes, and she's seduced."

"Watch where you're going!" Camille shouts.

Laughing, the guys keep walking. I turn to Wulf at the same time as he faces me, and for a moment, it feels like the world stands still. Maybe I can convince him for a private tour as well.

He clears his throat, and we spend the rest of the short walk to the conference centre in meaningless chatter. Wulf points out the various sights, most of them museums or old buildings that housed something important some time ago.

Then we climb Mont des Arts, passing the first of the many gardens we saw on our way to the hotel. A fountain sprays water into the air. Some musicians are giving an impromptu concert, drawing a little crowd. My face is stretched in a perpetual grin, as always when I experience a new place. I could almost pretend I'm here of my own free will.

On top of the hill, we get a pretty view of the park and the quarter around Grand Place. Wulf points out the central sights we can see, and talks about where the best eateries are.

"Don't," I chide him. "I'll be too hungry to suffer through registration."

He chuckles. "It only takes a minute, unless there's a huge queue."

"I'm sure we could use your celebrity bonus to skip the queue," I say, which earns me a poke between the ribs.

"Let's get it over with then." Wulf nods over his shoulder where a glass cube rises from a lower level. "There's the convention centre."

I could've guessed that judging by the amount of armoured spirit seekers entering and leaving the building. "Where are the rooms?" I ask.

"Underground. It's a massive space. One of the auditoriums seats a thousand people or more," he explains as we stroll over.

A thousand people. Surely, there won't be that many spirit seekers in attendance—or worse, at my talk. "Is that where we have to give the talks?"

"Depends." Wulf shrugs. "I have to, but I think yours is in the Silver Hall. That's only for two or three hundred."

"Two or three hundred people? I think I'm going to be sick." Yes, I wanted to talk to the spirit seekers, but giving my very first presentation in front of so many strangers? Why can't I just do little focus groups?

Wulf snorts. "Your videos are watched by nearly a million people."

"Yeah, but I'm not present when they watch them." That's a world of difference.

"You're going to be fine." He takes his arm away. "So far, you've captivated everyone."

Before I can complain that it only worked for one-on-one meetings, Wulf gets swarmed by a group of academy students, asking for autographs. I wait patiently on the side, while the others go ahead. A private sightseeing tour seems unlikely. At least not this close to the conference venue.

Wulf looks exhausted when he finally gets out of the throng. "Sorry about that."

"You have to give the fans what they want."

"They're not my—"

"Wulf!" And another session of joyful reunions begins. It's not even funny anymore.

When we finally enter the glass complex, the good mood from our walk has entirely evaporated. We ride the escalator, trying not to notice the frequent pointing and waving, as we slowly descend into the underground space.

I expected the worst when Wulf said the conference was mostly under the earth, but it's spacious and airy here. At least the entry hall is. Spirit seekers are going in and out or standing together in little groups talking. I see quite a few staffs, but most of them haven't bothered bringing their weapons. They're probably quite bothersome in the lecture theatres.

Surprisingly, we manage to get in front of the registration desk without further interruptions, and each receive a woollen bag with info material and our badges. Looks like I'm going to be Marika Csorba for the week. It's better than Marika Antonelli, I guess, and shudder at the thought.

"Is that an ancient staff?" The registration person asks Wulf. "Can I touch it?"

"Yeah, but don't tell anyone else."

The lad glows as he runs his fingers over the wood. "It feels so different."

"That's what a whole dryad does for you," I find myself saying with the biggest fake smile.

Confusion spreads across the young man's face. "What?"

Wulf takes my arm and turns me away from the table. "Let's not spoil all our exciting news beforehand."

As far as I'm concerned, I'm not going to say a single word about dryad wood in my presentation. There just isn't any space. I don't even know why I had to say it now.

Yet another call rings out. "Wulfie?"

Okay, that's a new one. I have to remember this. "Wulfie?"

This time, Wulf's face brightens. He lets go of my arm and embraces a buff spirit seeker with short-cropped blond hair. Their embrace is so hearty I know this isn't another fan.

"Miro." Wulf grins at the other man, then looks behind him, where a young woman stands, carrying one young child in front of her while holding the hand of a little blond girl. "Is that..."

The spirit seeker named Miro puts an arm around Wulf's shoulders, turning him away from me. I doubt he even noticed that we were together. "That's my wife, the beautiful Manya," he says with a distinct Russian accent.

The woman smiles at Wulf and says. "Good to finally meet you, Wulf."

Then Miro bends down and picks up the little girl, who squeals at her daddy's attention. "This is Katina, and the little sleepyhead is our Yelena." He says something in Russian to the little girl, and she shyly waves at Wulf.

"Priyatno s Vami poznakomit'sya," Wulf says, his tongue almost breaking around each word.

Miro pulls a face. "Eww, Wulfie! Have you forgotten everything I taught you?"

"Most of it. It just doesn't come up very often." Wulf chuckles.

"That's because you never visit." Then Miro finally notices me standing next to the group. He regards me with a puzzled look. "Did you want something?"

Remembering my presence, Wulf takes a step back to include me in the little circle. "Oh, that's Rika. She's... uhm..."

I'm curious about how he's going to introduce me to his friend.

Wulf seems to have trouble deciding, stalling for a few awkward seconds. Before he can come up with an answer, someone new joins us, and this time I know who it is.

"That's Wulf's newest infatuation," a familiar cutting voice says. Carina saunters over, positioning herself next to Miro with no care for his wife. "His little spirit girl."

"Well, better infatuated with me than with murderers." I didn't think I could top my fake smile from the registration desk, but I manage.

Poor Manya frowns, probably thinking she misheard. Miro looks from Wulf to Carina, and then me. "What?"

"Carina," Wulf says, his voice cold as ice. Good. At least, he hasn't forgotten how she betrayed us.

Miro groans. "Are you two fighting again?" He looks at me, slowly piecing things together. "Wait, are you Wulfie's girlfriend?"

We both say "no" at the same time, to which Carina snorts audibly.

"Okay, stop." Miro obviously has no patience for this drama. "What's going on?"

Carina crosses her arms, challenging Wulf with a glare. She obviously doesn't believe he'll come out with the truth in front of this guy.

But Carina's interference has hardened Wulf's features. "Rika's part of my team. She's a civilian consultant with an NAV of 512. Rika, this is Miro, our official number two, and the leader of Russia's spirit seekers."

"All of Russia?" I ask at the same time as Miro repeats, "512?" We stare at each other. I'd thought all spirit seekers were allocated to cities, but apparently that's not true in all countries.

"Civilian consultant," Carina scoffs. "You might as well call her a rogue at this point. You don't want to know what she did in Rome," she says to Miro, putting a hand on his arm. "Don't admire her too much. Her attitude will disappoint you. Her skills as well."

Okay. I'm out. Without a word, I turn around and walk away. If I don't, I might throw something at Carina.

"Rika!" Wulf comes running after me and makes me stop. Behind him, I can see Carina talking to Miro while his wife stands nearby, looking lost. "I'm sorry. Carina is completely out of line."

"What did you expect?" Worse, what did I expect? That I wouldn't run into a Vallesco on this conference? "I need to take a walk. Outside."

Wulf looks worried, but he nods eagerly. "Sure. Do you want me to join you?"

I watch Miro and Carina over his shoulder. The Russian spirit seeker is frowning now. Concentrating on Wulf again, I shake my head. "No, you go spend time with your friend. He seems nice." And it will probably be the last time Miro won't glare at me, now that Carina's getting to him. "At least save his wife from Carina. She probably wants to leave." It annoys me that his sister doesn't even seem to notice how abrasive her behaviour is.

"You gonna be okay?" Wulf seems reluctant to leave, and my anger loses its edge.

I sigh. "I'll be fine with fresh air and sunlight."

Suddenly, Wulf takes a step forward and pulls me close. He strokes my hair and smiles sadly. "She's got one thing right. You are my spirit girl."

My cheeks flush bright red. Hastily, I step back from him. There are too many eyes around us for such intimacy now. "Don't forget my waffles." I turn around and hurry away. By the time I've reached the escalator, Wulf has rejoined the little group, causing Carina to gesticulate wildly.

Why did I ever think coming here was a good idea? This week will be Rome reloaded. If not worse.

10

Being outside makes me feel instantly better. I exit the glass cube on the lower level and keep walking until my feet carry me to a huge park with wide lawns and neatly arranged trees in front of the Royal Palace. The trees were definitely not dryad-chosen, but the fresh air does wonders for me and I can finally breathe again. Even better, there's not a single staff in sight among the tourists strolling over the sand-coloured paths.

I make my way to a beautiful fountain that looks like a lily of water spouting from a lake. The water is level with the ground, so there's nothing to sit on. Instead, I crouch down and run my fingertips through the water. A soft wind sends ripples flying over the surface, and I look up to see Aeola floating near me. In the glistening sun, she's almost invisible.

"Why are you sad?" Aeola asks, picking up on my feelings.

Shrugging, I stare into the water instead. "It's Wulf." I keep my voice low to avoid attracting attention. "He belongs here. Everyone loves him and looks up to him, and though he says he hates it, he totally blossoms. He walks straighter, smiles more, and is incredibly patient with all their silly demands. I think I'm afraid he missed this."

"What do you mean?" Aeola settles a bit closer, so the wind picks up some of my strands of hair. "Is it bad?"

"It could be." My stomach cramps at the thought of Wulf. At seeing him with his friends, the ones who call him Wulfie. "Well, what if he thinks he's made a mistake? What if he goes back to them?" The danger was always there. As horrible as the Vallescos have been to me, they saved his life. "I can't do this without him."

Aeola snuggles close, cooling the air around me. "Yes, you can."

"But I don't want to." Losing Wulf means more than just losing his support. His word means something to the SSA, but I could battle on without that, leave the SSA behind, and focus on people not already indoctrinated by their war propaganda. It's *him* I don't want to lose. The way he believes in me. I felt safe on his arm when we walked over here, and I wish that could be every day.

"When are you gonna tell him?" Aeola whispers after a while.

I don't know why I haven't already. Before my kidnapping, I was ready to tell him how I feel. I'm even more sure now, but with everything going on, the timing's never seemed right. And recently, he's been withdrawing when the rest of us forge ahead. "When I'm a hundred per cent sure he won't choose the SSA over me." And not only for me, but for everything I stand for.

"Rika?" a familiar voice calls from behind me.

I turn and my mood lightens instantly. There's Rory, waving at me from a short distance. Next to him is a second figure. A little taller, hair more red, even though most of is hidden under a baseball cap.

"Eoghan!" I'm so elated to see him I fall into his arms instead of Rory's.

A fact Rory comments on straight away. "Okay, I'm getting a little jealous here."

I let go of Eoghan and gasp at him. "It's just..." Interrupting myself, I give Rory a hug. "Hi Rory. It's so nice to see you." But I keep turning back to Eoghan. "We thought you were dead."

Rory's little brother looks sheepishly at me. "I might've been."

"What happened? Henny's worried sick about you."

"Are they?" Eoghan asks. "Are they here, too?"

I nod. "Yes, I can call them. They're staying at a hostel somewhere in the city to avoid... well, you know who."

Eoghan's face darkens. "Yeah."

Rory loops his arm with mine and flashes me a smile. "Let's walk. Wouldn't want anyone to listen in." Then he gives the air beside me a nod. "Hello, Aeola. It's a pleasure to feel you blowing here. Especially on this hot summer day."

"Hello, Rory." Aeola makes sure she gives him an extra breeze.

"So, what happened? You went all radio silence on us," I complain, and nudge Rory. "You didn't say anything either."

Rory gives me an apologetic smile. "It was complicated. He got stopped by the police at the airport. I got Aileen on his case right away, but he's not an Irish citizen, so she couldn't actually do much for him."

"I only got released to British authorities a week ago," Eoghan says, looking dark.

"So, they kept you there for no reason?" This is horrible. Not as horrible as believing he was dead, but nonetheless.

Eoghan winces. "It was a flimsy charge. Battery, though I never hurt anyone, and aiding a dangerous fugitive. Piece of advice: never return to Italy."

A chill runs down my back. "Didn't exactly plan to." Looks like I was lucky to leave Italy by train so quickly. Dangerous fugitive does not bode well for my future. With a start, I realise that's what my mother was for so many years. "Maybe I should pick up travelling again."

"We won't let them take you," Rory assures me. "Remember, if you ever need a safe haven, Ireland will grant you amnesty. And we can get you there by boat or kelpie." He grins a little. "You'd find some spirit to take you."

"Let's hope it doesn't come to that." The warm afternoon has become cold to me, so I'm eager to change topics. "How's your wife?"

"Wife?" Eoghan asks, looking affronted.

Rory groans. "We're not married! She's talking about Liffey, the nymph that runs the Liffey River. We're... bonded."

"For life." I need this little silliness. Anything to shoo the dark thoughts away.

Rory gives me a death glare. "She's fine. Thanks for asking. She also sends her greetings. I updated her on what you're up to, and she's very pleased. If you ever need the help of a nymph, she's happy to put in a good wave for you."

"Aww." At least I've got all these spirits supporting me. Hopefully that means the SSA can't just come and pick me up in a raid like they did with my mother. "Well, send her my regards as well. May her waters always run clean." Then I lower my voice. "So, are you registered for this conference or are you here incognito?"

Rory laughs. "Eoghan certainly is."

"I did think about strolling into one of their big talks and telling them my truth, though," Eoghan says grimly.

"You're welcome to come to mine. Then I won't have to speak." It's one of the first talks, tomorrow, right at lunchtime.

Rory smiles warmly at me. "You're gonna be fine, Rika. And yes, I'm representing Dublin, and I'll be at your talk, supporting you."

"There's Alexander," Aeola points out.

We've walked back into the pedestrian zone in the city centre, sharing the streets with hundreds of tourists. A lot of them are taking pictures of the bronze statue of a little boy peeing into the fountain below. What their photos don't show is the gnome, who's trying to fashion himself after the iconic statue. He doesn't truly succeed though, being all edges where the Manneken Pis is chubby and round.

Aeola flies to him and alerts him to our presence. A moment later, the earth rumbles slightly, causing some sharp gasps, and Alexander pops out in front of us.

Eoghan immediately takes a step back. "Woah!"

"Took you some time," Alexander greets me. He turns to regard the statue. "I really don't know why they're making such a fuss about him. I mean look at that. All these costumes created for a lifeless statue emulating the waste production of humankind, and what do I get? A filthy sticker." He turns around to show me said sticker, proudly grazing his backside with the words 'Best currywurst in town'. As he does so, he finds something between his crevices. "Oh, fries. You want one?"

"No, thanks." I'm not eating some cold French fries out of his body crevice.

"Your loss," the gnome announces, crunching down on the fries.

I clear my throat to distract myself from the awful gnashing sound. "So, guys, this is Alexander. The patron gnome of Berlin Alexander-platz, which is not named after him, but he'll tell you lots of stories about the Alexanders he knew."

Eoghan stares at me, then the gnome. "I still can't get over the fact you can talk to them."

Rory, on the other hand, bows his head. "It's a pleasure to make your acquaintance. I'm Rory Mac Carthaigh or McCarthy, servant to the Liffey nymph."

Alexander stares up at him, squinting against the sun. "Yeah, you seem like a wetfinger boy."

"His fingers are perfectly dry," I find myself saying, making both brothers raise their eyebrows. I shake my head. "Don't ask. He's very opinionated for a gnome."

"How many gnomes have you talked to lately?" Alexander protests. He moves away from the crowd. "Come on, I'll introduce you to the locals. You'll get some opinions, then."

He's right about that. The first gnome, who jumps out of one of the cartoon murals to meet us, accosts us straight away. "Tell your spirit seeker friends we don't want them here. This is our city." She's a fierce little gnome who barely reaches my knee but makes up for it with jagged edges all over her surface.

"If I do that, they'll come looking for you," I tell her. Not to mention they wouldn't respect her wish. "They're only here for a week."

The gnome grumbles. "A week too long. What are you talking about? How to destroy and rob us of our treasures even more effectively?"

That describes it pretty well. "Well, some are... exchanging battle experiences. But that's not all. I'm giving a talk about positive spirit relationships, for example." And I'm pretty much the only one who will. "I'm sorry. We're trying to change things, but it's an uphill battle."

"Rika's right. We're trying our best, but it's a slow process," Rory adds.

The gnome sizes me up. "Wait. You're Rika. We've heard of you."

"Really?"

"Yes, because I told you about her!" Alexander snarls. He leans over to me. "Seriously, these gnomes don't have their gravels right."

The Belgian gnome gnashes her teeth and rolls her eyes 360 degrees. "I heard of her before that. The Earth whispers her name."

There can be only one reason the Earth would do that: Vesuvius. He's been tracking my progress. "Again, I'm sorry about the danger to you. If there's anything I can do to help..."

The gnome shakes her head. "No need. We can take care of each other. The spirit seekers won't see a single one of us." She shows me her glittering teeth. "This is our city. They won't get a part of it."

I exchange a confused look with Rory, but it doesn't seem like he has any idea, either. Then again, his understanding of spirits is still patchy. "How?"

"Because of the gnome parliament, of course." She rolls her eyes again, as if that should've been clear to me.

"There's a gnome parliament?" This is the first time I've heard of spirits organising themselves.

The gnome grows a few inches with pride. "Well, what do you take us for? Uncivilised rock grinders? The Gnomian Union regulates all spirit matters in Brussels and beyond. We have a well-functioning defence system that'll protect every spirit in our territory and hide them underground if necessary. As I said, your friends won't see any of us."

"Did you know that?" I ask Rory, impressed by the level of organisation and care for spirits who can't protect themselves that easily.

"La Senne, the river nymph, said the city was run by gnomes, but no. I had no idea what that meant." He laughs. "That's amazing. Is there any possibility we could sit in on one of your sessions...?"

"Madeline," the gnome offers. "And I fear not. While your curiosity may be sincere, we have very strict security protocols."

"Understandable."

Next to him, Eoghan clears his throat. Since he can't hear the spirits, the whole conversation must've been incredibly confusing for him. "If you don't mind, I'd like to pay Henny a visit. You said you've got their number?"

"Sure." I take out my phone and pull it up. Eoghan copies it into his equally new phone, and I send Henny a quick message that he's alive and well and in Brussels.

The phone rings the very next second. "Is it true? Did you find him? Is he there?"

"I'll pass you on." I hand my phone to Eoghan and watch him light up as he listens to Henny's worried questions. Then I return my attention to the gnomes. "You'll have to tell me more about this parliament." In my mind, I see countless opportunities. Spirits definitely talk to each other, but here they're organised. How many humans would dismiss negotiations with spirits because they see them as too foreign to comprehend? But a gnome parliament? That's something people can work with.

Madeline checks the cracks on her wrist. "I'd love to, but I've got a plenary session in five. You can put in your petition with any of the town's statues or murals. We'll get to it in time. Welcome to Brussels, Rika! Enjoy your stay."

"Thanks," I say, but the gnome has already vanished between the cobblestones.

"She's a feisty one, isn't she?" Alexander say dreamily. "I wouldn't mind sharing some fresh-cut rock with her."

Oh dear, a love-struck gnome. "She's pretty great. Sharp edges all around."

Alexander winks at me. "You know it. Well, catch you later, softies." And off he goes to harass Manneken Pis some more.

Rory and I are both stunned for a minute, then we break out laughing. "I never knew gnomes were so..." he looks for the appropriate word to describe the insanity of it all, "...human?"

"Well, they're ancient, so perhaps humans amuse them. You know, change it up a little every few thousand years." Of all spirits, I assume gnomes and salamanders are least affected by our hazardous effect on the planet. They were here long before us, and they'll be here long after we're gone.

Eoghan returns my phone. "I'm going to meet Henny and the others downtown. You coming?"

Rory nods, but I say, "I'd better get back to the hotel. We were planning to go out later." If Wulf still remembers.

"You want me to accompany you?" Rory asks.

I shake my head. "It's just around the corner, I think."

"I'll see you at your talk tomorrow," Rory says, then pulls me into a hug. "Take care."

"You too. Especially you!" I tell Eoghan, embracing him as well.

Thanks to Aeola, I find my way back to the hotel in no time. She wisely flies out of sight before we enter the street, though. Most spirit seekers can't see her, but there are too many elite seekers in town to risk it.

I don't see anyone from my team in the lobby, only groups of old friends and freshly made acquaintances. Watching the spirit seekers chat and laugh with each other makes them seem so awfully normal. So much so, even, that a part of me longs to be part of this community. But I know if I were to tell them about the Gnomian Union that runs the city, they'd grab their staffs and smash up all the statues in a heartbeat.

I'm deep in my thoughts as I wait for the elevator to come down when someone steps up next to me. "Hello, Rika."

The velvety voice causes my skin to break out in hives and accelerates my heartbeat. My throat constricts painfully and little beads of sweat form under my hairline.

Next to me, Dante looks immaculate in his expensive suit and Italian shoes. "I was hoping to have a chat with you."

I stare at him for three seconds. Meanwhile, the elevator arrives and the others waiting with me are pushing in. I am so not going to be stuck in a small box with the man who was the only visitor to my cell for weeks. Never mind the other thing.

Instead of stepping inside, I locate the staircase and bolt for it. *Run, Rika. Run fast.*

Behind me, I hear the door opening and closing before I even reach the first flight. "Rika, wait."

Yeah, sure. Not in your wildest dreams, Dante.

"I just want to talk." His steps are following me, gaining on me.

I keep running. Dante's talks are usually built to mess with my mind, and I'm not letting him do that to me ever again. Unfortunately, my foot gets caught on a step, and the next moment, my knee hits the edge above it. Pain shoots up my leg, cutting through the cloud of panic in my head.

"Are you okay?" Dante has caught up, extending a hand to me.

"I'm fine!" My voice is shaking as I bat away his hand and pull myself up on the railing.

He's got me cornered now. I stare at him, breathing hard, and pushing the throbbing pain in my knee to the back of my mind. *Think, Rika. You can't let him catch you again.*

But Dante raises his hands. "I'm not going to hurt you. I only wanted to talk."

He doesn't get that talking makes it worse. I'm sure my throat has swollen almost completely shut. My whole body is shaking, my hands gripping the railing so tight I might break it off.

"You must know I had no idea you were my daughter."

I gasp. "I don't have a father!" Yes! Words are good. Words are something I can count on to carry me through this ordeal.

Dante sighs. "I understand why you'd feel that way."

"No, you don't! My mother had all kinds of lovers. Sometimes many at once. Your chances are pretty slim. Anyone could be my father." I know he and my mother were in love during their time at the academy, but I want to hurt him. Anything to get away from him. Because one thing is for sure, I *am not* looking for a daughter-father relationship with the man who tried to murder me.

"Rika. The timing matches perfectly, and she had only one lover back then. We wanted to marry."

Is that supposed to make me all warm and fuzzy? My mother marrying a psychopath? Surely not. "You might have wanted to do that, but not my mum. She probably had a few on the side. She left you after all, didn't she?" Despite all my lashing out at him, the shaking gets stronger with each second. I need to escape him, fast.

"She didn't leave me," Dante stresses. "I helped her escape."

"And then you helped get her caught. And you kidnapped and tortured your daughter. Not to mention trying to murder me." Great. Now I've called myself his daughter as well. I can't think when I've been this frightened.

Pain flashes across Dante's face. He extends a hand and lets it hover way too close to my cheek. "I would've never done that had I known."

Once again, I stare at him, letting his words sink under my skin. "Do you want a pat on the back for that?" For a moment, my shaking subsides a little while my heart rate slows. "If anything, that makes you even worse."

"Rika..."

"You're fine murdering people, unless you're related to them. What a great guy. You want to get waffles, Daddy?" My face stretches painfully into a grimace. I don't think it's even a vague resemblance of a smile.

Dante pales a little, and for the first time, he doesn't look completely in control of this situation. He even shifts his weight backwards a little. That's my opening. I turn sideways and continue my mad dash up the stairs. Dante calls after me, but I don't stop, even though each movement of my knee is excruciatingly painful.

My panic-ridden mind refuses to acknowledge that there are no footsteps behind me. I run up all eight floors until I reach the corridor leading to my apartment. By then, I'm soaked in sweat and panting like a dog. At any moment, the elevator will open behind me, and Dante will step out. My hand fumbles with the card in the door. I can already hear the ping. He'll force himself into my room and lock me in there.

Finally, the door opens, and I all but fall inside and slam it shut behind me. Slowly, I back up, watching the door, waiting for the dreaded knock, knowing I'm trapped now.

And there it is.

"Rika?"

11

It's a female voice. Camille.

I have to tell myself that for at least a minute before I manage to inhale again. It sounds like I'm choking.

"Are you okay? Can I come in?" She knocks again. "I'm worried about you."

I'm worried about myself. My body's functions are irregular, as if my heart rate's all over the place. I can't breathe properly, making my head swim, and there's sweat running down my arms and back, but I'm freezing.

"Rika?"

Concentrating on Camille's voice, I take one step and then another. Slowly, I make it to the door. My hand touches the handle, and I freeze. What if it's a trap? What if this isn't really Camille? Or what if she's opening the door for Dante?

Get a grip, Rika! That doesn't even make sense.

With a sudden jerk, I open the door. Camille has her hand raised as if to knock again, but now she stares at me. I'm panting. Then she takes a step in and envelops me in her arms without second-guessing.

"You're shivering."

"Clo... could you close the door, please." Does my voice always sound this fragile?

Camille pushes the door shut. She takes my hand and pulls me into the bathroom. "What happened?" She takes one of the wash cloths, soaks it in the sink, and uses it to dab my forehead.

The cool touch gives me something to focus on. I sigh deeply and sink down onto the closed toilet seat. Camille pours me a glass of water and helps me drink it in small sips. Slowly, my body shifts into its normal rhythm.

Kneeling in front of me, Camille looks at me with worry in her eyes. "What happened to you?" she asks again, stroking the side of my head.

I take a couple of minutes to sort my thoughts enough to string them into something coherent. "I met Dante. He's here. In this hotel." Oh gosh! Dante is staying in this hotel, probably with the entire Vallesco family. They're all here. And that's probably how they planned it all along, by booking us these luxurious rooms.

"Hey, hey, Rika, breathe!" Camille's cupping my face now, forcing me to look into her eyes. Together, we breathe in silence. "There, that's better." She lowers her hands until she can grab mine. "Listen. From now on, one of us will always be with you when you leave this room. You'll never be alone. We won't let him close. I don't think he'll dare do anything right here in the middle of the conference, but we'll be vigilant."

Her promises help. I almost believe her, but then I was kidnapped from the middle of the citadel, and none of them ever noticed. "I... I need to tell you something."

"Of course. You can tell me anything."

I nod. Even so, it takes me a couple of attempts to actually follow through. "Dante isn't just a total piece of shit. Apparently, he's..." I've already said it once today. Why stop now?

Wulf and I never told the others what we'd learned in Rome. I wasn't ready for the questions. I'm not sure I am now, but Camille's rocking back on her feet, waiting for me to speak the blasted words.

"Apparently, Dante was my mother's boyfriend at the time she got pregnant."

"He's your father?" Camille's directness cuts straight through my overly complex explanation. "Wow. Does that make Wulf your...?"

"Nothing," I say promptly. "He's the foster son of Dante's sister, and I didn't even know him until March this year. So, this makes him exactly nothing. Just as the rest of the family is nothing to me." Oh dear. Contrary to Wulf, Carina actually is my cousin. And she knows it, too. "I'm going to be sick."

For the last few weeks, I've managed to push all this away from me, but now it's caught up. There's no way I can ignore all these implications with them hovering around me.

"At least, he decided to draw the line there. No killing family members, apparently," I quip, bordering on hysterical.

Camille winces. "Well, that's encouraging. He must be a good man, after all."

A short chuckle escapes my lips, and I instantly feel better. It means the world to me that we're on the same page.

More seriously, Camille says, "It's encouraging that he won't try to murder you here. I know what's been done to you is inexcusable, but that's one less thing to worry about."

Another knock sounds on the door. Camille and I tense up. Is that Dante now? She gets up and half closes the bathroom door. I hold my breath until I hear her say, "Wulf."

"I assume Rika's here?" He sounds so happy. It appears unnatural after what's happened.

Camille leans backward, catching my eye. "Can Wulf come in?"

I look a mess. My clothes are soaked with sweat, and I don't even want to see my face. But Wulf has seen me looking worse. I doubt it matters much to him. "Sure. Why not?"

Wulf enters my suite. There's a bounce in his step and a lightness in his voice that clashes with the whole gloom and doom I've got going on. "Did you have a chance to meet some people? I saw the Varga brothers on the way here. They're staying at a hotel a few roads down if you want to catch up with them later. In any case, how hungry are you?"

I step out of the bathroom in all my sweat-stained glory. "I'm pretty sure I've lost my appetite."

He doesn't get it immediately, although Camille's glaring at him. His eyes run over my face, taking it all in. "Are you sick?"

"I certainly feel queasy." Gosh, how slow is he today?

Camille loses her patience. "Rika was just accosted by Dante, here in the hotel."

Wulf's face falls immediately, worry replacing the buzz of socialising. "Did he do anything to you? Are you hurt? Are you...?"

"Well, I bumped my knee." Now that I'm saying it, I feel silly. I'm okay. Dante didn't hurt me, and he didn't attempt to lock me up either. Even the injury is all my own fault. "It hurts quite a bit," I add sullenly.

"Let's have a look at it," Camille offers.

Sighing, I sit down on one of the chairs and roll up my pants. I knocked that knee good. Two scraps of skin are now missing from my kneecap, and a bit of blood has seeped into my pants.

"I'll get the first-aid kit," Camille offers.

Meanwhile, Wulf sits next to me, leaning his ever-present staff against my table. "How are you?"

I shrug, non-committally. "A bit shaken." Understatement of the year, right there.

Wulf sees through it at once. He holds out his hand, and when I put mine in his, he squeezes it. "He can't hurt you. Not here. Not in front of all these people. And if he tries, I'll expose all his crimes at my talk. We'll see how he weasels himself out of that one."

Not too long ago, Dante was his man at the academy. He has an even closer relationship with my father than with his own foster parents. That he's ready to condemn Dante so easily eases the pain inside me. I never made the conscious decision, but suddenly I'm leaning over to wrap my arms around Wulf, burying my face in his shoulder. He doesn't spare a moment's hesitation and puts his arms around me, his right hand pressing my head against him.

"I'm sorry I wasn't there," he whispers.

"You're here now."

"Should I give you two some space?" Camille asks, sounding slightly amused.

I separate from Wulf and run my hands over my face. My hair is wet, as are my clothes. "Whew, I should get changed, and take a shower."

"Maybe with Wulf," Camille teases.

Wulf turns a delightful shade of red. He clears his throat and avoids my gaze. "I don't think Rika would appreciate that."

"Wouldn't I?" It's an absolutely bogus idea. I'm not in any state of mind where I could fully appreciate a naked Wulf in my shower. Now that I'm thinking about it, though, it has a certain appeal. If only to wash away all the bad memories the encounter with Dante has left on my skin.

Wulf stumbles over his words. "You... you what?"

Camille starts laughing. She tries to stifle it with her hand but fails to do so. "Your face! Oh my god, your face is priceless. Quick, let me take a picture." She pulls out her phone, which prompts Wulf to bat at it.

"Don't... Stop that!" He almost sounds whiny as he tries to get the phone from Camille.

Watching them, a smile blooms on my face; a real smile, full of joy. This right here is what I needed. Just three friends fooling around.

Wulf wins the battle over the phone, holding it triumphantly over his head, where Camille can't reach it. She crosses her arms and pouts. "Fine. I'll just take a picture later when you two are snuggling up again."

"When did we snuggle?" Wulf asks, making the mistake of lowering his hand in confusion.

Camille snags the phone from his fingers and hides it in her pocket. "You mean apart from your sleepovers outside? How about when you had your arm around her all the way to the conference centre? I've got some cute pictures of that."

Wulf turns bright red again. I feel my own face heat up. I never thought about how that would appear to others, I was just enjoying the intimacy of his touch. "Can I have those pictures?" I ask, innocently.

"See, Rika wants them." Camille grins.

Wulf looks back and forth between us, his face darkening even more. "You want them?" he asks at last.

"Do you want some quiet time now?" Camille asks.

I wave her off. "Not when I look like this."

"Oh, Wulf wouldn't mind," she says, cheekily.

"That's enough, Cami. Let Rika change in peace, so we can go for dinner."

"Uh, you're taking her out for dinner?"

Now, it's me who's blushing hard. "It's just waffles."

"Actually, my mother asked if we would join—"

"No!" The blood drains from my face, leaving me cold and sweaty again. "Absolutely not!"

Wulf looks taken aback. "This might be a good thing, Rika. If they get to know you—"

"They know me!"

"Not really. Not like I do." He looks to Camille for help, but she's crossed her arms. "We need to get my family off her case. This could be the way."

"Your father's the one who ordered my execution." I can't believe Wulf's still hanging onto the notion his family is in any way redeemable. "He threatened to sue you and put you in jail. And don't tell me he doesn't really know you, either."

Wulf shakes his head. "That was a quick shot. He didn't really mean it."

"Yes, he did. Just because your mother talked him out of it, doesn't mean he wouldn't do it in a flash if you crossed him again. Why are you so ready to forgive them?"

"Because they raised me," Wulf snaps. He runs his fingers over his face and calms his breathing. "I'm sorry. But if your mother wanted to make amends, you'd want to listen, wouldn't you?"

I'm glad he used my mother as an example, and not the father I never had. "Not any time soon." The moment I say it, I know it's not true. If I had the chance to meet her in a safe neutral environment, I'd still lunge at the chance. Problem is, there's no safe ground with the Vallescos. "I'm not going to eat dinner with your foster family." Petulantly, I add, "You promised me waffles."

Wulf stares at me. His lips move slightly, but he never says what he thinks out loud. At last, he lowers his gaze and nods. "Waffles it is." He doesn't sound particularly enthusiastic anymore. "Pick you up in half an hour?"

"Sounds good."

Without further ado, Wulf leaves the room. Camille waits until the door is closed. "They *are* his family."

"I know. And he can go for dinner with them, for all I care, but there's no way in hell I'm gonna tag along."

Camille sighs. "Well, I'd better get changed, too. I'll send you those pictures."

I'd almost forgotten about those again. Camille sends them through pretty much right after she leaves my room. Standing half-dressed in front of the shower, I scroll through them until I land on one on top of Mont des Arts. The city's spread out in front of us, the sun's high in the sky, and we're looking at each other, laughing, both grinning from ear to ear.

Will there ever be more than that? *Can there* be more than that with so many conflicting strings attached to the two of us? Or will his family inevitably tear us apart? I could've kissed him multiple times under the tree, but I never did. I just can't allow another Vallesco to hurt me again. Not even if his name is Wulf Bachmann.

12

Fortunately, our waffle dinner is a team event and not just the two of us. We stroll out of the hotel and immediately get derailed by a food truck offering fries.

"You need to try them," Wulf insists.

"But what about the waffles?" The others have already given in and lined up.

"We're taking a stroll. You'll be hungry again once we arrive. Besides..." Camille hands him a cone of steaming hot fries. Wulf sticks a little wooden fork in one of them and holds it up to my mouth. "You can't visit Brussels without having fries."

I blow on the fries, once again too conscious of his presence. "And waffles." Carefully, I bite off a piece.

"And waffles," he says, with the adorable grin that's almost as hot as the fries in my mouth.

"Ouch..." I draw in some air hoping to cool the piece in my mouth, and slowly, the pain dissipates. After that, the fries are good! "Oh my gosh, these are amazing!" They almost melt into my mouth, as if the entire potato's made of air.

Wulf's grin widens even more. "I know!"

After everyone's got a cone, we stroll towards the central quarter. The throng of tourists leads us down Rue des Boucher. It's a tight street for pedestrians only, lined with restaurants. Or "tourist traps", as Wulf calls them.

"Why don't we sit there?" Lukas asks, waving to two guys he obviously knows from his time at the academy. A lot of spirit seekers are filling up the place, though most haven't bothered bringing their staffs like Wulf has. "I want to try some craft beer."

"There's better in literally every other part of Brussels," Wulf says, strangely reluctant to stay in this crowded street.

Lukas shrugs. "Then we'll compare them. Come on, we'll just make a quick stop." And he's already off, clasping hands with his friends.

I check with Wulf, but he only sighs, and so we all follow Lukas in and get some drinks. It's surprisingly fun to spend time with the others this way, even though I skip the big craft beer comparison. The only thing missing is Aeola, who would've had a blast with the different smells in this place, but there are too many spirit seekers around. In fact, there are even some I know.

"Iván! Rebeka!"

The couple stroll up, arm in arm. I get up to hug Rebeka and wave at Iván. When he turns to shake Wulf's hand, I see Szirom's dagger-like wood in the back pocket of his pants. "How are the trees coming?" I ask him promptly.

"Very good. We've been taking good care of them," Iván says. "I can't talk to them like you, but I think we've reached some kind of peace. At least, it feels pleasant to walk under them."

"That's great to hear. Any more trouble?"

Rebeka shakes her head. "The SSA's left us alone for now. Which is good because with the funding cut, we don't actually have that much time to devote to... let's say patrolling." She winks at me.

"Such a shame, really," I answer, then chuckle softly. "You want to join us? We're going to get waffles." Eventually, that is.

Iván slips his hand a little lower on Rebeka's back. "We're actually on a date. Had to get rid of József before." He grins. "Poor guy always wants to tag along. But I left him with some Russian seekers who were very solemn, so they can have serious discussions all night long."

"Well, in that case, we'll see you at the conference tomorrow."

"We'll definitely come to your talk," Rebeka says. Then she leans forward and lowers her voice to a whisper. "How did you get them to put you on the schedule with *that*?"

"Long story." Rebeka was the first to tell me to stay away from the SSA. That I haven't managed to do so is slightly embarrassing.

Iván pulls her away again. "You're gonna rock!"

I wave after them and watch them saunter down the street. Suddenly, my nerves are tingling again. I completely forgot about my talk. "They're going to kill me tomorrow, aren't they?" What was I thinking, offering a presentation on spirit communication to a bunch of active spirit seekers?

Miriam reaches over the table to take my hand. "You'll be fine. I don't want to toot my own horn, but you have some stellar slides. You've got this." She looks at Lukas.

He shrugs. "Delivery could be a bit better, but honestly, you're better than half the talks will be. At least nobody will fall asleep during yours."

"That's a plus, I guess."

"And we'll all be there to support you," Wulf says, smiling gently at me.

My heart flutters at the sight, and I quickly pay attention to my soda.

"We can do another practise run in your room later," Leon offers.

"Yes, room party!" Lukas hollers.

Camille promptly takes his glass away. "That's enough beer for you." Her gaze lingers a little too long on the glass.

"What's going on over there?" Wulf asks, looking over his shoulder down the street.

People are hurrying down the street in our direction. A ringlet of smoke rises into the sky.

"Au feu! Au feu!" shouts are multiplying.

We're still watching the crowd when a loud shriek cuts through the evening. Moments later, a fiery shape emerges from between the houses.

She's glorious. And frightening. Shaped like a bird of fire, an enormous spirit soars through the darkening sky, leaving behind a trail of smoke.

"What's that?"

Instead of answering me, Wulf jumps up and grabs his staff. "You stay here!" And off he goes, running towards the mayhem.

None of us thought to bring our weapons. They're all safe in our hotel rooms. Lukas is ready to rectify that. "Give me your keys, I'll get our staffs."

"I'm coming with you," Miriam announces.

Still struck with awe, I drop my hotel key into Lukas' hand without tearing my eyes away from the beautiful spirit. She's now banking in the sky. Then she comes swooping down the street, her wings setting the marquees of the restaurants on fire.

"Get down!" I shout.

Camille, Leon, and I duck moments before the spirit soars over our heads. Panic breaks out on the street. People are scrambling for safety, shrieks and shouts filling the air. Because of the tight quarters, people shove each other and fall. Some spirit seekers are running towards the first outbreak, not knowing the spirit has already moved on.

A smell reaches my nose. It's not normal smoke, but something more pungent, more volatile. "Gas."

Panicked, I look at Camille. "It's one of the polluted ones!" As frightening as that is, it makes a lot of sense. The Gnomian Union wouldn't allow one of the spirits under their protection to show themselves in front of so many spirit seekers. Nor would a fire spirit of this size appear in an area like Belgium, which has no volcanoes of any sort.

"What do we do?" Leon asks, looking frightened. "You can't talk to them."

"I know!" I don't think I'd be able to talk to this spirit even if she wasn't polluted. Shrieking birds of fire usually have little time to listen.

Camille assumes command of our tiny group. "Right now, we're waiting for our staffs. Rika, keep an eye on the spirit. Maybe you can guess what it's going for next."

"She."

"What she's going for next." Camille nods, then checks the street for an update.

Restaurant owners are telling people to evacuate, but only a few are willing to leave their premises behind. A couple of people bring buckets of water outside, trying to douse the flames. Since the spirit fire hasn't fully taken hold yet, they're partially successful. At one point, I see Wulf sending a few spirit seekers to the other end of the street. Miro's joined him, and the two split the defence of Rue des Bouchers between them.

Meanwhile, the firebird is circling in the sky. Her piercing shriek hurts my ears. She makes one round, two, then swoops down again, near where Wulf is waiting for her. As his staff hits her left wing, a plume of fire explodes in the air. Dark smoke envelops the scene.

"Wulf!" Without thinking, I run towards him.

I don't get very far with the crowd pushing against me, away from the explosion site. People run into me, knocking me aside. I get pressed against a wall, trying to catch my breath, only to realise there's no air for me to breathe in. None I want, at least.

Black smoke surrounds me, unnaturally wrapping itself around me like a blanket. It's a gas, but it feels so slick. "Aeol—" I inhale a handful of smoke and double over. Coughing, I fall to my knees, trying to flatten myself against the ground.

For a moment, there's fresh air, but then the smoke lowers itself instead of rising. Someone steps on my arm, and I try to make myself as small as possible, protecting my face from the smoke. There's a vicious presence in it that feels like a spirit and yet doesn't.

Dark tendrils try to sneak through my arms, aiming for my airways. They crawl past the scars on my arms, almost caressing the dendritic lines. My skin burns as if it's on fire. This thing is out to get me. Not anyone. Me.

"Rika." I hear a voice, but when I try to answer, only a sputtering of coughs come out.

And then it's inside of me, setting my insides aflame. I writhe in pain, breathing in more and more of the vicious smoke as I try to get away from it. There's no escape from it. It's attacking my lungs. Stars dance in front of my eyes as my brain screams for oxygen.

Just then, the ground opens up below me, and I'm falling. Something cushions me as I land in complete darkness. A wrathful shriek sounds above me, but it's muffled by layers of earth. Earth. Oh my god, I'm stuck under the earth, in a cold, dark, airless space.

But I'm wrong. There is air, surprisingly lots of it, brought to me by a familiar presence.

"Aeola?" I croak.

"Hush. Let me get this out of you."

I'm still coughing, unable to control my convulsions. Aeola takes care of that. Gently, she fills my lungs with clean air, pulling out the toxic carbon monoxide the smoke has deposited there. The pain recedes, and as I take deep breaths, my world clears again.

There's someone else with us, another friend. "Alexander? Did you swallow me?"

"Well, the ground swallowed you, but I asked it nicely."

"Thank you." I'm grateful. I truly am. And yet, the darkness, and knowing there's nothing but stone around me, makes me cry. It's like I'm back in my worst nightmare, trapped in the Castel Sant'Angelo.

"You need to bring her up again," Aeola whispers gently.

"Oh, come on, sylph. You can stick it out a bit longer," Alexander nags. "The place is crawling with spirit seekers. It was pure luck I was able to sneak in to get her."

I sit up, carefully stretching out my hands to figure out the extent of my confinement. It hardly goes beyond the space my body takes up.

"Ugh, get out of my nose!" Alexander scoffs.

"Sorry," I say, my voice breaking even on that one word.

Aeola blows soothingly over my cheeks. "Alexander, please."

"What if that black stuff is still there?" Not even he's calling it a spirit, which should concern me, but all I can think about is how I'm going to die down here.

"It's gone." I don't know how I know, but I do. It's like the weight of its presence has lifted off my shoulders, and not just because Alexander's shielding me from it.

He crunches down on something, but then I feel myself rise through the ground again.

The fire spirit is still soaring through the sky, but the smoke has lifted. Aeola hovers around me just in case.

"Rika!" Camille bends down to help me up. She's got Grune's staff in her hand and is breathing hard. "Is that...?" Pointing the staff at Aeola, she wavers.

"Aeola." Protectively, I wrap my arms around the air spirit and whisper to her. "Fly fast."

She shoots out of my embrace into the sky and out of sight.

Camille lowers the staff and hands it to me. Nearby, a second one, her own, is leaning against the fence. "I saw that smoke spirit choking you. But don't worry. I took care of it. It's gone."

"You did?" Slowly, I take in the information: the spirit—or whatever it was—is gone, defeated by Camille, whose pupils are unnaturally wide. "You took drugs." To save me.

"I destroyed that spirit," she says, a grin jumping onto her face. It doesn't find much purchase, appearing and vanishing again at sickening speed. Finally, worry wins out. "You must've inhaled so much of it. How are you even okay?"

"Aeola took care of it."

Camille nods. "I should still get you out of here. Just in case." Longingly, she looks at the fight taking place further down the road.

Some of the spirit seekers are dousing the flames with a special liquid, which does real wonders. It even helps diminish the beautiful firebird. And there's Wulf, leading the charge, swinging his staff masterfully.

Next to me, Camille is shivering. As worried as I am about Wulf, it looks like he and Miro have it all under control. Camille? Not so much. "Yes, let's get out of here." I loop my arm through hers, making it seem as if I need her help to keep me steady. "Thanks for having my back."

Camille's already dilated pupils widen even more. "Of course. You've got mine. I got yours. That's the way it is."

I only wish she had it without having to take any drugs.

13

We all meet in my room to debrief. Wulf is the last to join us, soot still smearing his hair and the edge of his face, having had only had time for a quick wash. Camille's been jittery ever since we returned, walking up and down the room, talking about the firebird. "It was magnificent. So beautiful."

"It was toxic," Wulf says, while Miriam glares at Camille.

"You mean, it was one of the polluted spirits?" Leon asks. "Because once it came closer, I didn't feel too well."

Lukas snorts. "Yeah, I didn't feel good about all that fire, either."

Camille turns, nearly losing her balance and points at Wulf. "But it wasn't as toxic as the smoke that swallowed Rika."

Concerned, his head jerks around to me. "You were swallowed by smoke?"

I'm curled up in one of the comfy chairs, Aeola in my arms. Although she claims she got all the carbon monoxide out, my throat is sore and itchy, making it hard to suppress the need to cough. Nevertheless, I shake my head. "I wasn't swallowed. But the smoke attacked me. It sought me out, and I don't think it was truly part of the firebird. It was with her, yet had its own consciousness." I've never experienced anything like it. "It was like a spirit of smoke and hate. It hated me."

Aeola unfolds a little to stroke my hair. "It can't hurt you anymore. Camille destroyed it."

"Camille destroyed the smoke spirit?" Wulf asks, to clarify.

Smugly, Camille declares, "I did. Smashed it with Rika's staff until it went 'poof'. It totally went straight for Rika."

Miriam's been sitting in the chair next to me, glowering at Camille. Now, she gets up, shoots her one more death glare, and leaves the room without a single word.

"What's wrong with her?" Lukas asks.

Camille only shrugs. Everyone's too focused on the attack to notice what's really going on.

"So, what does this mean?" Leon asks. "There were at least three-dozen spirit seekers out there. Why did it go for you?"

I check with Wulf. We're both thinking the same thing, but can that be true? "Well, we do know the polluted spirits are modified and released by the SSA. And we also know who's number one on their hit list."

Wulf winces. "It could be incidental. The polluted spirits are all completely out of control. They have no self-control and are purely hate-driven. So, unless the SSA has a spirit that hates your guts, I don't see how they could train one to go specifically after you." He gives me a weak smile. "And spirits generally adore you."

His last words fly over my head. I've suddenly had a horrible realisation. One too horrible to be true. And I'm not the only one. Aeola blows ice cold against my skin. "It couldn't be him."

Only Wulf hears her words. "Who do you mean?"

"Huh?" Lukas asks, looking back and forth between us.

The way the smoke caressed the scars on my arms. *His* mark. I shudder. My right hand flies at my left arm and digs its nails into my skin. Suddenly, I want to rip these scars out.

"Don't!" Aeola cries, blowing gently against my hand.

It takes all my effort to pull my hand away and dig my fingers into the armrest instead. Where my nails punctured my arm, the muscle throbs in pain. With both hands clutching my chair, I notice everyone looking at me. "It's... It can't be. He... That smoke was too weak. If Camille killed it..."

"What are you saying?" She puts her hands on her hips and raises her eyebrows. "It had to be a weakling spirit or I wouldn't have managed it? I'm a good spirit seeker. In fact, I'm a 300-plus seeker."

Wulf looks like she's just broken his heart. So, now he knows. "Cami, you were always a good seeker. The NAV isn't everything."

"Easy for you to say, Bachmann." She never uses his last name and certainly not in such a derisive way. It stuns Wulf into silence. Camille doesn't care. "I saved Rika's life today. You wanted me to keep fighting, didn't you? Well, I did today. And I took care of a smoke spirit no one else even cared to notice."

"It's a piece of the Erlking."

Everyone stares at me. Lukas and Leon wide-eyed, Camille confused, and Wulf deeply concerned. "Are you sure?"

I shake my head. "No. Yes. I have no idea." My skin is crawling. It hasn't forgotten the old promise. "But that's the only spirit who hates me. And Dante knows I caught him." Oh, why did I tell him about that? So much for not killing his own flesh and blood. "He must've chosen to combine a piece of the Erlking with the firebird to bring me down."

"Wait, wait!" Lukas puts his hands up. "You all really think the SSA would bring a powerful spirit—two powerful spirits—to Brussels and release them right on the eve of the biannual conference? What for? Why would they do that? To get Rika killed? They had no idea she'd be having a drink right there."

"He has a point there," Leon admits. "Unless they're spying on you."

I cross my arms. "I wouldn't put it past them. The Vallescos might've been so miffed about me refusing their dinner invitation that all bets were off." It isn't until Aeola blows at my arms that I realise I've started scratching them again.

Wulf shakes his head. "Lukas has a point."

"Or you want him to have a point."

"Who's giving out points?" Camille asks, confused.

"Nobody." I sink back into my chair and glare at Wulf. "So much for reconciliation."

He doesn't respond immediately and massages his temples again. At last, he comes up with a lacklustre explanation. "What if it doesn't have anything to do with you?"

"Really?"

"Hear me out, please." He wrings his hands. "If this is really what we think it is and the board released the firebird, then they did it in the most controlled environment. The spirit attacked Rue des Boucher at dinner time, when dozens of spirit seekers were around to subdue it. As for the Erlking, we've already found out that they're basically transplanting bits of other spirits into their... experiments. That wasn't truly him, just a part of him."

A part that split from the firebird's consciousness to seek me out.

I don't want his words to make sense, but they seep in nonetheless. "So, it's like Dublin, then? Not a punishment but a demonstration of spirit seeker might."

Wulf nods slowly. "Yeah. Lots of chaos, but a swift victory for us. There's damage, so the danger was real, but it didn't turn into a tragedy. Thanks to us. And with no small help from me." He doesn't sound particularly proud of it.

An uncomfortable silence spreads as the realisation sinks in. From all I've learnt about the SSA, that's indeed a tactic they'd use to assure continued support and trust. However, that only changes things slightly. I know it's terribly self-centred to keep harping on about it, but I didn't just imagine the touch nor the hate. It didn't appear like the Erlking, not even to Aeola, but if he's been altered and was no more than a piece...

I'm just about to voice my doubts when Lukas breaks the silence. "So, what were we supposed to do? Refuse to play their game and let that street burn? Sorry, but if that's their evil plan, I'll choose people's lives. Every time."

Wulf flashes him a proud smile. "I wouldn't choose any differently, but..." He glances at me.

"What?" I ask when he doesn't continue. "Do you think I'd let people die?"

"I know you wouldn't."

Why does he always have to be so infuriatingly sensible? "So, they win." I scoff. "They endanger people, and you save them. All is well."

"Until we can't save them," Leon says, before Wulf has a chance to protest. "Because that's what's going to happen, isn't it? If their blackmail is successful, if they can keep us in line by using our chosen line of service, they're gonna use it time and time again. Nothing will ever change, and people will continue to die. More and more people, the way we're angering spirits."

"There's only one solution," Camille says, beaming at all of us. "We go on strike."

Everybody stares at her. Then Wulf clears his throat to ask her, "What?"

Her eyes gleam. "Better even. You go on strike. At your talk, you lay down your staff. You return it and go on strike. And we follow. Yes, people will get hurt, but there'll be more if we don't rise up."

My stomach churns at the thought. Wulf shakes his head, looking caught between disgust and disbelief. "I can't do that. I can't stand by and let people die." He looks at me as if asking for absolution. "You know I'm always happy to try it your way first, but... but I can't put my staff aside. I'm not willing to take that risk."

"I'm not asking you to." This was Camille's idea. I remember my own dilemma in Budapest. I couldn't fight with those horrible, mutilated staffs the spirit seekers use, but I couldn't just stand by and watch either. "I'm fully aware that it's sometimes inevitable to fight. Especially polluted spirits."

"Well." Camille slaps her hands on her chair's armrests. "If even Rika is unwilling to do what's necessary, I'm out." She stands up. "Sometimes you have to do things that don't seem right to make things right."

Camille gives each of us a pointed glare and walks out of the room. She's almost at the door when Wulf mumbles, "Sure. Let's all take drugs to boost our ability." His words carry well enough that the door slams shut.

"Wait! Did she...?" Lukas only seems to realise it now.

I raise my eyebrows at him. "You never considered it?" He's the one obsessed with raising his NAV by all means possible.

Lukas sneers. "Do I look like a junkie to you?"

"You'd be surprised how different junkies are." I sigh. The last thing we need right now is for Camille to go on a drug binge. I might owe her my life, but I'm not letting her pay for it with hers. "Sometimes, I wish the Erlking would've just done away with me, then everyone could live happily ever after," I find myself muttering.

"Don't say that!" Aeola hisses, outraged.

Both Wulf and Leon stare at me, absolutely horrified, but Lukas nods happily. "Oh, yeah, we'd all be dead, except Wulf here, smashed by the storm, along with what? A tenth of Berlin's population? Who cares about a few hundred thousand? Definition of happy ever after right there."

I pull a grimace at him, suitably grounded once again, thanks to his snark. "I meant the whole SSA and Camille and—"

"Lukas is right," Wulf interrupts me darkly. "You did way more good than harm." He scoffs and amends his words, "You didn't do any harm. What Camille does is her problem. You never forced her to take drugs or caused her issues with the SSA. And as for the agency, a little harm sounds exactly like what we need."

"Are you gonna confront them?" I ask, not willing to be any clearer.

Again, Wulf doesn't immediately answer, and I groan. He sighs. "Can I do it my way?"

"What *is* your way?" So far, he's done everything he always does. Jump straight into battle, assume command, greet all his old friends, toy with the idea of attending dinner with his manipulative family. If he's looking for an inside angle, he's got the inside aspect of it down, but the angle might as well be zero degrees.

"By talking and trying not to jump to conclusions," he starts, but I won't let him continue.

"Great. Sounds awesome. Good luck with that." I get up from my chair, making sure Aeola doesn't fall. "Meanwhile, I'll be over here, being all paranoid for no reason."

"Rika…" Wulf starts, having the audacity to be annoyed.

Lukas takes the opportunity to launch himself up as well. "Time for me to go. You can continue fighting, but I'm tired. Good luck with your talk tomorrow. If you're still gonna do it." He makes a dismissive wave. "Doesn't really matter." He leaves the room with a slight limp.

Behind him, Leon also gets to his feet. "Do you want to go through the talk once more?"

I can see by his stance he's not really looking forward to it, either. And neither am I. The talk seems to be the least important thing at the moment. After everything that's happened today, will the conference just begin as planned? It feels surreal. "I'm too tired for it."

"Okay, raincheck in the morning, then?"

I nod, and he leaves as well, bidding Wulf goodnight on the way. In an effort to make things more awkward, Wulf doesn't follow suit but remains seated, waiting patiently until the room has quieted down again.

At last, he speaks. "You know I didn't mean it like that?"

"Do I?" I'm still standing in the middle of the room, looking rather stupid compared to his calm, collected demeanour.

What makes it even worse is the hurt that flashes over Wulf's face. "You don't trust me?" he asks, his voice uncharacteristically meek.

Great. Now, I'm the Big Baddie. How dare I have my doubts when all I've got from him are pretty words and no action? Well, one action. But returning Vesuvius' eggs to the fire spirit is fading more and more in light of his recent reactive course. "Can I?"

"A hundred per cent." He gets up. "Rika, I would never do anything to hurt you..."

"On purpose," I add, sourly.

His face falls. "When did I...?" Letting out a giant exhale, he shakes his head. "Just because we have different opinions or different ways to approach things—"

This time, it's Aeola who won't let him continue. "You're the one who doesn't trust her! How many times does she need to tell you that your agency is destructive? That they do more harm than good? Even if you ignore all the pain they create for us spirits. And it's not just Rika. You put more trust in those who raised you, even though you're aware of the horrible things they've done, than anyone who tells you differently. Not Rika, not Rory, not the Travellers. You hear them out, but you don't listen."

I bet Wulf's never been berated by a spirit. Her anger creates an air current in my room, battering down the pretty flowers and setting the pictures askew, but it isn't vicious. It's not trying to attack Wulf or hurt him.

But it does. The look he gives me after Aeola has inhaled her little storm again speaks loudly of his pain. "That's not true."

I cross my arms, unable to resist him otherwise. "Well, that's what it feels like sometimes."

"I just—"

"—have to consider multiple things. I get it. You have a lot of ties and strings and relationships that are important to you. I don't have that. All my relationships are fairly new and based on the same person I am today. You've changed, but people like Miro and so many others haven't found out about that yet." I watch him for a moment, noticing how his eyes aren't truly meeting mine for longer than a heartbeat. "And you haven't told him, have you?"

"Not yet."

Even though I expected it, it hurts. It cements everything Aeola said and justifies all my doubts. "Yeah."

"I will," Wulf stresses.

"I know. You'll do it your way." I don't even mean in a bad sense. It is what it is. I know what I've got in Wulf, and now I know what I don't have in him.

"Rika…"

I'm surprisingly calm as I take his hands. "It's okay. That's just how we are. Always at odds with our methods." Hey, this is better than when he was still anti-spirit.

Thankfully, Wulf lets it stand at that. His gaze hardens a little, but more in a way of distancing himself. This hasn't exactly been going the way he wanted. Nor my way. Instead, he changes the topic. "Do you really think that smoke spirit was a part of the Erlking?" He looks to Aeola for confirmation as well.

Oh, yeah, another thing where I jumped to a conclusion. "It didn't feel like him," I admit. "But that could be the alteration."

"It didn't appear like a spirit at all," Aeola clarifies. "More like... a part." The wind in my room suddenly rises again, as she gets a new idea. "Like the black staffs aren't truly dryad wood."

Wulf and I share a glance, equally horrified. "So, it could've been a part of him?" I ask.

"As I said, they could've used parts of him to supplement the firebird. That explains why Camille could simply defeat it."

"Oh, don't tell her that."

Wulf winces at the suggestion. Then he cocks his head. "I know you're gonna hate me for saying it again, but this would mean that this wasn't an attack on you. They never released the Erlking."

I let go of him with a groan. "Fine. Maybe I *am* paranoid."

"Can we agree on PTSD instead?" he asks.

I hadn't considered that. Now that he says it, it makes a whole lot of sense. Of course I'm traumatised after everything that's happened to me. My reaction to Dante's assault at the elevator should've been a dead giveaway. Gosh, was that really today?

Rubbing my face, I shrug. "Maybe. All I know is I do need to go to sleep now if I want to make the most out of my talk tomorrow." If all goes well, tomorrow might be even bigger than today.

"You've got this," Wulf says. "Sorry, I... I'm sorry I don't make you feel like you can trust me. It might not seem like it, but I'm yours."

Any other day, I would've swooned. A small part of me still soars at the admission, but at the moment, I'm too emotionally exhausted to do more with the information than file it away. "Okay." Bringing him to the door, I add, "And for the record, I don't hate you. Far from it."

He gives me a tired smile. "That's good to know. Will you be okay alone in the room?"

"Is that an attempt to get into my bed?" I ask, more out of reflex than intent. Before he can answer, I add, "Don't worry, Aeola will stay with me."

"Okay. Well, I'm next door. Shout and I'll come running."

Fine! That's pretty heart-warming. Why does he always worm his way back into my heart?

Annoyed with myself, I open the door for him. "Goodnight, Wulf."

"Good—"

Further down the corridor, a door slams shut.

We both check outside my room to look for the source. There, in the soft orange of the night lights, Camille stands with what looks like all her belongings strewn around her. Her face is tear-streaked. She's barely holding it together as she finds our gaze.

"Miri broke up with me."

14

It turns out that when Lukas and Miriam returned to the hotel to get our staffs, Miriam found Camille's stash. The one she'd promised me she'd throw away weeks ago. Though part of me is as angry at Camille as Miriam is, I invite her into my room. She just saved my life, after all. With her coming down from her drug-related adrenaline rush and me fighting with Wulf, we're both too exhausted to talk much about what happened.

The next morning, there's an awkward silence between us. Camille has a hangover, which serves her right. I really hope her break-up with Miriam slaps some sense into her. I should have been as resolute as Miriam instead of falling for Camille's promises. But now that she's starting to realise what's on the line, I can be a true friend. No more covering for her.

"Did you throw it all away?" I ask, after I've dressed.

"Miriam did," Camille replies in a meek little voice.

I eye her summer jacket. "All of it?"

She sighs. "Go for it."

In the pockets I find two little pills. Touching them makes my toes curl, but I carry them to the toilet and flush them down. "Any other hidden ones?"

Camille looks at me with bloodshot eyes. Her head moves from side to side, but then determination sets in, and she produces a handful from various pockets of her jeans. This time, it's her who flushes them away. "I'll stop for real this time."

I rub her back and give her a smile at last. "You will."

If she'd hoped Miriam had cooled off overnight, she's sorely disappointed. As soon as we go down for breakfast, Miriam announces that she's finished, takes her tray, and leaves. The rest keep their heads down.

"How are you feeling about your talk?" Leon asks in a quiet voice, as if he doesn't want to disturb anyone.

Now that he's reminded me, my nerves are fried. In less than four hours, I'll be standing in front of two or three hundred spirit seekers and telling them what they've been doing wrong all these years. They'll either throw rotten eggs at me for sullying their sacred profession or start a revolution. After everything that happened last night, I'm not sure I can handle another day of endless drama.

The worst thing is I have no idea what to do if it goes well. What if they listen? What if they believe me? I don't have a plan for what happens next. Are they gonna tell the other seekers who missed my talk, or will I have to publish a paper, like Miriam? Will they demand a new leadership? Leave the SSA altogether?

"Rika?"

Oh, that's right. Leon asked me a question. "I think I'm good. I might throw up later, though."

Leon laughs. "Yeah, I know that feeling. Whenever I had to do a test, I went to the toilet five times or more. At least you don't have to talk in front of a thousand people, right, Wulf?"

Wulf's reading the news and only looks up now. "What?"

I can't even imagine that many people in a single room. While I need to reach as many as possible, I'm glad I'm not in one of the big rooms.

"Your talk?" Leon asks, slightly amused. "Are you nervous?"

"Why would I be?" Wulf frowns, then his eyes meet mine. "Oh. I mean, sure, it's always a bit nerve-wracking, but I'm well-prepared, and in the end, it's just a talk. Not a life-or-death battle."

It feels like, for me, it is a life-or-death battle. I certainly won't get another chance like this. But before it's my turn to shine or fall, we all have to attend the keynote lecture at 9 a.m. Or rather, the address from the SSA Board.

It takes place in the Gold Room, which is so huge that a camera and giant screen are needed to see the people in front. All 1,200 seats are going to be taken by spirit seekers from all across Europe, and a few European Union delegates and journalists. This conference isn't just a giant class reunion, but also an opportunity for the SSA and the EU to rethink policies. Some of those delegates might be at my talk later. In fact, I hope they are, even if the thought of speaking to them scares me to death.

Wulf gets swept away, but the rest of us find seats somewhere at the back, far away from the speakers. I recognise a few second-years from my fighting classes in the crowd, but no one I'd care to reconnect with. Wiola is in a gaggle of young spirit seekers at the far end of the room. And though, by all rights, Tiago should've been here as well, there's no sign of him. There must be some reason for it. Surely, they're not suspicious of him if they let Wiola come.

I recognise three of the nine board members on stage: the Vallescos and Dante. Two of the other six look like they could be from Italy as well. In fact, there's a distinct lack of diversity, though at least the male-female ratio isn't abysmal, with three women. If these people are worried about what might come out of this conference, they don't show it. I see them laughing and joking with each other while they wait for the room to fill up.

The lecture hasn't even started yet, and I feel my skin crawl. These are the men and women who've decided to not just create polluted spirits but release them in strategic places. There's an excited buzz among the spirit seekers, many of whom were drawn into battle last night, thanks to the board's new programme. I see one guy with second-degree burns chatting with his neighbour, already putting his recent injuries behind him, not knowing he'd be without pain if not for the people he so desperately wants to hear from.

I'm almost of a mind to skip this keynote address when the room quiets down, and Humberto Vallesco gets up. His microphone is now turned up, and I get a close-up of the man who so casually ordered my execution. And lied straight to my face beforehand.

"Welcome! It's a pleasure to see so many of you here. We as the board appreciate the time you've taken to come and learn about new ways of fighting spirits. We'd also like to acknowledge all the hard work you've done in keeping our world safe. That can't be said enough. You're the reason our children can sleep safe and sound, knowing that there'll be no storm ripping their house apart or fire burning it to the ground."

Oh dear, back patting and fear mongering. This is going to be a long hour. It looks like everybody's lapping it up, though. Tell people how important they are, and they'll stop thinking.

Humberto drones on and on about the important work that's been done by the spirit seekers, including the *frightening* incident last night and, of course, Wulf's groundbreaking mission in Naples. There's no mention of enhanced spirits. No admission that Vesuvius isn't where he's supposed to be, but free and united with his offspring. I half wish the rogue seekers would pull off a serious prank just to stop Wulf's father from talking.

As the hour comes to an end, I feel like I've had to sit through another brainwashing session. Especially when his final words are: "Every time has its unique challenges. We fought spirits when others went to war and even during times of economic hardship, when we could barely pay our seekers a fraction of what they're worth. Today, we have those who turn away from science and empirical data because of anecdotal evidence. There's a craze for alternatives, just for the sake of them. Instead of medicine, people take globules or go to witch doctors. In terms of spirits, people return to the '*old*' ways." He puts air quotes around the word old. "Primitive religions are on the rise. People call each other witches or druids nowadays, and some will defend spirits. They'll try to tell people how all we need to do is appease spirits. As if a sacrificial feast would stop a volcanic eruption." His little joke earns a roaring response. What a clever little man he is.

I want to poke his eyes out, or better, cut out his tongue. My talk hasn't even started, and he's already made fun of it.

Humberto continues, "We know better than those charlatans because we know spirits. We're the ones who can feel them, hear them, and see them. And people know that. They might think there are cheaper, less dangerous avenues, but there aren't. So, don't let these New Age people discourage you. You do work that's not just valuable but indispensable. We've been doing this for centuries, and we'll be doing this for centuries more."

I'm fuming. My pulse is rushing. It's just as well there are at least thirty rows between me and the podium, as my stare would surely burn holes in Humberto's Armani suit. Such a neat little piece of propaganda. Yes, let's never evolve, never progress. It's not like that ever did anything good, right?

Camille pulls on my arm. "Come on, Rika. Let's get out of here."

The lecture's over, and people are already moving, but I'm frozen to my spot. I'm so angry I want to jump up on stage and tell him how wrong he is in front of everybody. "Did you hear that?" I ask, getting up reluctantly.

Camille gives me a pitiful look. "Yeah, it was pretty bad."

Well, at least, his propaganda didn't work on everyone. For a short moment, I was worried my team would fall for his argument. But as I meet up with the rest of the group outside, even Lukas shakes his head angrily. "Why are they inviting you to talk at this conference if they're warn everyone off trying new avenues?"

That question is answered the moment I enter the Silver Room shortly before my presentation. After the keynote address, I couldn't listen to anything else on the program. Instead, I went back and forth with my slides, trying to decide whether I should make the science in them even more pronounced or make the whole text glaringly New Age to spite the Vallescos.

It doesn't matter either way because there'll be no one to listen to it. Three hundred people can fit into the Silver Room, but a minute before the designated start time, fewer than twenty have found their way into the lecture theatre. And about half of those are my own team, Rory, Eoghan, and Rebeka. Not even Wulf's found time in his busy schedule to make it, despite his promise.

This is a farce. I could've met these few people outside in the park and had a picnic.

I was aware there were other talks scheduled against mine, and I'm also keenly aware it's lunch time. But twelve people who aren't on my side already, one of them the ever-sneering Wiola? Out of more than a thousand? This can't be happening.

It only gets worse when the door opens one last time and two figures slip into the back row. Alena Vallesco and her brother. My father. They're the last people I want to see here. The last I want to embarrass myself in front of. Dante's sight alone sends my pulse rushing and my head swimming. He may be far away, but his focus is on me.

"You should start now," the room technician lets me know. It's already 12:02.

My words are all gone. The first slide is up behind me, but I have to read it to even remember what I'm supposed to talk about. Communication with spirits. That's right. Now, how do you communicate with humans?

"Hi, uhm... For those who don't know me, uhm, my name's Rika Csorba." My eyes flick back to Dante, as if I need his permission to call myself by the name I've always gone by. "And I'm from, well, I'm currently in Berlin."

Gosh, how can I even fumble my own introduction? Desperately, I search out a familiar face. My friends are all looking at me encouragingly, so I'd better get my game face on. The problem is, I don't really have one.

"Today I want to talk to you about talking..." Nice, doubling up like an idiot. "About communicating with spirits." I turn to look at the slide. Is there anything else I needed to say beforehand? I can't remember, honestly.

It only gets worse after that. Even to my own ear, my presentation sounds painful, reduced back to the bare minimum. At one point, I'm practically reading from the slides, flicking through those with pictures faster than anyone has a chance to understand them. I completely mess up Miriam's scientific correlation between spirit attacks and human technological advance, missing out on the big conclusion. My words are getting all fumbled up and I even call Aeola a nymph halfway through the talk.

By the time I reach the final slide, it's only 12:26. "Uhm... any questions?" I ask, hoping desperately that no people means no questions. My friends seem stunned. They probably figured that pretend questions won't make this any better. But there are Alena and Dante to consider, and they're probably going to tear me to pieces now, to drive home their anti-spirit agenda.

Instead, a guy on the right, who's sitting next to Wiola, raises his hand. "So, what do you talk about with spirits?" He can't even end the question without snickering. Wiola and the rest of his posse chuckle as well.

Ignore them, Rika. Just answer the question. "Well, you can talk to them about whatever you like, but the idea is to find out what bothers them."

"Well, I can tell them what bothers *us*. Like them killing our people," Wiola replies promptly, getting some more laughs from her friends.

Lukas' scowl deepens, but he, like most of the others, remains silent. Only Rory turns around and asks, "Did you know that we kill, or rather capture, about ten to twelve times more inactive spirits than spirits who ever do serious harm to a human?" Now, see, that's a well-formulated argument.

I should be able to deal with such hostility. I've done it many times in my life. But my quick-fire wit is gone, and all I can do is stand there and grimace. "Does anyone else have a question?"

They don't. Not even Alena and Dante bother to take me down. It's not like it would be worth it in front of so few people and after I've done such a great job at embarrassing myself. "Well, thanks for coming."

As I turn off my presentation, Camille jumps up and turns towards the auditorium. "You should all check out her YouTube channel. On there, you can see what communication can actually achieve." When the group of troublemakers wave her off, she repeats, "You should give it a chance. Might teach you some communication skills with humans as well."

My presentation has bored them so much they're not even rising to the challenge. Turning their backs on Camille, they leave the room.

Camille turns around to me. "You did well."

"Yeah, sure." No amount of first-time jitters can excuse how I've floundered our one and only chance.

I pack up my things as quick as I can and turn around, only to come face-to-face with Dante. Panicked, I check the room. His sister is nowhere to be seen. She's probably off to tell her husband how badly I've done.

"Are you ready to grab some lunch?" Dante asks, as if we discussed it earlier.

Is he going to follow me around the entire conference? I don't want to be anywhere alone with him. "I—"

"I know a little restaurant nearby. It'll be my treat."

Yeah, I had enough of Dante's treats to last me a lifetime. "No, I—"

"Sorry, she's already got a date with me." Rory steps up and hooks his arm into mine. "We've got so much to catch up on." He turns to look at me with the full power of fake cheeriness. "You good to go? Cause I'm starving."

Gratefully, I nod. "Me, too."

Dante makes a face as if I called him a murderer in front of the entire SSA, but steps aside as Rory leads me past him. "Then perhaps another time."

Or maybe not. But I'm too distraught to say that aloud.

Now that the presentation's over, I'm shaking all over. My breath hitches in my throat, and I blink incessantly to avoid breaking down.

Rory pats my arm and leads me up the stairs. "It's alright. You survived. We'll get another chance." At least he's not pretending I did well.

The others join us outside the room, and Camille envelops me in a tight hug. Lukas keeps his mouth shut, which is the best he can do. I'm sure he's got about thousand pointers for me after that catastrophe. But what's done is done. I've missed my chance. I haven't even managed to convince the twelve spirit seekers who bothered showing up.

We meet the rogue spirit seekers and some Travellers in the Royal Park near the fountain. Eoghan has already updated them, so I'm spared from having to recount my failures. Instead, Pavel embraces and comforts me. "It's alright, little spirit. Those aren't your target group."

The others have brought food, so we sit down on the lawn and have a picnic. Slowly, the fresh air, and Pavel's and Aeola's presence raise my spirits.

"So, what happens next?" Lukas asks, having reached his maximum time of non-confrontation. "This can't be it, can it?"

"Well, I had an idea." Inga looks first to Bijan and then Leon, who nod at her. "Why don't we do our own conference?" Upon my confused look, she elaborates, "We call it a fringe program. And it's gonna be free and open for all. Plus, we use our YouTube channel."

Miriam, who's sitting between Bijan and a Traveller named Annina, sits up straight. "We'd need a conference centre. Or are you planning an online conference? Then we need proper recording gear."

Bijan grins. "Leave the conference centre to me. And don't worry, I'm not going to hack us into there. Might just let the SSA pay for it. It's the least they can do after sabotaging Rika's talk."

"You think they sabotaged it?" I ask, feeling like I did a bad enough job entirely on my own.

"Scheduling you at lunch time against the technology update and the board Q&A in the hall? And just to make sure nobody goes, they tell everyone what a bogus idea talking to spirits would be." Bijan shakes his head. "Rika, there's a reason that room was close to empty, and it had nothing to do with your ability to give an engaging talk."

"Which you're capable of!" Camille insists, putting her hand on mine.

I'm not sure I believe her, but perhaps if the interest had been real and Dante hadn't been there, I could've done a better job. Maybe it's not just my fault my talk wasn't the great turning point. "A full conference? What am I going to talk about?"

"You're going to do your talk, but focus on the spirit relationships you've established," Inga replies. "In fact, yeah, scrap the whole science bit. We can do that in other instances. You focus on what you've learned from Grune and how that applies to our current situation."

Leon looks at me encouragingly. "You just need to talk, no slides."

"Sounds doable." I hope. Right now, I never want to talk in front of people again. "So, who else is going to talk?"

"I could do a talk on the NAV improvement," Miriam offers. "Doing the science-y bits."

There are so many ideas once we get started. And all of them are focused on positive spirit relationships. Rory's going to do two bits, one about the history of the Aos Sí and the other about his union with Liffey and Dublin's new policies. Rebeka offers up Iván the moment he joins us to talk about the real battle of Budapest. There are other bits about the Travellers and their unique relationship with spirits, about the secret behind staffs, and a visionary future lecture on how life could be if we worked with the spirits and not against them. Even Pavel seems more at ease with this new plan.

"I want to do one of those talks, too," Aeola announces, the wind around us growing slightly agitated.

No one hears her, of course. But that's exactly why she should speak. "Guys!" I wait until I have everyone's attention. "Aeola wants to speak, too."

As expected, it takes some time for the information to sink in. But then an excited buzz arises, and a million questions pop up.

"What's she gonna talk about?"

"Does she need slides?"

"How's anyone gonna hear her?"

Bijan is beyond excited. "Major draw right there! Let the SSA top that. An actual spirit addressing us. This is going to be so cool."

I love their enthusiasm, but it surprises me, as well. So far, all attempts at improving spirit-human relationships have been coming from me. I've been trying to teach humans to listen and respect spirits. Aeola and everyone else have been going along with it, but they've never expressed a wish to be an active part of it.

"Are you sure?" I ask Aeola. "There may be a lot of spirit seekers. Some will probably come just to capture you."

"Wouldn't you defend me?" Aeola asks, sounding slightly amused.

I have no idea what's so funny about it. The SSA is vindictive. They'd totally call for a mission if they were pointed to a target. "Of course I'd defend you. I'm just worried."

Aeola smiles, her breeze playing affectionately with my hair. "That's only fair after you worried me so much. But, Rika, how can I let you fight our battle by yourself? If we want a better world for us spirits, we have to be willing to take risks. That's what you taught me."

"I did?" We might as well be alone out here for all the attention I pay everyone else. Aeola's had such a profound effect on me. To learn that I've had the same on her makes me appreciate her even more.

"Every day. Even when you were scared." Her words warm me in a way only a hot summer breeze can. "Especially then."

The only person missing from our planning session is Wulf. He calls me when we're all on our way back to the hotel after deciding to skip the afternoon sessions.

"What's this fringe program?" he asks, sounding tense.

Bijan and Leon have already put everything up online and started advertising. Judging by this phone call, it's working.

Instead of answering, I ask Wulf a more important question. "Where were you when I needed you most?" Okay, that might be a bit dramatic, but he promised to be there.

There's a sigh on the other side. "I couldn't make it. My father asked me to sit in on a meeting with the EU delegates. You know, discussing the current state of affairs and how people are responding to the SSA."

"How wonderful for you." I'm of half a mind to hang up on him just for that. "Back in Daddy's good graces, then?"

There's no denial. "I thought it'd be helpful to see where the EU stands on all this," he says, sounding only slightly dismayed.

"And?"

Wulf answers promptly. "It gave me a lot to think about. I learnt that the raised spirit attacks are a great concern to the EU. They're worried we might never get on top of it. A couple of ideas were thrown around, such as supplementing the research fund and adding people with a low NAV to our ranks. Some interesting ideas in regard to changing training methods." I'm just about to tune out when his voice becomes sharper. "And then they found out about the fringe program. Congratulations!

You're definitely not in my daddy's good graces again," he adds, and I can only imagine how dark his frown is.

"Was I ever?" Being liked by Humberto Vallesco is really at the bottom of my priority list. "You know you weren't the only one who missed my talk?" I ask, keeping my voice smooth while I'm fuming inside. "After that keynote address and the clever scheduling your mum did, not even twenty people attended." I'm not telling him how much I blew it. It's bad enough I couldn't even present my arguments to twenty people. "If the SSA doesn't want to hear what we've got to say, that's fine. There are plenty of others who will."

There's a long silence on the other side before Wulf speaks again. "You really want to do this the hard way?" he asks at last, his voice tired. "My mother still wants to meet you for dinner. Can't we at least try to talk to my parents without ruining all they've worked for?"

I stand still, letting the rest of the group get ahead of me. "What happened to 'I'm yours'?"

"I am," he replies immediately. "I just wish there was a way to bring you and my family together. To make them see you the way I see you. To make them fall in love with you the way I did."

Leaning against a wall, I sigh. Aeola looks at me with concern, but I wave her off. "That's never gonna happen." It's not like I don't pick up on the hurt in his voice. Isn't it normal to want all the people dear to you to get along with each other? "Wulf. You've tried talking. It doesn't work. And I'm so sorry about it, but you can't keep sitting on the fence. It's me or them." It feels stupid to say it like that, but even as I speak, I know I'm right. The way his family's acted towards me, there can be no reconciliation. "You can't really be in love with me and support those who try to hurt me in every way possible."

"Rika—"

"I'd understand if you chose them." It hurts to say it, mostly because it's a lie. I wouldn't be able to understand it at all, but I've never been caught between two stools like him. "I have to go now. The others are waiting."

Wulf tries to stop me, but I quickly break off the call. If he chooses the Vallescos, it'll rip my heart out. There's no way I can deal with that kind of pain now.

Just as I'm about to put the phone away, I get a message: *Sorry I wasn't there for you. I'll do better.*

If only he could.

15

So far, there's been little interest in our fringe program. We've managed to procure some rooms at the Science 14 Atrium and put our event online, starting tomorrow, but as it corresponds with the SSA's advanced training camp following the lecture series, very few have signed up. At this point, it'll probably be a repeat of my disastrous talk.

A talk which is very well attended is Wulf's on Wednesday morning. I'm early enough to snatch up a seat somewhere in the middle, perfectly obscured by hundreds of other spirit seekers. Yet it's just my luck that I'm acquainted with the one who slips into the seat next to me.

"Oh, it's you," Carina greets, sighing greatly as she sits down. I bet if there was anywhere else to sit, she'd have taken it, but the seats behind her are already blocked. The Gold Room is packed. Every single seat is taken. Some people are even occupying the stairs to hear Wulf talk.

I ignore her snide little comment and look for Wulf. He's talking to Miro and two other seekers in the front row, looking awfully relaxed.

"I saw your little side programme," Carina announces. "Who decided on that line-up? I don't know any of those people." When she doesn't get the reaction she wants, she purses her beautiful lips. "I hope you're not really thinking of bringing a spirit to a gathering like that."

The people around us have caught onto our one-sided conversation and are now taking notice of me. "Are you really having a talk given by a spirit?" a young woman asks.

Forcing myself to smile at her, I nod. "Yes, it was Aeola's idea. You should come."

Next to me, Carina snickers. She leans forward to the woman, infringing on my space. "Don't bother. Unless your NAV is near 500, all you'll hear from that talk is the wind whistling through the seats."

"I'll be transcribing for Aeola."

"So, you're making it up?" Carina asks, her lips curling into a smile. "Anything to support your little idea."

The young woman doesn't really care about Carina's vicious remarks. She looks at me with awe. "Is your NAV near 500?"

"Above, actually." If I've learnt one thing about spirit seekers, it's that they value their NAV above anything else.

"Above 500?" The woman's eyes widen. She looks at Carina for confirmation. "Is that true?"

Carina folds her arms and leans back into her seat. "According to an unofficial test."

"By Wulf," I add, willing to play all my cards if that'll get one more person to our fringe programme.

"Well, she's Dante's by-blow," Carina announces, "so a high NAV is somewhat expected." That revelation sends the woman gossiping eagerly with her seat neighbours.

And thus, the news of my high NAV, my only value among this crowd, has been eclipsed by the one connection I don't want to be associated with. "Nicely done," I commend Carina, who smiles smugly at me.

"I hate this as much as you do, Rika, but you *are* family."

I snort. "Oh, no. I'm staying far away from your kind." Frankly, it frightens me that Carina would think of me as family. We might technically be cousins, but that doesn't negate what's happened between us. With a lowered voice, I say, "Don't forget Dante tried to kill me. Twice. And you didn't exactly step in."

For the first time, Carina looks flustered. She leans towards me, lowering her voice in a rushed whisper. "I didn't think he'd do it. He just wanted to stop Wulf from making a mistake. He never would've gone through with it."

"Oh, and I accidentally fell into the Colosseum, through a locked gate, after your father sent me there?"

"Why would he do that?" Carina pulls a face, deciding I can't possibly be believed.

I shake my head and lean back. "Because I'm oh-so dangerous. With all my radical ideas."

"You *are* dangerous!" Carina protests, a little too loudly. People are looking again, but this time Carina shoos them away, and they seem to know her temper well enough to heed her wishes. Again, she whispers, "What you're doing is extremely dangerous. I don't condone what Dante did to you. That's not okay, but you need to stop riling people up against us. What if someone important actually listens to you and stops the spirit seeker programme? The next deaths in that country are on you."

"I'm not trying to get rid of all spirit seekers. Not all spirits can be talked down, but a lot can, and why would you choose to aggravate them if you could find peaceful solutions that save spirit and human lives?"

Carina snorts and shakes her head in disbelief. "You're delusional."

"No, you are!" I no longer care that we're in the middle of a fully packed auditorium. There's still so much talking going on that barely anyone hears us, anyway. I know how important Carina is to Wulf—and he to her. Maybe she really isn't as deplorable as her older relatives, but she's certainly the poster child for wilfully shutting her eyes. "How can you still defend your parents after what you saw in the lab?"

Flustered, she drums her fingers on the tiny table. "I have no idea what you saw, but I saw my brother coming up with an ingenious way to pit spirits against each other." Her breath catches slightly, a sign that this topic is still sore to her.

"So, what spirit was going to attack Rue des Bouchers?" I prompt her. When she doesn't answer, I decide to probe a little further. "I didn't know your brother—"

"That's right!" she hisses. "You didn't know Piero. You think he's some kind of monster, but he's not. He was the sweetest and kindest soul who ever lived. And you know what's the worst?"

I keep my mouth shut, not willing to fight over the memory of her dead brother with her.

"He would've liked you." A faint glistening mists Carina's eyes. "He would've welcomed you with open arms. You're family, Rika, whether you want to be or not. So, stop playing up and give my mother her stupid dinner."

There's so much I have to say about that, but just then, a hush falls over the auditorium. It's time for Wulf to begin. Or rather, for my father to introduce him.

"My dear fellow seekers and honoured guests," Dante says, his voice carried by a microphone. "This man here needs no introduction. You all know Wulf Bachmann. A spirit seeker like him comes along once in a lifetime. For ten years, he's served our community, keeping not only Berlin safe, but helping all across Europe in times of need. His latest and probably largest feat took place this year when he led a team of elite spirit seekers into an active volcano and came out victorious."

Roaring applause greets this well-known announcement. None of them notice the shadow that flickers across Wulf's face at the mention. It's gone in a flash, replaced by a gracious smile, but I know how fake it is.

And so does Carina. "He's always hated the fame," she whispers.

Weird to have something in common with my cousin. "Now even more than before." Even weirder is knowing Wulf released Vesuvius and Dante was there to witness it.

Dante, however, smiles like the proud mentor he pretends to be. "I can't wait to hear more about this success and the challenges we're all facing. So, give it up for Wulf Bachmann!"

Another round of applause sounds. Once the auditorium has quieted down, Wulf gives Dante a curt nod and gets started. "Thank you all. I'm not sure I deserve all those accolades, but I'm going to try to give you a complete picture of the challenges I've faced and those that are yet to come."

Surprisingly, his first slide isn't too dissimilar to mine. It's Miriam's correlation between spirit attacks and industrialisation. "It's a well-known fact that spirit attacks have become more frequent and more deadly since the onset of industrialisation. Both have accelerated in the last few decades, correlating with climate change. Even the best-case model predicts even more deadly storms and frequent attacks. What does that mean for us? We need more spirit seekers, better technology, and a miracle."

My heart sinks as he reiterates the same old phrases the SSA's used. More soldiers, better strategies. If he knows it won't be enough to stop what's coming, why does he repeat it?

"One of those miracles was supposed to be the Vesuvius mission." Wulf changes his slide to one showing the ten spirit seekers who entered Vesuvius. Two of the pictures have a black ribbon across them. I know who Piero Vallesco is even before reading his name on the slide. He has the same eye colour as his sister, but a softer, warmer face framed by dark brown curls. He looks much younger than the almost thirty years he was when he died, like a cuddly teddy bear. The other one who died is a ginger boy named Oliver Reed, with lots of freckles covering his youthful face.

There's no smile on Wulf's face at the moment. "I know you're all expecting a glorious description of how the ten of us entered Vesuvius, found his inner sanctum, and caught a spirit so powerful he's been raining fire and blood on Italy for thousands of years. And I'll give you the details, but it was far from glorious." According to the excited murmurs in the auditorium, the people beg to differ. "Two of us died. We lost Oliver Reed in our first confrontation with Vesuvius. If you read the mission report, you saw that he broke protocol, but I'll be honest with you: no protocol would've saved his life once Vesuvius got his hands on him. He grabbed Oliver and threw him into a lava pool before the rest of us even got there."

The entire auditorium has quieted down. They came here for the victory, not for the losses it was bought with.

"We lost an ancient staff in the same battle. And all we could do was flee. I sent three people home at that point, and to this day, I wish we would've all gone with them," Wulf admits.

My heart goes out to him. By now, I know how he takes each failure personally. Whether it was his fault or not, to him, being commander means bearing all the blame.

"But we pushed on, eager to fulfil our mission. It took us more than a week before we got another chance. By that time, we'd been lost in the maze of conduits under Vesuvius for days. Every one of us wanted to go home. But that's not what spirit seekers do. We don't give up. So, when we picked up Vesuvius' energy levels, we launched a double-pronged attack. Three of us stayed in the tunnel while the rest of us tried to get to Vesuvius from behind." Wulf takes a deep breath, searching for something or someone in the audience but failing to find them. "We never got that far. Vesuvius wasn't confined to the tunnels like us. He could melt through the stone and bring rocks down on us." Wulf spreads his hands on the table, looking more serious than ever. "And by sheer accident, we had come too close to what we dubbed Vesuvius' eggs." He pulls up a picture of the three flowing lava eggs. Thankfully, there's no blackness pumped into them yet. "He caught us mid-split. And my brother paid the price."

Next to me, Carina inhales sharply. Tears are glistening in her eyes. I realise she must be back underground, seeing her little brother die.

"We managed to get away from Vesuvius, and by then it was clear that we'd completely underestimated this spirit. Not even our ancient staffs were a match for him." Wulf seems eager to move on from the topic of his dead brother. "So, how did we beat him, then? Or as Miro is protesting right now, how did *I* beat him." A few chuckles meet his little attempt to lighten the mood.

Completely disregarding his slides, Wulf comes to the front of the wide desk and leans against it as if he weren't in an auditorium of 1,200-plus people but talking to his friends. I'd envy him his casualness if I didn't feel sorry for how he's earned it.

"It's true," Wulf says. "I did send everyone else back home with Piero. I had one last plan, one last vanity, and I was willing to die for it."

Curious, I lean forward. There are these little things in his talk that don't quite add up. There's humility, and then there's beating yourself up. What's he doing?

"I went back for the eggs. It took me a long time to find them. About two weeks, I was told, when I came back out. One thing we learnt in our time down there was that temporarily coating our staffs with nymph water made them just a tad more effective against fire spirits. I had two bottles of nymph water left when Vesuvius found me. I fought him with one of them and my staff, and I thought I'd weakened him enough, but I was mistaken. Not even Piero's specifically designed trap was sufficient to hold him."

Wulf shakes his head, lost in the memory for a moment. "I thought I'd die there that very minute, but a lucky fall brought me right to the eggs. I seized my chance with the last water bottle in hand. It was a wild guess, but this giant, powerful spirit was scared for his offspring. So scared he didn't dare to get close to me. So scared he even heeded my command to bring me back up. If I'd had to walk, it would've taken me days. I would've had to sleep, and he could've killed me easily, but he was too afraid to think straight." He pauses to let that information sink in.

I doubt anyone makes the connection. These people need it spelled out for them.

Fortunately, Wulf does exactly that. "I think that was the biggest takeaway from this mission. Spirits aren't soulless. They care for their own, and they can be negotiated with. Or in my case threatened." He slaps his thighs and gets up, quickly glossing over this moment of thoughtfulness. "But it worked. I got Vesuvius to follow me to Rome, where he was subdued by the SSA, who used his eggs to keep him under control."

A picture of the Colosseum and the built-in protections shows on the slides. The SSA didn't solely rely on the eggs, but in the end, they were all that kept him confined. "I survived a volcanic eruption and brought home not only an S-class spirit but his eggs to be examined."

A round of applause forces Wulf to pause for a moment. Nobody seems to notice how tense he appears. On the large screens behind him, I can make out small beads of sweat. He's far from done with his talk.

"Surely that should've been my greatest triumph," he says, sounding everything but. "So, why then did I leave Rome as fast as possible?" He lets the question hang in the room.

Around me, I feel the confusion ripple through the crowd. What's he planning?

"I'll tell you why." Wulf returns to his conversational tone, facing the crowd awfully relaxed. "I didn't understand it at that time. But I felt horrible. Everyone was praising me, but what had I really done but threatened to kill a bunch of babies? If I'm putting it like that, it doesn't sound very heroic, does it?"

My heart beats faster, so fast I slip to the edge of my seat. Is he going to tell everyone how he released Vesuvius now? Is he going to out himself as the traitor his father believes him to be? I almost want to stop him. People don't take well to fallen heroes. The crowd will tear him apart.

"One of the reasons I ran home was that I learnt of an A-class spirit attack which had taken place while I was gone. I was worried about my team, though I was aware they'd won. How, I couldn't fathom. There were a couple of gaps in the report that made little sense. Mostly because they left out a critical person." Somehow, his eyes find me in the crowd, as if an invisible string is connecting us. "Someone had stepped in for me. A young woman with zero training but an unrivalled natural attunement. Rika Csorba."

I wish I could melt into my seat. People are turning around, trying to find who Wulf is looking at. Not many do, but those who find me raise their eyebrows. I realise now that some of these people *have* seen my videos. They recognise me.

Fortunately, Wulf keeps talking. "Rika had the most peculiar outlook on spirits. She even claimed to be friends with a sylph." His casual tone invites a few laughs. Yep, they totally saw my videos.

But Wulf's half-grin vanishes quickly. "I didn't take her seriously. I was grateful that she'd helped defeat the Erlking, but talking to spirits? Being friends with them? That made me angry. Let her talk down a volcano and we could speak." Now a real smile flashes over his face. "She did, though not immediately."

Now, he's got them curious. More people try to catch a glimpse of me, and I feel like I'm on the podium with him. It makes my skin crawl.

"Instead, we were called to Budapest to help the team there with some unnaturally strong spirits." Wulf pulls up a new slide. I've never seen one of these, but it seems to be the official mission report. "I want you all to do the maths. It doesn't add up. Look at the energy. The Danube was flowing upstream, taking down fortified bridges. You're gonna tell me that eight spirit seekers with only one ancient and seven normal staffs were able to stop that? I know I'm good, but I'm not that good."

Only a few laugh at that. The rest are too busy adding up the numbers. Wulf continues, talking about the battle as if it were nothing more than afternoon tea. "In fact, I would've drowned. So, why didn't I? How did we manage to hold Széchenyi Chain Bridge? And defeat five spirits the world had never seen the like of? More on that later." He waits a moment until he's sure he's got everyone's attention. "The answer is dryads. Dryads and Rika Csorba."

My palms are sweaty. It's as if every single person is looking at me now. People are intrigued, but more so, they're confused.

"When the spirits threatened Budapest, Rika went to the dryads of Margaret Island. She'd already made their acquaintance beforehand. And that night, she convinced them to help us." Wulf shakes his head as if he can't believe he's saying this. He pulls up a new slide with a different equation. "That night, eight spirit seekers and more than a dozen dryads fought together. As a team. Led by Rika Csorba. And as for me, I fell from the bridge and would've drowned if it weren't for Rika's sylph friend. She provided me with air until I dispatched the nymph trying to kill me."

At this point, multiple murmurs arose. I try to find Dante, but I can't see him anywhere, nor any of the other board members. Wherever they are, they must be horrified.

"So, you really *can* talk to spirits?" someone asks loudly. "How?"

Wulf points towards me. "Those are questions Rika can answer much better than me. But I've done it with her help. I've talked to spirits. It's definitely possible."

I shrink into my seat, not quite ready to face the entire spirit seeker force. Meanwhile, the room buzzes with whispers as people try to figure out what this all means.

After a moment, Wulf raises his hands to quiet down the auditorium. It takes about a minute before the agitation settles enough for him to continue. "Shamefully, I have to admit I wasn't happy with what went down in Budapest. It went against everything I learnt. Everything I'd been taught. On top of that, I owed my life to a sylph. Many of you know my parents were killed by sylphs when I was nine. And now another one had saved my life, and Rika Csorba had been right. I was furious. But more importantly, I was in denial."

At this, I sneak a look at Carina. She has her fingers wrapped around her armrests. Her face is almost entirely white, her lips moving quietly. If I didn't know better, I'd think she's close to passing out.

"We returned home, and only a day later, the citadel was attacked," Wulf continues. "A powerful dryad named Grune, like the forest in Berlin, came to our citadel and attacked us in our own courtyard. And in my worst moment, I sent Rika into that mayhem without even a weapon. She wanted to talk to him, and so I let her. And what happened next was a miracle." With his hands, he pictures the scenes. "Branches came slamming down, missing her by only the width of a hair. Every centimetre of her skin was pelted with acorns. And still, she continued. And she put her hand on the trunk of the big oak tree and... moments later, the attack stopped. An A-class spirit, brimming with anger, stopped his attack because she was willing to listen to him. Because she recognised his pain and was there to soothe it."

Once again, he lets the words sink in. This time, no one talks. Everyone's waiting with bated breath for him to continue. Even I'm holding mine.

"You can't watch something like that and continue to deny what you saw. Since that day, I've seen her do it again and again. I've seen her talk down Vesuvius in the Colosseum when he was determined to kill her. I've seen her bond with river nymphs and feisty little gnomes." Again, people are talking, but Wulf remains unfazed. "That. That is the miracle we need. That's how we can move forward. How we can find peace."

It's too early. Most of the seekers are still processing what Wulf claims I can do. They haven't drawn the conclusion yet.

Wulf picks up on it as well, and he pulls up another slide. This time it's a picture of his staff and mine. "There's more," he says. "Not only has Rika discovered a way to settle spirit attacks peacefully or mitigate them entirely. She has single-handedly solved the problem with our weapons. You've all learnt this at the academy. Our staffs are barely powerful enough to be of use. But we had three ancient staffs, two after Vesuvius. Now there's a fourth. Though, it isn't exactly ancient."

I hear multiple gasps, and now the tingling of my skin is in anticipation. These spirit seekers will have their minds blown in a minute.

"It took a spirit seeker with an NAV above 500 to figure out the reason we were unable to recreate the ancient staffs was because we had no idea what we were doing. We cut off dryad wood and shaped it into what we thought was the most efficient fighting form. But what we really did was ruin the wood. The ancient staffs weren't made. They were gifted. And after helping Grune get rid of yet another of these strong, polluted spirits, he gifted Rika with her own staff. A staff made from his wood. And it's just as powerful as the one I'm using."

Wulf snorts. "We could've had powerful weapons all this time if only we'd been more open to spirits. If only we'd seen more in them than the enemy. It turns out Rika isn't the first person in the world to build intimate relationships with spirits. Druids have done it before her. In the past, spirit seekers, if we want to call them that, bonded with powerful dryads, or nymphs, or other spirits to defend the people—and the spirits—under their protection."

He shakes his head, sounding almost sad when he speaks next. "The board asked me to talk about the biggest challenge for us spirit seekers. It isn't spirits. It's not even those unnaturally powerful spirits we've so far encountered in Budapest, Berlin, Dublin, and now here in Brussels. The biggest challenge for the 21st century spirit seeker is the same as for everyone else: it's climate change. It's how we've treated the world, disconnected from nature—and from spirits—that's forced us into this era with more frequent and deadly attacks than ever before." He pulls up his summary slide, which reiterates the graph. "There's a correlation between the pollution of air, water, and earth, and the retribution we feel. We caused these attacks. But hopefully, by working with the spirits, by learning to listen to them, we can reverse this effect."

For a moment, Wulf waits, seemingly catching the eyes of every single spirit seeker. Then he stands up straight. "Any questions?"

It turns out there are a million of them. I can't even listen to the first few; I'm that jittery. I should've never doubted Wulf when he said he wanted to do it his way. He's just told all attending spirit seekers and the press what I wanted them to hear. And better than I could've ever said it. Change has to happen now. Something has to. They can ignore a little unknown upstart like me, but they can't ignore their hero. And judging by the questions, people might be struggling to process everything, but they're curious.

"But how do we figure out whether spirits are malicious or righteously angry if it takes an NAV of close to 500 to understand them?" Someone on the far left asks.

Wulf repeats the question for all to hear and pulls up some bonus slides. "That's an excellent question. And fortunately, there's yet another advantage to Rika's method. One of my team members, Leon Harting-Ueda came to me with an NAV of 112. Pitiful, really. He barely noticed when spirits were around. When he met Rika, he changed his entire attitude. Instead of being frightened of spirits, he was eager to learn more about them. From them. This is the NAV test he took last week."

Not a single person remains unimpressed. Wulf smiles openly now. "Leon's NAV's improved by more than 150 points. At this moment, the exact process is still very much trial and error and we haven't quite found out how to effectively improve someone's NAV. There seem to be different methods that work for each person, but the key is our attitude to the environment and the spirits who live in it. I'd probably say even my NAV has improved slightly since Rika taught me how."

"That's not fair!" someone in the front shouts, and laughter bubbles up. People are excited, buzzing really.

Next to me, Carina rises, demanding a microphone. She's still awfully pale. After it's handed to her, she takes a deep breath. "Wulf. Is it true that Rika Csorba freed Vesuvius and returned his eggs to him?"

The exalted mood quickly flips. All attention is back on me, even though Carina refuses to acknowledge me.

Wulf looks serious. "No. That was me."

My breath quickens, worry rising in my chest. *Please don't let every-thing fall apart now.*

"You're probably all wondering why I'd do such a thing." Wulf takes a deep breath. "I told you how I felt about it. How it just didn't feel right. At first, I pushed those feelings away. I did what I had to do to save my life. But, guys, I threatened a spirit's babies. As necessary as it was down in the volcano, it felt terribly wrong once I got out of there. I told you how Rika talked Vesuvius down. They struck a deal. I sealed that deal. I made amends and I returned those babies, and in return, Vesuvius promised to go dormant for the rest of humanity's lifespan. If we keep our end of the bargain and stop poisoning every centimetre of this earth," he adds, then looks up at Carina. "So, yes, I made that deal. I wish we'd talked to him earlier. Maybe then two of our dearest friends would still be alive."

For a moment, Carina looks as if she's going to throw the micro-phone at him. Instead, she drops it, causing terrible feedback that hurts everyone's ears. Then she pushes through the row, forcing people to get up quickly or raise their legs. The whole auditorium seems to hold their breath until Carina has left the room, slamming the door behind her.

Then, the questions and buzz arise again. At one point, Wulf defers to the fringe programme for everyone who wants to learn more. And to me, something the people around me take immediate advantage of.

"When did you learn to speak with spirits?" the woman from before asks.

"When I learnt to speak with humans. My mother taught me how. It's all a matter of expressing how you really feel."

A guy to my left leans over, frowning slightly. "Is your mother Magdaléna Csorba? The spirit teacher?"

There's no point in keeping that secret anymore. "Yes, she is."

"Why did she never teach us that?" he asks.

Well, what do you think? I want to say, but this isn't the place to throw around accusations. "I have no idea. We lost touch eight years ago. We only reconnected recently."

"Is Dante truly your father?" the woman asks again.

I'm bursting with so much optimism that even that question can't throw me. "Apparently. But we don't really know each other. As far as I'm aware, my mother and he attended the academy together."

Slowly, the crowd moves towards the exits. Once I reach the stairs, my friends manage to jump in and gently guide people to the fringe programme instead. Meanwhile, I make my way down to the podium against the throng.

There, people are crowding Wulf with even more questions. He answers a few before noticing me at the side. With a few more words, he excuses himself and makes his way over to me, looking somehow guarded. "I'm sorry for putting you in the spotlight."

I can barely contain my giddiness. "I should thank you for that."

His shoulders relax and a smile graces his lips. "Well, you belonged there. I thought your point of view needed to be heard."

I can't keep still any longer. Instead, I throw my arms around his neck and press my lips onto his. Someone whoops nearby, but I don't care. All my gratefulness, my nervous energy, and the love I've harboured for him so long flows into that kiss. He chose me. In front of more than 1,200 people, Wulf Bachmann chose me.

16

Coming out of the room is insane. There are supposed to be other talks, but people are more interested in flooding Wulf, and to a lesser extent me, with questions. Miriam pulls me into a big hug, grinning from ear to ear. "So many people are signing up."

"To the fringe programme?" I'm still buzzing from Wulf's talk and the kiss.

Miriam nods, excited. "Yes! Some of our talks are already fully booked. Yours and Aeola's were the first ones to go. You might have to do a second one. Or we'll have to put up screens outside."

"Let her breathe," Leon laughs, then hugs me as well. "Are you prepared for this?" he asks, his lips twitching with a smile. "There's going to be a lot of interest in you. Wulf just introduced you to the entire SSA."

Around us, there are quite a few fingers pointed at me,

as people show their friends who I am. A few are waiting on the side, looking eager to talk to me. "I have no idea!" I admit.

There's also the SSA board to consider. Surely, they won't just take this without comment. But right now, I can't think of any danger. It all gets swept up in the excitement. We did it. Wulf did it!

Most questions I get are related to the spirits I've conversed with. "Can all spirits be talked to, or how do you figure out who's safe and which one isn't?" someone asks.

"Well, you can talk to all of them, but they're not always willing to listen. A lot of them have been conditioned by centuries of battle to fear humans, especially spirit seekers. It usually takes a token of faith, like putting down your staff, for them to give you a chance," I explain.

Naturally, that frightens them. "Are you crazy, or what?"

I laugh. "Sometimes. It might be my NAV, but I can usually feel whether a spirit is angry or frightened, or absolutely hates my guts. I tend to stay away from the latter ones."

"Definitely sounds like an NAV thing. How high is yours?" a man wants to know.

"According to the test, 512."

"But," Wulf is suddenly at my side, "as Rika reminds me every once in a while, I wasn't really impartial when I tested her. I likely graded her far too low. We might need to reinvent the NAV scale."

They're as excited to see him at my side as I am. "Can one really get better?"

"Leon?" I turn to call him to us. "It worked for him, but so far, he's the only one who's had any sizeable success." As Leon reaches us, I bring him up to speed. "Hey. Perhaps you can tell these folks how you improved your NAV."

He seems happy enough to oblige. "Sure. It was a bit unintentional. Personally, I think it's a matter of finding out what's limiting your NAV in the first place."

Nearby, I see Camille listening in, a shadow passing over her face. Her hands are trembling.

I walk over to her and put a hand on her shoulder. "If the drugs have shown us one thing, it's that there's potential for more. We just need to find how to get you past your limits naturally," I whisper.

Camille winces, then forces a smile. "It doesn't matter, does it?" She reaches out to Wulf, who's followed me. "That was a great talk. The way you controlled the crowd. Also, incredibly brave."

Wulf snorts. "I only told them the truth, and not even the whole thing. If someone's brave, then it's Rika." His hand finds mine, and I can hardly keep myself from bopping on my feet.

"Well, everyone knows that," Camille says, sounding somewhat distanced. The smile she gives me is gone in a flash. "You're the one who started it all."

"And you're stronger than you think you are." I hug her and whisper once more, "Stop being so hard on yourself."

Some of the people around us start moving towards other lectures, but there are enough who are sitting out the next round. One of them is Miro, who strolls over like some sabre-toothed tiger, exuding danger while seeming completely relaxed.

"There's the woman of the hour," he announces.

I can't help myself and giggle. Then I point at Wulf. "He gave the talk."

Miro rolls his eyes. "Yeah, but all I got from that was that you blew his mind. To be fair, it doesn't take much to do that to Wulfie."

For that, Wulf boxes him in the arm.

I think it's the first time I've met someone who's truly Wulf's peer. Nobody in awe of him, nobody falling over himself to impress him. Miro might not get the same amount of adoration as Wulf, but his NAV is almost as high.

He jerks his chin towards me. "So, Rika, tell me. In Russia, we have big problems with the tundra spirits. Especially in winter. They never attack en masse, but are rather guerilla-like. I've got thousands of kilometres of front to defend, and they can strike anywhere. If I were to talk to them, I wouldn't even have an idea of where to find them until after they've struck. And also, I might be able to do that talking thing, but I can't be everywhere at once. So, what do I do? What do I tell my seekers to do?"

Oh, wow, he's going straight for the jugular, wanting my professional opinion. "That sounds really tricky, but I can't give you on-the-fly advice. I know too little about the situation in Russia, the people and the spirits." I remember the beautiful but dangerous ice spirit I met in Rome and wonder if he's still living in the freezer section of an Italian supermarket. "It might be the melting of permafrost soils that sets them on edge or something else entirely." If gnomes can form a union, then perhaps those tundra spirits are more organised than Miro realises. "I would have to travel to Russia and get a lay of the land, talk to other spirits, question the winds. I fear it's a case-by-case method." What am I talking about? Moments ago, there wasn't even a method to begin with.

Miro nods, deeply in thought. He might've been joking before, but this is serious business for him. So many lives depend on him, as he leads the entirety of Russia's spirit seekers. "It's a date then. You two will visit us this fall."

"Will we?" Wulf asks, amused.

"Well, I want Rika there," Miro declares. "And I'm happy to pay you for your expertise and reimburse you for all your troubles." Then he nods towards Wulf. "And if you can convince that guy to come along and finally make good on his promise to visit, I might even pay you extra."

"You don't need to bribe Rika to get me to visit," Wulf protests.

Miro pulls a funny face. "Yeah, I'm not so sure that's true. It's been ten years."

"When have you ever come to Berlin?" Wulf asks.

"Touché." Miro grins and moves in to pat Wulf on the back. "Alright, I'm gonna head out, meet Manya and the little ones for some sightseeing. Dinner at Thierry's or are you two planning a private celebration?"

One thing's for sure: I'd much rather have dinner with Miro and his family than the Vallescos. But a private celebration doesn't sound too bad either.

"Meet you at seven?" Wulf asks, deciding on the former.

"I'll book us a table." Miro backs away, raising his hand in greeting. "See you later."

By now, the foyer has emptied considerably. Wulf turns to face me, looking somewhat nervous all of a sudden. "So, were you going to catch one of the other talks?"

"Were you?"

"Not really. Shall we take a walk outside and find you some waffles?" he asks.

I grin wildly, still tingling from his touch all over. "It's like you know all my sweet spots."

Wulf laughs. "I hope I do." He puts an arm around my shoulders and leads me out of the conference centre.

We get waffles from a street vendor not too far from the conference centre. They're round and much thicker than the ones you get in Germany. Sugar in the dough has caramelised on top, while the inside is delightfully gooey. Even with nothing more than powdered sugar, they're divine.

As we walk down the cobbled streets of the inner city, my mind is buzzing from processing Miro's proposal. "I should take Miro up on that offer, shouldn't I? I've never been to Russia, but I met a tundra spirit in Rome, and we got along well enough."

"Of course you did," Wulf laughs. He nudges my shoulder. "You know you might have to do that for every team?"

"What? Travel the world and teach people how to work with spirits?" The moment I say it out loud, it becomes a vision. "You know what? I think I'd like that a lot."

Wulf nods, mirroring my excitement. "It does sound perfect for you. And exactly what we need. You get to travel and implement new ways for communities to deal with spirits, fostering human-spirit friendships. You'll be much in demand once word gets out."

I stop walking to take his hand in mine. "And will you come with me?" If this is what lies in my future, I might not see as much of the friends I've become so fond of.

He puts his other hand to my cheek. "I'd follow you to the end of the world."

My heart beats faster, so fast my breath hitches. "Would you?"

Wulf rubs some powdered sugar off my cheek, a soft smile gracing his lips. "Well, after that kiss..."

"It was long overdue, wasn't it?" Suddenly, all I want is to kiss him again. I might never want to stop.

Wulf's smile turns into a grin as he nods. "Oh, yeah. We might have to catch up on all those lost opportunities."

"Sounds good to me." I let go of his hand and put both of mine on his waist instead, pulling him towards me.

Wulf takes a step closer, cupping my face in his hands. Then his lips brush mine, softly at first, almost hesitant, but that changes quickly when I open mine. The world falls away as I focus on the touch of his body against mine. There's only him and me, and where we both connect. My stomach flutters when his tongue touches mine, and I grab his waist tighter, wanting more of him.

All the waiting, the dancing around each other, and distanced yearning has been worth it. This is better than any kiss I've ever shared. I feel his love flowing into me as I give him all of mine. And I know that he's wholly mine, just as I'm his.

17

After having dinner with Miro's lovely family, I may or may not have spent the night in Wulf's room, talking and kissing all night long. No, don't worry, we weren't rushing things after waiting for so long, but it just proved too hard to say goodnight. Instead, I slip back into my room sometime in the morning to take a quick shower and change my clothes, choosing a light summer dress for the first day of the fringe programme. I bought this one on a whim after the Travellers showed up and have had yet to find the courage to wear something so impracticable and flashy. After years spent on the greyscale, I feel like a peacock in my blue and yellow dress.

All awkwardness slips away the moment Wulf picks me up for breakfast, though. He takes one long glance at me and leans in for a kiss, as if he hadn't got enough of those last night. "Wow," he whispers, then kisses me again.

I laugh. "It's just a dress."

"A pretty dress," Wulf jokes and offers me his arm. "Shall we get some breakfast? I could use some coffee."

"Could you?" Grinning, I loop my arm into his and let him guide me to the elevator.

Downstairs, we load our trays with breakfast waffles—the square type, this time—and fruit and get a big pot of coffee. Wulf starts feeding me little bites, stealing a kiss now and then. I know it's ridiculous, but I could have this every day of my life and never tire of it.

"I hope we're not intruding on anything?" a female voice, dripping with acid, says.

I jerk away from Wulf and sit up straight. Opposite us, Carina and her mother sit down with their own trays. Carina stares daggers at both of us but her mother is smiling.

"Good morning, you two," Alena says. "It looks like you had a good night's sleep." She smirks. "Or lack thereof."

Confused, I check with Wulf. Did he know about this ambush? But Wulf looks as tense as I do. "What is this?" he asks.

"Well, you refused my dinner invitations, so we invited ourselves to breakfast," Alena explains, pouring herself a cup of coffee from our pot. "I hope that's okay with you."

Carina talks in rapid-fire Italian to her mother, obviously complaining about something. Next to me, Wulf grabs his butter knife tightly before responding likewise. After a short moment, Alena raises her hands. "Enough, you two. It's not polite to talk in a language not all of us understand." She smiles comfortingly at me. "It's a real shame you never had the chance to learn Italian, Rika."

"I know plenty of other languages," I answer, my face muscles straining under a fake smile. Why can't we have at least twenty-four hours without Wulf's meddling family?

Wulf jumps straight to my defence. "Yes, Rika is a true polyglot. And that's not counting her speaking with spirits." Someone's not taking any prisoners today.

But if he'd hoped to unsettle his mother, he's sadly mistaken. She remains in a good mood. "How wonderful. Did your mother teach you?"

"Yes," I answer carefully. Since the mother-daughter team has arrived, I haven't been able to eat a single bite. I suddenly feel every hour of missing sleep as I wait for the hammer to drop.

"I guess that's to be expected from a pair of Travellers like you." Try as I might, I can't detect the derogative undertone I'm so used to.

I decide to probe my luck. "So, how come I haven't seen her at the conference? As a teacher, I'd assume she'd be all over this."

Alena sighs. "You must be so disappointed to miss her, but Magdaléna didn't want to come. I'm sorry."

Try as I might, I can't keep the disappointment at bay. My eyes strain with the effort of staying dry. And not even Wulf's hand on mine can soften the poison dart my mother's voluntary absence has deposited in my flesh.

"But enough of that," Alena says, eager to move on. "There are a lot of things we need to discuss."

Here it comes. For some reason, I'm much calmer now I'm about to go into battle. "I assume you're not too happy with Wulf's talk or the interest our fringe programme has garnered?"

Alena laughs, shaking her head. "Quite the opposite. Your father might be sulking," she tells Wulf, "but that's mainly because you jumped this on him." She rolls her eyes. "You know how much he values tradition. He struggles with all these changes more than he cares to admit. And as for you, my dear," Alena says to me, "I wouldn't have invited you to speak if I didn't want to hear from you. Your fringe programme is frankly genius. I wish you'd spoken to me about this earlier, but I guess time was against us. I wasn't even aware of all these new developments, or I would have scheduled them myself."

"You would've scheduled a sylph talk?" So far, my scepticism wins, but all her kind words are beginning to wear me down. Maybe Wulf was right and I should've given his family a proper chance.

"I would've been intrigued if you'd suggested it." She thinks a little about it, which I appreciate. "But yes, I think I would've. Contrary to my husband, I believe in progress. The world is changing. There's no doubt about that."

Wulf and I share a nervous look, both unsure how much of what his mother says is real. At last, he clears his throat. "You want to discuss some things? How about we start with what Dante did to Rika? Kidnapping her, locking her up in a cell, subjecting her to brainwashing and psychological torture, not to forget locking her in with Vesuvius under the impression that the spirit would kill her."

Thanks, Wulf, for reminding me. I needed that cold shower to wash off the niceties. "And I'm not the first person he's done that to. I've heard of several others who've been either tortured into submission or... shall we say, conveniently vanished?"

"That's utter bullshit," Carina protests. She moves to get up, but her mother grabs her wrist with an iron grip and forces her back down.

"I fear it's true, my dear," Alena says. "The evidence is mounting up."

Carina snorts, but a firm look from her mother makes her relent. "I guess."

Satisfied, Alena continues, "You must understand that it's a hard thing to believe of one's own brother, but perhaps I shouldn't be surprised. He's always been rather... radical with his methods." She looks at Wulf with pity in her eyes. "I'm not saying he wasn't a spectacular spirit seeker, but... I'm sorry, darling." She reaches out to him and squeezes his hand.

Wulf shrugs it off, but I know that it bothers him more than he's letting on. Dante was his hero once. "So, what's the board going to do about it?"

Alena leans back. "What we have to do. Gather evidence. Go to the police. And fire him, of course. A man like that shouldn't be anywhere near our students." Her harsh words leave her breathless for a second. With a few blinks, she manages to keep her composure. Then Alena looks at me. "I'm terribly sorry for everything he subjected you to."

"He wasn't alone." As much as I abhor Dante, he could've never pulled it off alone. I think of Agnes and her gun pointed at my face. And Gian, my personal bodyguard, who knew exactly what was going on. "Your husband told him to bring me to Vesuvius. And he knew where I was held."

Carina looks pale. Her lips are moving, her head slightly shaking. A small part of me feels sorry for her. I've already accused her brother of being a terrorist; now we're coming for her uncle and father.

Wulf, meanwhile, nods. "And he was the one who called me immediately and threatened Rika with a lawsuit if she should ever go to the police. He knew."

"And he threatened you and our entire team with retribution if we didn't take down the YouTube channel," I remind him. Humberto Vallesco didn't just go after me. He went after his own foster son.

"Because that YouTube channel is so harmful!" Carina bellows, drawing the attention of several other guests. She leans forward to hiss at us. "Have you read the comments? People are calling the SSA liars and warmongers. They want to disband us. We've had reports of teams being harassed. How are we supposed to keep people safe if they don't want us to?" I open my mouth, but Carina jabs her finger at me. "And don't come at me with your communication bullshit. Yes, that may work for you. I'm not questioning your successes. But you're only one person. And those people calling for the SSA to be abolished? They can't talk to spirits. So, what'll happen next? Spirits attack and there's no one to talk them down and no one to defend our communities. Voilà, mass catastrophe accomplished."

Out of breath, she leans back again, waiting for me to challenge her. Next to me, Wulf shifts uncomfortably. They're the same doubts he had over our public campaign. "I get it," he starts gently. "It makes me uncomfortable, too, but maybe public pressure is exactly what we need to make the important changes. Tio Dante and Father have damaged the SSA almost beyond repair. I've been saying this for years. There's so much nepotism and manipulation going on. It's not okay to have a board comprised almost entirely of old SSA families." I remember there was talk of putting Wulf onto the board.

"That's how legacy works," Alena reminds him softly. "All these families have been working hard their entire lives. They haven't just shown up at the academy and gotten their education. They've been trained since they were children. Just like you, Carina, and Piero were. If you raise your children to take over your business, why would you give it to someone else, who barely knows enough about the history and tradition of your business."

"Because the SSA isn't a family business. It's a multinational defence force that should have a multinational board. A true multinational board, not just some straw members for show." Judging by Wulf's agitation, this is an argument he's had several times.

Alena raises both her hands in defeat. "Alright, alright, one thing after the other. I hear your concerns, Wulf. And yours, Rika." She looks sideways at her daughter. "And even yours. This can't all be solved over breakfast. So, what do you think about coming to Italy after the conference, and we'll discuss this with the board, draw up new strategies, and—"

"Absolutely not." The mere thought of returning to Rome sets my skin on fire.

Exasperated, Alena lowers her hands. "Rika, we want to work with you, not against you. Your mother will be there." The possibility is dangled in front of my nose like a carrot. "But to move on, we need you—"

This time, Wulf interrupts her. "I barely got her out of Rome last time. If you want to meet, it has to be on neutral ground."

Alena leans back. Slowly, she nods. "Neutral ground, very well." There's a hint of hurt in her voice, probably because Wulf no longer sees his hometown as a safe place. "You pick. Are you okay with that?"

I honestly have no idea. Am I okay with that? Alena is practically offering us the SSA on a silver plate. Sure, they won't agree to everything. Who will step back from their position of power? Part of me feels like this will be a giant waste of time, a show more than a change. But it's a pretty big show. A chance to set things right, of a magnitude I would've never believed possible. Is it really doubt that's holding me back, or am I just scared? "What of my... father?"

"The board will take immediate action against him," Alena says promptly. "And anyone that's been involved with him."

"Including your husband?" Wulf asks.

Alena winces when he refuses to acknowledge his own relationship with Humberto. "I will look into it, yes."

Carina inhales sharply when she hears that. "We've only got Rika's word on his involvement!"

"And mine," Wulf says, his face darkening.

Carina looks at him, bewildered. "How do you think Piero would feel if he knew you were tearing our family apart?"

It's a cheap shot, and I quickly put a hand on Wulf's thigh to comfort him. His face is set in stone. "Piero would've never stood for such deplorable actions. I didn't think you would."

"I'm not condoning what he's done. But, Wulf. He's our father. And just because this tramp," her eyes are glistening with tears as she points at me, "wriggled herself onto your team and now the SSA... Why are we listening to some wannabe seeker who came out of nowhere?"

Any sympathy I might have had for Carina evaporates with her words. I know very well how pretentious it is that the entire world should change its ways just because I say so, but this isn't about me. Not truly. "I'm just the messenger, Carina. The things that are wrong with this world, that are wrong with the SSA and our understanding of spirit seeking, have been wrong for centuries. I may be the only one saying it out loud, but that doesn't make it any less true."

Wulf nods. "And that's why we listen, why I listen. Because what Rika says, it's true. The evidence is there. You might be able to close your eyes to it, and frankly, I understand that. I've been through it. All this is overwhelming, but it's necessary that we stop hiding behind what we know and learn more about what we don't. We can't keep going on like we have."

"And we won't," Alena says with finality. "I'll let you finish your breakfast. Pick the place, I'll organise the rest." She and Carina get up.

Even though they're gone, I've no appetite left. I want to believe this is a good thing. I not only owe Wulf as much, but also the spirits who are counting on me and everyone else. If we can get the SSA on our side, we could move much faster. We could train spirit seekers to become spirit advocates as well as good fighters. It wouldn't all be on me. But if that's so great, then why do I feel like I'm selling out?

18

I decide to push away all thoughts about the SSA as I attend the fringe programme. We might not have to worry about the SSA if this goes smoothly. Contrary to my talk, the side conference is incredibly well attended. It takes place at the Science 14 Atrium, which immediately wins my heart with the carpet of greenery hanging in the reception space. It's light and open—and completely packed with people.

"Rika!" Miriam pulls me to the side after spotting me. "There you are. We're completely sold out. We even had to shift things around to open some places for EU politicians. Turns out they're very interested in alternative ideas. So, go get them!"

As exciting as all this is, it's also scary. "I don't even have slides."

Wulf puts his hands on my shoulders and squeezes them. "You don't need slides. Just talk from the heart."

It turns out that just talking without any proper preparation is my sweet spot. Perhaps it's because I already know everything I want to tell them. And how. This time around, I'm not trying to appeal to the spirit seekers. I'm not catering to their narrative, trying to convince them how advantageous it would be to try my way. Sure, they want a higher NAV and more effective staffs, but those are only the side effects, not the main selling points.

Instead, my entire talk is structured around building up empathy towards spirits. I tell them how I used to watch spirits with my mother and how they helped me survive on the streets. There's a long bit about meeting Aeola and how, from our friendship, my understanding blossomed. And of course, I recount my meeting with Grune and all that he's shown me.

"Grune called it being a 'true spirit seeker'. Someone who spoke for the spirits and established positive human-spirit relationships that would foster both sides and protect them from harm, be it evil spirits or mindless destruction by humans. What I'm telling you isn't new. I didn't come up with this. Did you never wonder why we call the NAV the 'natural attunement value'? It's because we're attuned to nature. We're aware of the spirits and their needs. But we lost our way. Instead of guiding our communities, we perverted our talent and used it to turn spirits and humans against each other."

I'm aware these are uncomfortable truths. To find out you're not the hero but the bad guy doesn't go down easy. But it doesn't have to define the rest of your life. "It's not too late to change our ways. The spirits haven't completely turned against us. They want peace and protection as much as we do. And you only have to look as far as Ireland to see it's working. I don't want to take too much away from Rory McCarthy's talk, but the spirit seekers over there have been practically bored because their druids' work has lowered hostile spirit activity by almost a hundred per cent. And that's simply due to the respect shown to the Aos Sí. Now, they're establishing an active working relationship with Liffey, Dublin's river nymph."

Time has flown by. It's almost time to open the room for questions. "So, if you're interested in spirit advocacy, check out Rory's talk. It's my hope we can duplicate Dublin's efforts in every major city. It may not always be that easy. Each spirit is different. Each spirit community has their own rules and needs. That's why it's important for us to take a step back and try to truly understand the dynamics at play. Make friends with local spirits, take time to listen to them, and if you can, help them. Creating sustainable relationships is the only way forward. We need to stop this war against nature or we'll face even worse disasters."

For a moment, the room is silent, digesting my last words. Then something wonderful happens. People are applauding. They actually appreciated my talk. A smile of relief slips onto my lips, and I feel myself relax. "Are there any questions?"

Just as with Wulf's presentation, there are countless ones. It looks like almost every hand is up. A couple of them are asked in disbelief. How did I know I could trust the spirits? *Well, how do I know if I can trust humans?* Am I really saying that most spirits only want to be left in peace? *Of course, they do. Most people do, so why not spirits?*

Some go beyond that, referring to things Wulf told them about. How did I convince the dryads to assist in the battle of Budapest? I refer them to Iván's talk, since it's a long story, *But in short, I appealed to their own need to keep the trees they care for safe.* Did I honestly talk down Vesuvius? *Yes, and it was the scariest thing I've ever done. If a little salamander named Glut hadn't spoken in my favour, it wouldn't have been a success.* When one asks how I even got in that position, I gloss over it.

One of the politicians asks an interesting question. "Would you say there's a connection between climate change and increased spirit activity?"

"I'm not a scientist, but I believe there is. It's quite obvious when you look at the data. And the thing is that elevated sea levels, higher temperatures, and melting of permafrost soils are all things that directly impact spirit habitats. Climate change is threatening them just as much as us, maybe even more so. I think you'll find that many things bothering spirits, that make them anxious and aggressive, are issues we face as well. I—"

There is much more I want to say, but Leon rushes in and interrupts me. "You need to come," he whispers. "I think Alexander's here, and some of the higher NAV seekers have seen him. They're getting ready to fight him."

Great. I have to deal with some self-important idiots, so we don't have an earthquake on our hands. "I'd love to chat more about all of that, and I promise, there will be plenty of opportunity to do so. Thanks everyone for coming today."

I quickly follow Leon before anyone can stop me. A small crowd has gathered in front of the conference centre. Three gnomes are standing outside, crunching their teeth. Alexander is one of them, having turned out all his glimmers today in a bedazzling interpretation of a suit. Next to him, Madeline is tapping her foot while a third is half submerged in the ground. In front of them, Lukas has positioned himself, his staff held in a defensive pose. However, it's not the gnomes he's guarding himself from, but the four spirit seekers who've brought their weapons with them. I recognise one of them as the guy from my disastrous talk. One of the others is Wiola. She's the one able to see the gnomes.

"You can't even see what you're defending!" she accuses Lukas. "Don't come crying to me when they break your legs in a pothole."

"Don't come crying to me over some broken arms if you don't back off soon," Lukas retorts.

My heart almost wells over. Lukas is standing up for a group of gnomes and he can't even see them behind him.

"Your posturing is all very charming," Alexander says, "but let me have a go at them. They'll be picking gravel out of their skin for days to come."

Alright, time to step in before things get nasty. "What's going on?" I ask, pushing my way through the crowd.

Wiola turns to me, looking me up and down. "Can't you see it? Gnomes are trying to sneak into your neat little conference and probably kill everyone inside."

"Or they're curious about what's going on. Alexander is a friend. And every gnome from the Gnomian Union is my guest," I declare.

The guy from my lecture snickers at first, then starts laughing out loud. "What are you on, Csorba? That's some excellent stuff. Gnomian Union? Who the fuck comes up with something like that?"

"Knowing her, she probably organised some gnomes in a union, riling them up against us," Wiola announces loud and clear for everyone to hear. "Just like she led a bunch of spirits in the destruction of the academy. Because that's what you do, right? All spirits have to be free, doesn't matter how much damage they do. Spirit rights over human rights."

"I'll let you know that the Gnomian Union precedes the European Union by a total of seventy-two years," Madeline announces, justifiably angered. "You're not the first creatures who learnt how to conduct business the proper way."

"Softies," Alexander mutters.

I don't know what Wiola heard in the gnome's words, but she moves forward quickly, swinging her staff.

"Don't!" I shout, but I'm too late to stop her.

She sidesteps my outstretched hand and swipes her staff at the gnomes. Before the wood hits the stone, Lukas brings his own staff down, blocking her attack. "You want these gnomes?" he asks. "You'll have to go through me."

It's obvious that Wiola doesn't think much of people below her NAV, but Lukas isn't a spirit. He fights just as well as any of the higher attuned spirit seekers, and he's giving Wiola a run for her money. That is, until the others join in.

Even Lukas can't hold himself against four. And now they're getting dangerously close to the gnomes. Below us, the earth starts rumbling.

"Stop it!" I shout and throw myself in the middle. I get a hold of one of the staffs only to have it ripped from my hands and smacked against my thigh.

"Get out of the way, spirit friend," one of the guys snarls.

Instead, I spread my arms wide, blocking Lukas' left side. "Come on. Hit me, oh brave spirit seeker!" I tease. "Defenceless spirit or human, it's all the same to you, isn't it?" I know I'm begging to be beaten up. I've seen the speed in which these staffs are wielded. One good hit and he could break my arm or knock me out.

Before it gets that far, others join the scuffle. Leon has found himself a staff and is fighting side-by-side with Lukas. Two other familiar faces come to my help: Eoghan and Henny. Henny steps in front of me, forcing me backwards between the gnomes while Eoghan closes the circle. Sure enough, Wiola stares at him, her face blotchy from exhaustion.

"Eoghan? So, it really is true? You're with her?" she asks, pausing her attack.

He snorts. "More like I went to prison for helping Rika escape Rome. All legal, I'm sure."

I leave those two to hash it out and turn my attention towards the gnomes, who are now tightly protected by friendly spirit seekers. The unknown gnome has vanished completely underground. Madeline stares stalactites at me. "This is not proper conduct."

"And I'm deeply sorry for this unwarranted aggression. We should've have been more vigilant with our security." To be honest, I hadn't even thought about spirits attending, apart from Aeola tomorrow.

"Bringing staffs to a co-spirit conference is a serious offence." Madeline is still trembling and so is the ground immediately beneath her.

I nod hastily, noting the seekers around me are still locked in battle. "I'll let everyone know they should leave their staffs at home or hand it to wardrobe upon arrival."

Madeline regards me with a severe look that makes me want to crumble on the spot. Then Alexander leans over and whispers something to her. Annoyance radiates off her. Whatever he's telling her isn't to her liking, but the trembling stops and the earth quiets down. "Very well. I acknowledge that there will be growing pains and this is your first major event. I accept your apology, spirit seeker."

I didn't know how much was riding on this until she'd absolved me. "Thank you. We'll do better. I promise."

Turning around, I notice more people have come to our aid and the scuffle has been resolved. Eoghan has taken Wiola to the side and is trying to explain to her why he chose to leave the academy. From the looks of it, Wiola is not having it. She keeps pointing at Henny and me and stomping her feet. The others spirit seekers fled the scene as soon as the tide turned against them.

"Wiola has always sucked up to authority," Henny explains, rolling their eyes. "She thinks the SSA is the greatest. It doesn't surprise me at all that she'd go to battle for them."

Put that on the list for the SSA to fix. None of their students should have to choose between following their destructive course or the people they love. "Why did Eoghan never clue her in?"

"Because he needed her to be exactly as she is. Stubborn, misguided, egocentric," Henny explains. "He was only in the relationship for the cover she provided him. Couldn't find a more devoted follower." They sigh, still watching the couple fight. "Looks like Wiola finally got it."

Just as they say that, I can hear Wiola shout, "I hope you rot in prison!" Then she storms off, pushing through the crowd. Eoghan looks at us and shrugs with a sheepish grimace.

I can't help feeling sorry for Wiola, but Henny laughs. "I'd better go and soothe his broken heart."

This isn't my business, so I leave them to it and find myself faced with Lukas. "You okay?" I ask, noticing him rubbing his arm.

"Just a few bruises." As usual, he hates to admit he's actually hurt. "And yourself? Jumping in without a plan, as always."

"You know me." The amusement over his half-hearted animosity is quickly swept away by unfamiliar admiration. "You sided with the spirits."

Lukas looks uncomfortable. "Well, I couldn't let those upstarts ruin everything we've worked for just so they could flex their muscles."

"How did you know the gnomes were there?" I ask innocently. It's entirely possible he didn't figure it out until Wiola announced it, but somehow I doubt it.

Naturally, he bristles at the perceived slight. "My NAV isn't that low! I know when spirits are around." Then he shuffles his feet. "I sensed the same pompous energy as when we did that weird food ceremony."

I can't help the grin, and neither can Alexander. He shuffles closer to Lukas and affectionately pats his leg. "He sensed me! I might have to adopt this one. He's hard as granite but with a soft mica core."

"What?" Lukas barks when I burst out laughing.

"Sorry." I try to stifle my laugh but fail miserably. "You might have to change your name to Alexander." Lukas' bewildered stare only makes me laugh harder. "Sorry! What I meant to say is that Alexander appreciates you vouching for his safety."

Lukas breathes in deeply through his nose, nostrils flaring. "I guess I could play bodyguard to a few gnomes."

This time, I manage to contain my laughter. "Thank you. Alexander, would you like to join the conference now?"

Alexander grabs Lukas' leg just above the knee. "With the greatest pleasure."

I indicate for Lukas to turn around and enter the building. As Lukas walks away, I can see him stiffen. "Is he touching me?"

"He wouldn't dare," I manage to say, shortly before bursting into giggles again.

Next to me, Leon is similarly amused. "Looks like his NAV is improving, huh?"

"I think so." Taking a few calming breaths, I turn my attention to Madeline. "Do you want to come as well? It would be an honour to have representatives of the GU at our conference. I'll make sure you'll have seats in the front row."

Madeline smiles at me. "Don't worry about that, dear. We can provide our own seats."

Filled with curiosity, I follow the gnome back inside.

The gnomes are making sure everyone is aware of their presence, even if they can't be seen. They've changed the layout in the front, creating a bunch of small rock chairs for them to sit on. It's really not more than a little knob on the floor, but it has quite the effect. I see some tense faces, but most regard them with curiosity.

As for the talks, they go great. Miriam and Inga have done a fantastic job curating the topics while Bijan makes sure each session is also live-streamed. Among the attendees are spirit seekers, but also politicians, journalists, and interested members of the public. Online, the crowd is even more diverse, and Rory and I spend a lot of time answering questions popping up in the feed.

At the end of the day, Wulf finds me, leading a group of important-looking people to me. He introduces them as members of the European Parliament, and I recognise the one lady who asked about climate change. Her name is Carole Dubois.

"May I congratulate you on this truly ground-breaking programme?" she says as she shakes my hand.

Talk about a step up on the social ladder. Half a year ago I was living on the outskirts of society, seemingly forgotten by everyone; now I'm shaking hands with the shapers of today's world. Yeah, I'm flustered. Very much so. "Well, that praise is for the conveners. They organised everything."

Carole checks with Wulf. "But it's my understanding that none of this would've been possible if it weren't for you." She smiles at me. "Aren't you the one who came up with this radical new approach?"

"As I said in my talk, I'm not the first one..." I catch Wulf's eye, who nods encouragingly at me. "But I guess, yes. I'm the instigator of this movement."

"A movement is exactly what we need," the man on my right, Adrien Moreau, says. "I'm sure you're aware of how climate change is becoming our biggest challenge. We used to look at climate change and spirits as two different issues, but now I see they're actually closely related." He looks at me to confirm. "You're basically saying that the changes we forced on the world are what drives those spirits to extreme reactions, right? And so, they retribute by releasing floods and storms."

I find it hard to follow him, but I believe we're on the same page. "That's always how it's been. We're essentially fighting about the same habitat." Suddenly, I remember a discussion I had with Dante of all people about the overpopulation of the planet. "It's a complex topic, but as you're surely aware, humans are literally everywhere, and so the spirits are being pushed further and further into a corner."

"And then they lash out," another woman whose name I've already forgotten concludes. "That makes a lot of sense. In that case, fighting them is like throwing timber at a burning house."

"Pretty much." My stomach's doing somersaults, I'm that nervous and excited. These people get it. They get why the SSA needs to change course.

Smiles greet me all around. Then Mrs Dubois announces, "Ms Csorba, we would like you and Mr Bachmann to speak to the European Parliament. We're planning to create a new initiative centred around positive spirit relationships to combat climate change. And seeing as you're the expert, we'd like to involve you intimately in the conception. We're aware you might have other responsibilities, but we hope to make you a convincing offer."

I'm so overwhelmed, I would've said yes on the spot if Wulf hadn't had stepped in and said, "We'll think about it."

"Of course, take your time," Mrs Dubois says. She gives me her card and tells me to call her once the conference is over.

They're just about to turn away when I regain control of my senses. "Wait." Curious, they turn around. "Two things. First, I hope you're all planning to attend Aeola's talk tomorrow. I think it's important to gain a spirit's perspective."

Mr Moreau nods emphatically. "Yes, we're looking forward to it. That's certainly a first in human history."

"Good. She's awesome. I mean... an expert on spirit matters." Gosh, if I want to work in such high-level environments, I'd better watch my tongue. "I'd also like you to meet Madeline." I look around and see her talking to Alexander nearby. By the looks of it, Alexander is regaling her with stories of his famous past while Lukas keeps guard with a sour face. "Madeline!" I call out to her. "Could you come here for a moment?"

The gnome sees me and comes rolling over. "What is it?"

Meanwhile, the politicians are all looking confused, unable to see what Wulf and I do. Well, they're in for a treat. "May I introduce you to Madeline? She's a local representative of the Gnomian Union, which, as she informed me, predates the European Union by seventy-four years."

"Seventy-two," Madeline corrects me.

"Seventy-two." I can tell I blew their minds. The politicians are all staring at the spot where Madeline stands and at each other. "I know. Spirits are a lot more organised than we credit them for. There are a lot of individuals, but they also have kings and queens, leaders, and even unions. Madeline, why don't you tell us a bit more about what kind of issues you're tackling at parliament?"

Before she can launch into a lengthy account, Miriam calls to me. Immediately, Wulf steps in. "I'll translate for Madeline. You go and see what Miriam wants."

Wow, having a supportive boyfriend is awesome. I don't have to tear myself in two. "Thank you." I turn to the politicians. "It was lovely to meet you all. I'll be in touch." Maybe. Hopefully. If I can get over the creeping imposter syndrome that wants to tell me I'm way out of my comfort zone.

I all but rush towards Miriam, hoping she's not going to introduce me to the next group of important people. A woman's standing next to her. She's short and round, her hair a vibrant pink, which makes me instantly like her. "Hi."

"Hey, Rika." Miriam pulls me closer. "This is Téodora Sanchez. She's part of the SSA research team, the staff expert."

Okay, scratch that like. "Really?" I ask, tense.

"Look, I know what you're thinking," Téodora tells me. "How can I call myself a staff expert if I didn't even understand what I had under my hands for twenty years? Miriam's talk was revealing. My NAV is just shy of 320, and I was wondering if I could check your staff. And no, I'm not going to cut it or anything. I only want to get a feel for it."

"I'll be with her the whole time," Miriam assures me. "It's just what you said, right? You need to feel your way? Well, I can't, but perhaps Téodora can."

Giving my staff to someone employed at the SSA makes me uncomfortable. I want to tell Miriam to forget it, but she's beaming with excitement. "No cuts!" I tell them, then force a smile. "I have to go get it from my room."

Miriam beams at me. "We'll wait here."

"Thank you so much!" Téodora says, clutching my hand. "You'll get it back first thing tomorrow morning."

I'm not entirely sure I'm happy with that, but I force myself to trust Miriam. And just because someone works at the research programme of the SSA doesn't mean they're a bad person. Apparently, not even Piero Vallesco was, though the jury's still out on him. Good intentions sometimes have terrible consequences.

"Who was that?" Camille slides in next to me, whispering harshly. "With Miriam?" Small beads of sweat are lining her hairline.

"Téodora Sanchez. She's a researcher at the SSA," I explain, feeling slightly ambushed.

Camille purses her lips. "Making plans with the enemy again. I see."

Stopping short, I take her hands. They're clammy and cold. Signs of withdrawal. "Talk to her, Camille! You know she loves you more than anything. More than her research."

"Not anymore," Camille admits in a little voice. Her hands are trembling in mine. "I'm staying off the drugs, but it's hard."

"I know. And we're here to help you. One day at a time. Have you told Miriam you've stopped?"

Camille sighs. "I don't think she'll believe me. Not after I lied to her for months." She's got a point there. She lets go of my hands and stares into the distance. "Well, now that Wulf's torpedoed the SSA, I can finally leave and give rehab an honest try, I guess."

"That... that sounds sensible." Somehow, I never considered what going against the SSA would do to our team. In my mind, the team would stick together, but now I realise how naïve that thought was. "Will you come back?"

"I don't think so," Camille admits, then quickly adds, "Which doesn't mean we won't stay in touch. Please stay in touch!"

I lean forward and hug her. "Of course I will. And once you're clean and ready to face the world again, I'll help you make friends among the spirits."

Camille laughs. "I can't see them, Rika. Not without... Not when I'm sober."

"See? I don't believe that! The potential is there. The drugs are only a crutch." Suddenly, I'm certain of it. And just like that, the wheels in my mind start turning. Drugs and alcohol lower inhibition. They loosen us up, making us lose control. And Camille is always in control when she's sober. She's always so disciplined. Maybe too disciplined. "I think I've got it."

"Got what?"

"I've figured out why a change of attitude towards spirits had so little effect on you. Your limitations have nothing to do with fear or indoctrinated hate, but the pressure you put on yourself. Nature can't be controlled. Not really, but you always need to be in control of everything or you beat yourself up." As she starts frowning, I continue with haste. "That's why the drugs help. When you're high, you no longer feel the need to perform, to never disappoint anyone. You can just be yourself. Well, your intoxicated self."

Understanding wipes away the irritation. "That makes sense, in a way." Despair blooms on her face. "But how do I stop putting pressure on myself?"

I admit, "I don't know. I'm not a psychologist."

Camille sighs greatly. "I really have to do this the hard way, don't I?"

"Well, not too hard," I attempt to joke.

She only grimaces. "It sounds great in theory, but how's that supposed to work? I need discipline to get off the drugs. And if I'm all disciplined, I can't loosen up. If I want to stay sober, I'll have to do without spirits."

Though I want to argue, she's right. "Spirits aren't everything. There are so many people in the world who can't see spirits. And it doesn't mean you need to stay away from them either. I know a lot of Travellers who respect and honour the spirits without an NAV like yours. Just think of the Aos Sí and druids."

"What are you saying?"

"I'm saying your health is more important than raising your NAV. You don't have to see spirits to be a good soldier. And you don't have to be a soldier to be a good human. Wulf might not see it that way, but there's more to life than being a spirit seeker. And with the world changing now, there might be lots of ways to repent, if that's what you need to make peace with the last ten years."

I see the hope light up in her eyes. "You think so?"

My arm sweeps in an arc, trying to encompass the buzzing crowd on the verge of change. "Oh, yes. We'll find something for you. As soon as you're feeling better." Once again, I take her hands and squeeze them.

Camille nods. "Who'd have thought this coffee-stained street girl would change my life one day?"

Laughter bursts from my lips. "Well, this coffee-stained street girl certainly never imagined you'd change hers."

My heart swells when a real smile slips onto Camille's face. She pulls me close and we hug each other for what feels like five minutes.

Soothingly, I pat her back. "It'll all be well now."

19

I arrive back at the hotel, feeling every minute of sleep I'm lacking. The day's been exciting enough to keep me awake, but now the buzz is leaving me, I feel exhausted. Yawning, I wait for the elevator to arrive at our floor. As lovely as the rooms are, getting there takes ages. And I still have to walk back with my staff.

At last, the ping sounds, and the doors open. Someone's standing in front of the doors. I almost stumble back into the elevator when I recognise him. Almost, because Dante grabs my arm and pulls me out into the corridor with him.

"We need to talk. Now," he announces, before opening the door to some supply closet and pushing me inside.

Darkness envelops me as I hit the wall, sending cleaning supplies tumbling to the floor. A moment later, the light flickers on and I become aware of my tight surroundings. The little closet is smaller than the elevator. My bed surely wouldn't fit, and Dante's closed the door behind him.

This can't be happening again! My breath hitches in my throat. My pulse is racing. My fingernails dig into my palms in an effort to keep me from crying out. The walls are too close. Dante's too close. There's no air. "I can't breathe."

"Yes, you can," Dante says, almost gently. "This won't take long. I promise."

All my mind hears is that it won't take long to kill me. How's he going to do it? He's stronger than me, so there are a million of ways. One thing's for sure, I won't make it out of here alive. "Please, don't!" The words are choked by tears.

Dante comes closer, reaching out a hand. "Rika."

I bat his hand away, retreating as far as I can, only to slip down the back wall and cower in front of him. *Fight,* a voice inside me says, but my body refuses to heed its advice. There's no escaping him.

He stops short before taking a step back. "I'm sorry. I wish I didn't have to do this."

A whimper escapes my lips. He didn't want to give me to Vesuvius, either. But he did it anyway. "Then don't!" I shout, only to break down in tears.

Dante has this awful expression on his face, full of empathy. It's all lies. I know this. I've learned that the hard way. Oh, why didn't I ask Camille to come back with me? Or anybody?

"Look. I understand that you have no interest in me as a parent. I get that," he admits.

Him being my father is the least of my problems right now. It sounds like he's given up on that, though. We're back to murdering me.

"The things I've done to you can't be excused. And I'll have to live with my choices for the rest of my life. I know now what they've cost me."

"Poor you," I manage to shake from my lips. Poor little Dante has to live with the choice of killing me.

He sighs, then lowers himself to a crouch so we're on the same level. "You're aware I wasn't acting alone?"

If he's going to say someone else made him do it, I'm going to scream. Instead, I nod.

"But they're gonna throw me under the bus. I'll be going to prison for doing what I was told." Dante raises his hands in a gesture that reminds me of his sister. "I'm not saying I'm innocent. I did some horrible things, and I'm ready to face the punishment. I truly am."

What's he talking about? Is this how he justifies killing me? By following his stupid orders and turning himself in afterwards? I'll still be dead.

"Rika, there are things you need to know. You want nothing to do with me. I get that. But I've been where you are. Going up against the SSA. You realise how that ended, huh?" His forehead is creasing heavily, and for the first time, I see something else on his face. Fear. "You've met my sister. She's so kind and understanding, isn't she? Well, she was that to me, too. Thanks to her, I even became director of the academy. I only had to betray everything I believed in. Everything Léna taught me. And it led to this mess where I convicted the woman I love and almost killed my own daughter."

Slowly, his words are lifting me out of my panic-induced stupor. Is this the kind of speech people give before they kill you? No, they just do it. But then again, Dante's always been a masterful manipulator. It's his smooth talking I fear more than his threats.

"Alena's only invited you here so she can get Wulf back. He's the one she cares for. Her decorated son. Her prized tool. Two talented kids of her own, and she'd throw them both in a ditch for that unfortunate boy. That Piero died only gave her another weapon. A mother's tears are oh so powerful, aren't they? Even you're falling for it, and you know better than to trust any Vallesco."

"What are you saying?" My voice is still shaking, but his words intrigue me. They feed the doubts I already had. And though I shouldn't trust him, my scepticism welcomes him. "Why would she let me speak, then?"

Dante snorts. "That's simple. So everyone can see you fail. You saw what happened at your original talk. That was a classic Alena move. Build you up high, so the fall breaks your neck."

"But we've got the fringe programme. She had nothing to do with it. And it's a success. Delegates from the EU want me to develop a programme that basically renders the SSA useless." There's no way Alena Vallesco could've foreseen that, master schemer or not. Nothing can stop the movement now.

"You garnered more interest than she thought you would. But as I said, the higher you're up, the harder the fall." He takes a deep breath. "You know about the altered spirits. They've brought them. They've brought the most powerful one they could manufacture. And they're gonna set him free. Then everyone will see that all you can give them are pretty words. Because not even you can talk down one of them."

My insides are curling into each other. Who have they brought? When will he hit? "Then stop them!"

"I'm trying to. But they're ahead of me. Did you see the police in the lobby?" I was so tired I didn't notice. "They're looking for me. That's why I was waiting for you here. I wanted to talk to you. Gian informed me when you'd be going up. I guess you didn't see him either."

Which is a good thing. He frightens me almost more than Dante.

Dante leans back, resting his head against the door. "I've prepared files to support your claims. It's all in there. Go up against them. But make it out of Brussels alive first."

That's not going to happen, right? They'll scare people, yes, but kill them?

"Carina is innocent," Dante says. "Of course, they've been grooming her, but she hasn't actually been privy to any decisions. She had no idea about her brother's research, either. As for that matter, Piero himself was wary of his new project. We talked about it before Naples. He was of half-a-mind to scrap it for fear of what monsters it would create. But of course, he died before he could do that. And your mother is nothing but an innocent victim, of course."

I turn my head to the side so he won't see the hurt in my eyes.

But Dante knows me too well. "Whatever you blame her for, it's my fault. I did this to her. To you."

"Why isn't she here, then?"

"For the same reason Tiago isn't here, despite being a second-year. They don't want anybody beyond your team who might sympathise with you here. Everyone on the board, especially Humberto and my sister, are ruthless. They'll do anything to protect the SSA's interests."

"Then why didn't you stop them earlier? If you're aware of all this, why play along?" *And for spirits' sake, if you're not going to kill me, let me out of this room.*

Dante snorts, rocking back on his heels. "For the same reason Wulf was ready to throw you out on the streets, or Carina pushed you harder when you stood up to her. We're humans, Rika. We run in one direction until we hit a wall. It's different for each of us."

"I'm not like you." *In more than one instance.*

To my horror, Dante smiles kindly at me. "No, you're not. You're like your mother. Spirited." He chuckles, but then his face turns dark. "And breaking her like I tried to break you is something I'll never forgive myself for."

Wary and stunned, I watch him get up. If he's looking for forgiveness, he surely won't find it in this tiny supply closet.

Dante opens the door, letting some air in. "Goodbye, Rika."

I keep my lips pressed together, which makes Dante sigh. He turns around and leaves the room. His steps are receding, and still I'm sitting pressed against the wall, shivering more with each passing minute. The elevator pings, and then he's gone. If what he says is true, it'll deliver him straight into the arms of the police. They'll take him away. Alena will have kept her promise, and I'll be safe from him. She might even turn her husband in, though she only said she'd look into it. And then it's my turn.

I bite the back of my hand to keep from crying. How did I end up back here in the dark?

20

Though every fibre of my body yearns to leave the room, it takes Wulf and Camille finding me before my muscles remember how to move.

"What happened?" Camille asks, while Wulf kneels next to me.

As he scoops me up, I wrap my arms around his neck and break apart. I have no idea what he and Camille are talking about until I'm back in my spacious, light-filled room, folded into Wulf's embrace on the floor, a soft breeze on my face. It's the fresh air that pulls me out of it. Aeola blows away my tears, planting a kiss on my forehead.

Camille hands me a cup of tea, looking worried. "I should've gone with her," she tells Wulf.

"That's not important now." He cups my face, searching my eyes. "Was it him?" When I bring myself to nod, he hugs me tighter. "You don't need to worry about Dante anymore. He was arrested an hour ago."

Somehow, the confirmation only makes me cry harder. "But it's not just him."

"I know," Wulf says. "But the rest will follow. My mother..."

I put a finger on his lips. "She might not be as innocent as we think she is." Pain flashes in his eyes. We're back at this again. "Dante said he's going to send me files. Proof." It's only now I realise he doesn't even have my number.

"Did he?" Wulf asks.

When I check my phone, it tells me there are a lot of messages, but none of them from Dante. Why did I believe him? I feel like an idiot now. All those pretty words were lies, just like always. He deserves to rot in jail. Or maybe he never had the chance to send them. Then again, he knew about the police. Yeah, I'm for letting him rot in prison all the way.

"Oh," comes from Wulf. He's staring at his own phone.

"What is it?"

Wulf's face has fallen. He's gone almost paper white. "He sent it to me."

To his golden boy. The one he helped groom. "Is it..."

Wulf scrolls through the files, opening some at random. "Cami, can you get Bijan? We need to put this on a secure drive as soon as possible. The moment my parents learn of it, they'll get it taken down."

"On it." She puts the tea down and runs from the room.

"Your parents?" I'm almost too afraid to ask. He didn't just say father.

Wulf takes a deep breath, now shaking himself. "This details the polluted spirits program. It has the signatures of all board members on it. And there's more. Files on missing seekers." Each word is choked out by this point.

I know that it's out of my hands now. I don't have the files. Wulf has. One click, and he could delete all of it and pretend he never saw it. "What are you gonna do?"

He lets out a painful whimper, his eyes glassing over. His hand with the phone sinks, and for a moment, he buries his forehead against my chest. I put my arms around him, stroking his back. If he deletes it, I'll never forgive him, but I understand how much it'll cost him if he doesn't.

"This will send them to prison," he cries, shuddering under my fingers. "Carina will never speak to me again."

There's nothing I can say. All of it's true. They raised him. No matter what they turned him into, they took care of him in his greatest moment of need. "I'm sorry."

Wulf looks up at me, tears streaking his face. "I'll do it."

Surprised, I jerk up. "What?"

With each word, he claws his way back to confidence. "It has to be done. The SSA is broken beyond repair. It doesn't matter what I do, it'll always be based on shaky foundations. Sometimes, you have to tear something down to build something new." His face hardens as he looks into my eyes. "I'm ready to tear the SSA down."

Frantically, I run my fingers over his face, wiping his tears away. "You'd do that for me?"

"I'm doing it because it's the right thing to do." He pulls me close to him, burying his face against my shoulder. "But you're everything to me. And I can't wait to make the world a better place with you."

Once again, I pull his face up in my hands, but this time to kiss him. With him at my side, I feel like I can do everything. He's all the strength I need, the rock I can launch myself from to fly.

After everything that's happened, it's weird to go back to Science 14 the next day. Dante's warning still rings in my ears, but there's nothing I can do about it. Wulf has stayed true to his word and handed everything over to the Belgian police. With luck, they'll act fast enough before the Vallescos get wind of it. Until then, we have to finish what we've started.

To make things more comfortable for Aeola, her talk takes place in Orban Square in front of the conference building. While I'm all nerves, Aeola exudes confidence. To make matters worse, Bijan tells me, "You're gonna be on live TV. Okay?"

Live-streaming is one thing, but live on TV? How did I find myself in the middle of a historical event?

"You ready for this?" Miro asks. After much discussion, we've agreed we need a neutral person to verify my translation. Wulf is out of the running since too many people saw me kissing him, but Miro was happy to take over. Just like Wulf, this kind of attention doesn't seem to bother him.

"I'll manage," I reply, wishing desperately I could make my words come true. Perhaps Aeola could blow some confidence on me.

Miro cocks his head and grins. "Nah, relax. You just repeat what she says and we're good."

Then it's time to begin. Inga greets everyone and explains the set-up, introducing Miro, Aeola, and myself. "We're still working on making spirits visible for everyone, but I think there are enough spirit seekers here to confirm the presence of our sylph."

"That's right," Miro announces. "Ready when you are, Aeola. Rika."

I hold out my hand and Aeola wraps a strand of her hair around me. "Take it away."

Aeola smiles warmly at me before she faces the crowd. As she starts speaking, I make sure to translate each word of hers for the crowd. "Hello humans. I am Aeola, daughter of the Erlking, most commonly found blowing over Berlin. I'm here today because Rika assured me you'll listen." As I translate her words, I can't help but be awed by her confidence. "I'd never thought much of humans. Instead, I grew up in fear of them. My father told me, like he told every air spirit, that nothing good ever comes of humans. And then a human saved my life. Though she was almost freezing, Rika dropped everything to pull me out of the river. Without her, my father's wrath would've torn me apart."

The touch around my wrist is an exact replica of our first one. I would jump into an icy river at any time for Aeola.

"But why was my father angry? Why are so many of us angry? I want to explain this to you in the hope that you'll do better. Because you need to do better." Aeola hasn't told me what she wants to say, but now I feel the intensity like an electric shock going through me. She's not here to inform people, but to appeal to them. "We sylphs are angry because you pollute our air. You blow waste into the sky, thinking nothing of it. Have you ever been filled with toxic smoke? It's disgusting. It hurts! And it does horrible things to us."

It isn't hard to match my voice to her emotions. Everything Aeola feels runs through my veins as well. "And we're not the only ones. I know of rivers so polluted the nymphs there are sluggish and grey. So, they wash it all away with a flood. And you cry out and call us evil. We need to be stopped, you say, but it's you that needs to stop. You need to stop throwing your garbage into the sea and blowing your fumes into the air. Don't come for us with your staffs when you cut down every tree that grows in your way! Stop mindlessly destroying everything!"

She's darkened, trembling with anger. It's an unfamiliar side. Usually, when we're together, she's a calm breeze. Now I can see the storm inside of her. "This is our world, too. Just because you can't see us or hear us when we cry out in pain doesn't mean we don't have a right to live. So, do better! Listen to Rika and people like Rory, and do something. Help the dryads regrow their forests! Let the volcanoes breathe! And clear the air! We don't want to fight any more than you do. We only want to survive. Is that too much to ask?"

Judging by the rows of shocked faces, it might be. It's certainly more than they bargained for. Next to me, Miro's no longer smiling. If I didn't know better, I'd say he looks ashamed. He escapes my gaze and clears his throat. "Everything has been translated correctly."

A breath of relief washes through me. Aeola smiles now that she's got this off her chest. "We want to work with you. Being with Rika, seeing what she can do and what she can inspire others to do, has given me hope. I used to think the world was dying and there was nothing left in it but hate and destruction, but that's not true. It's not too late to turn things around if we all work together. So, let's—"

Wind rises around us, sending leaves spiralling to the ground. The hairs on my arms rise in response.

Miro checks immediately with Aeola and then announces. "This storm isn't her." He blocks his microphone and whispers, "Are other sylphs coming? What's going on?"

Aeola looks as surprised as he is. "I didn't call anyone."

"It's him," I say, pointing to a dark storm cloud that's quickly enveloping the roofs of Brussels. I know this storm, know the electric static that sends my pulse racing.

The wind's picking up quickly, now blowing against the large screen behind us. Equipment falls to the ground and hats are sent tumbling down the path. People are jumping up from their seats. I almost keel over with fear.

"I thought you caught him," Aeola gasps.

"I did." And now he's coming for me.

The Erlking has been released back into the world, stronger than ever.

21

The most frightening thing about the storm is that this is just him. There are no other sylphs wrapped up in the Erlking's train, adding to his force. And yet, the entire sky has darkened and winds strong enough to rip branches from the trees are blowing towards our meeting.

People are running for cover. Some are screaming, some are stunned. And far too many look at me. As if I have all the answers.

Aeola's pulling at me, but my feet are stuck to the ground. I can only stare at the horrible swirl of darkness sinking down on us. My brain refuses to comprehend what's happening. I faced the Erlking. Faced and defeated him. It's not fair that he's back. And so much stronger than before.

A terrible bang jolts me from my paralysis. The screen behind me has fallen. Thankfully, not on top of me.

By now, some sort of order has been established. Miro and Wulf are herding people into the surrounding buildings. Aeola's still dragging me, and this time, I give in and follow her lead. We make it halfway across the park before the wind rips my feet out from under me. I hit the ground, and the next second, a branch lands on my legs.

Pain stabs me in half a dozen places. My elbow hurts, my face stings, and my legs feel numb. I look over my shoulder to confirm one thing: I'd be dead if that had hit my head.

"Get up!" someone bellows and drags me to my feet with no consideration for the heavy branch. Carina is there, with one of the ancient staffs in her hand. She hauls me over to the entrance, all the time berating me. "Stop being so damn useless!"

"Sorry," I mutter, more out of reflex than actual intent. "What are you even doing here?"

"Saving your ass, apparently. You still need that sylph?" Carina nods toward Aeola.

I rip my arm out of her grip, bringing some distance in between us. "Yes!"

"Well, good luck keeping her safe," Carina says, already turning away from me.

"This isn't her fault!" I shout after her, but the wind presses me backwards, and I follow Aeola's pull, which brings me inside the Science 14 building.

The entry hall is packed. Spirit seekers are grabbing their staffs from reception and heading back outside. Civilians are being ushered into the lecture rooms to make more space for everyone. A triage centre is in the process of being set up with far too many people already waiting to be seen. I see blood and shocked faces. I'm strongly reminded of Central Station, and sure enough, there's a glass ceiling above us.

Someone pushes me deeper into the crowd with no space to go. A spirit seeker takes a swipe at Aeola, and I bring my arm up just in time to block the hit. "Ouch!"

"There's a sylph," the panicked seeker yells at me.

"It's not her, you idiot!" I bellow back, cradling my hurting arm. "She's a friend."

He looks at me bewildered, then shakes his head and runs after the others. I pull Aeola into my arms and cradle her there while she blows cool air onto my arm. "Sorry about that," I mutter.

I hardly get four metres in before Mrs Dubois and the other politician from yesterday accost me. "What's happening? Why are the spirits attacking us?"

Oh dear, I'm not prepared for this. Unfortunately, Humberto Vallesco is there to give them an answer. "Because that's what spirits do. You heard the sylph. They're angry." He sneers at Aeola huddling in my arms.

"You did this!" My voice sounds awfully screechy. I want to throw myself at him and claw his eyes out because all of this is his fault. "You released that spirit!"

Humberto snorts, looking at me as if I'm the crazy one. "That's ridiculous. This is a wild spirit. Probably attracted by all the fuss she's made."

"I caught that spirit!" My heart is pounding. Too many things are happening at once, and control is slipping through my fingers faster than quicksand.

"I thought you talked to spirits," Mrs Dubois asks me in confusion. Just yesterday, she wanted to start a spirit program with me.

Once again, Humberto shakes his head. "It's impossible to talk to a spirit as strong as this one. Once they're set on destruction, nothing can stop them. Well, almost nothing. The SSA has been dealing with these kinds of situations for centuries."

He's got their complete attention now. The other woman—I think her name was Sanne Willems—nods and looks distraught. "Then do it. Please, you have to stop this storm."

"No!" I'm too horrified to understand what I just said.

Humberto's eyes gleam a little before his face hardens. "No? You'd rather let the spirit reign free in the city? Maybe you want to talk to it? Well, be my guest. Talk that storm down. Please, for the sake of all of us, do it."

That's impossible, and we both know it. I couldn't even get through to the Erlking before he was caught. Now, he's like every other polluted spirit, corroded by hate. It'll be impossible for him to think of anything but death and destruction.

When I don't turn around and run outside, Humberto huffs smugly. "That's what I thought." And with that, he dismisses me, gently guiding the two women away as he tells them how the SSA will take care of the storm.

I stand there feeling like I've been run over by a truck. In my arms, Aeola shivers. "What do we do now?"

There's nothing we can do. If I go out and join the fight, everyone will think I'm a fake. That I say one thing and do another. If I protest, people will die. And even without my interference, people may still die, proving once again how dangerous spirits are, and that the only thing that can protect us are the spirit seekers. The real ones, not my band of spirit friends.

"There you are." Wulf and Miro have found me, apparently having completed the evacuation. Frantically, Wulf checks me for wounds.

As far as I can tell, there are only scrapes and bruises. Even my legs are able to hold my weight. Miro and Wulf seem to be mostly unhurt, as well. "Are you okay?"

"Yeah. Don't worry about it. Now, about the Erlking—" Wulf starts.

"I'm sorry, Rika," Miro interrupts. "I think there's a lot of merit in your ideas and definitely more to think about. But this is reality, and as long as spirits are capable of such destruction, we cannot back down. My family is out there. They're stuck in Grand Place, visiting the tower. If it collapses..." He checks with Wulf, who puts a gentle hand on his arm. "We're gonna go back out and fight this thing, right?"

When Wulf nods, a whimper escapes my throat. They're absolutely right, but I feel like the floor has been pulled out from under my feet. Everything we've worked for, all our efforts, it's all going down the drain. "This is what they want." Looking over my shoulder, I see Humberto Vallesco organising the spirit seekers.

Wulf scrunches up his face, looking close to tears himself. "I know, but... people will die if we don't do anything. We'll get them afterwards." He gives my shoulder a quick rub. "You stay here."

"And what? What am I supposed to do?" I feel like passing out. Moments ago, hundreds of people looked up to me; now they want me to step aside and let the big guys handle it. But what can I offer? I'm a mediocre fighter at best. Talking to the Erlking is useless and scares the shit out of me. So, what then?

"I... I have no idea." Wulf looks eager to be on his way.

I'm holding him back. My shoulders are sagging. It's time to admit defeat. "Go," I say at last. "Go and save the world." Subconsciously, I press Aeola closer to my heart.

Wulf looks as if he wants to say something else, but instead, he steps forward and presses his lips to my forehead. "Stay safe, you two." He turns around, and he and Miro rush away.

They don't get far. The rest of our team has assembled, all of them with staffs ready to fight. "Where do you want us?" Camille asks.

Wulf takes one look at her shivering, clammy self. "In your state? Right here."

"I can fight!" Camille protests.

"But you can't guarantee me you won't take drugs to do it," Wulf says harshly. "You're benched. I'm taking your staff."

Camille is so surprised, she lets it slip from her hands when he grabs it.

Wulf turns around, dismissing her for more important matters, and hands the staff to Henny, who left theirs back in Rome. "Lukas, Leon, come on! We've got a storm to diffuse." Together, they join up with Carina near the door.

When Camille turns around to face me and Miriam, her face is taut. "I'm clean."

Miriam holds her gaze, but her shoulders are trembling. "Cami..."

But Camille won't have it. She spins on her heel and strides away, quickly getting lost in the crowd.

With a shudder, Miriam releases a breath. She turns around and hands me my staff from the coat room. I never managed to bring it to her and Mrs Sanchez. "He did the right thing. And I'm not just saying that because I'd be worried sick if she goes out there."

"I know." The wood sings in my grip, and I'm reminded of Grune. He gave me this staff as a sign of trust, but also to defend myself and those in my care. This weapon and my high NAV are telling me I should be part of the battle. Surely, people's lives matter more than my values. But they're not just values. If the SSA is allowed to continue as they always have, other people will die. Maybe even more. "They released him." This is their fault!

Aeola's wind against my cheek is ice cold. I catch indignation and fear in the gentle breeze of her being.

Miriam sighs. "It seems like it. And they made him nice and strong. His spirit energy is off the charts." She sounds bitter.

"We've got the proof."

"Not for this," Miriam says, looking at me with pity. Even she knows there's nothing we can do about it right now.

Why am I so hung up on this? The SSA has won. *Accept it, Rika.* I went up against them and lost. It's just as Dante told me it. They built me up and now all I can do is fall.

Miriam looks up to the ceiling where dark clouds are pressing down on the glass. "We should get people inside the lecture theatres. If the ceiling breaks, we're not safe out here."

I agree, "It's like Central Station." The scars on my arms are crawling now, reminding me of the hateful words once spoken to me. Aeola reaches out to me and wraps her hair around my wrist, much the same as she did back then. I have no doubt the Erlking's going to seek me out again. I already had a taste of his hate five days ago at the Rue des Boucher. That was just a tiny part of him. Now that he's back in his full glory, I know I won't survive another lightning strike.

Miriam leaves me as well, trying to usher people out of the atrium. I'm left standing, numbly observing the mayhem around me. Wulf and the others are heading out, risking their lives to protect everyone else. Humberto Vallesco is still running the show, assigning spirit seekers to the three teams outside. His wife is talking to the politicians, placating them. Camille is pacing through the atrium, driving herself mad. I don't see anyone else I know, which means they must've found shelter somewhere else.

Or they're injured and dead in the park.

My stomach turns at the thought of Rory lying bleeding under a tree. All his spirit advocacy couldn't save him from this storm. He'd always believed that, in the end, a battle with spirits was inevitable. That after all the appeasing and respecting has failed, you'd have to pick up your staff and fight. Just like a true spirit seeker.

"What are we going to do?" Aeola asks, still cold against my cheek.

I grip the dryad wood tighter, feeling its life force run through my fingers. "I don't know." I just know one thing: I can't stay here, cooped up behind the lines, watching the Vallescos and the Erlking ruin our future. "We need to get out of here."

"Yes!" a familiar voice says.

I spin around to see Camille, her eyes wide. "Wulf said—"

"Wulf isn't the one with the highest NAV," Camille snaps, then takes a deep breath. "I'm sorry. What I'm saying is I can't stay here while the Erlking storms. Are you going to fight him?"

I'm almost afraid to shake my head. "He's too powerful for me."

"Then what's your plan?"

"I need to check on the Travellers. Make sure they're safe." My gaze finds Humberto Vallesco and his confident display of leadership. "I bet he won 't mind if a few Travellers die today."

"Or homeless," Camille says, easily following my thoughts. When I smile, she nods, determined. "You lead the way, Rika. I'll follow."

"Me, too!" Aeola hisses, gaining in strength. "I'd follow you to the ends of the world."

We stride over to the door when an all-too-familiar shape blocks our way. Gian. "You planning on going somewhere?"

My skin crawls worse than with the Erlking's whisper. The words are stuck in my throat. How many times did I try to escape only to be hauled back by him? He's Dante's man through and through. Fortunately, I'm not facing him alone.

Camille takes a step forward, putting her body between him and me. "There's a battle to be fought, right?"

"Your father said it would be too dangerous for you," Gian says in a surprisingly uncomfortable way.

I'm stunned. No matter what happened, he was always confident, never fazed. Now he can't even meet my eyes. Meanwhile, his words are trickling into my brain. "Wait! You..." I shake my head. Dante's man through and through, even after his fall. "I don't need *your* protection. Or *his*." Self-confidence oozes back into me. For once, I have the upper hand in our interaction. "Let's go, Camille. Aeola."

Camille gives Gian a death glare, and he shuffles back, visibly relieved he doesn't need to save my life after he made it miserable for so many weeks. I loop my arm into Camille's and make for the door before anyone else can stop us.

And with that, we join the throng of spirit seekers and slip back out into the storm.

22

The wind outside is so strong it presses my body against the wall. The spirit seekers fare little better. The moment they stop swinging their staffs, the storm pushes them back, its energy unrivalled. Meanwhile, branches, leaves, and garbage are whipping through the air. A blown-over traffic sign skitters over the ground, producing a horrible screeching noise.

Ahead, I can see Wulf establishing a route across the park, using the largest trees as cover. The Erlking isn't here, so the spirit seekers are trying to get to him. Miro and Carina are doing a similar thing, trying to connect our hide-out with the building on the opposite side of the park where other spirit seekers are trapped. They have to cross the road, hiding behind cars, which are being pushed by the wind despite their weight.

"Let me..." Crawling along the wall, Camille and I make our way to the corner. By SSA standards, I should be out here, putting Grune's staff to use, but there are enough spirit seekers around to follow Wulf's lead. We need to check on other people.

The Travellers who followed me to Brussels have put up their camps in Parc Maximilien. They may not have found shelter. And as Camille mentioned so aptly, there will also be a lot of homeless and refugees, who are yet again subjected to the wrath of the storm king. There are too many vulnerable people, while the spirit seekers are all concentrated in one spot. I may not be able to stop the Erlking, but I'll defend those nobody thinks of.

"Can you feel where he is?" I ask Aeola, who does her best to take the brunt of the storm off us.

"I think he's blowing from the northwest," Aeola says, pushing away a nasty-looking branch.

Great, that's the direction we're going. All the more reason to find the Travellers. "We need to go northwest," I yell at Camille.

Just then, a terrible crack sounds behind us. The glass ceiling!

"Miri!" Camille cries, bolting back the way we came.

With the purest of luck, I manage to grab her hand and jolt her back. "She's fine!" While I can't be a hundred per cent sure, I know she was aware of the danger. "She was urging everyone to go into the lecture theatres."

Camille breathes heavily. Every now and then, she glances over her shoulder at the building. I let go of her, leaving her the option to run and check on her beloved. But Camille shakes her head, and together we set one foot in front of the other.

"There she is," a sylph howls, then shoots out of the sky to grab me.

I bring my staff up just in time, tearing through her flimsy body. Her howling shriek makes my skin crawl. I know I shouldn't feel bad about the demise of a spirit loyal to the Erlking, but my stomach didn't get the memo. With a heavy feeling, I push on, Camille on my heels.

It isn't the last sylph who tries to attack us. As we battle our way through the city, multiple spirits delight in my presence, taking the opportunity to measure themselves against the dryad wood. So far, the staff has torn through each of them, but my arms ache, and my body is sore.

"Where are they all coming from?" I ask Aeola as I hand over my staff to Camille so she can take over for a while. When the Erlking was released, he was alone. Now it seems for every sylph or storm sprite we break down, three more appear.

"His wind's calling them," Aeola says, sounding like an oppressive rain cloud. "Can't you feel it?"

Perhaps I was too occupied with keeping on my feet as the storm tugs me this way or that, but I didn't feel it until Aeola mentioned it. It's a deep vibration that sends the air swinging. Like an earthquake in the sky, it sends out inaudible waves in all directions. And the sylphs follow, drawn in by his power.

"He's gonna destroy the whole city." And probably others in his wake. "They've created a monster."

"That's for sure," Camille huffs.

But the SSA is the least of our worries right now. It's as Wulf said: people's lives are more important. Most humans have made it somewhere inside, but I see people huddling in doorways and gaps between houses, and even a few who are trying to cross the city like I am. Worst of all, I see people injured, some lying on the ground unmoving. They've been hit by bricks torn from the roofs or poles ripped from the ground.

We watch the storm blow off three roofs, sending down a shower of tiles and bricks. A car is slammed into two others, glass shattering. Then the rain sets in, and water whips the streets. Within seconds, I'm soaked, and I curse the decision to wear another pretty dress this morning. A dress that's now slapping against my thighs.

Aeola protects us from the worst, but then lightning hits the lantern next to me, and the flash-over almost gets me. Maybe going out in the storm was a bad idea. Oh, who am I kidding? It was a decision made in panic.

"Whoa!" Camille gasps, holding onto my arm.

Above us, a thunderina cackles, teasing me to raise my staff.

"Not very likely," I say, wheezing.

For that, a second bolt of lightning strikes the house behind me. Sparks hit my skin, burning through the thin fabric. The rain washes the sting away, but the danger remains.

Aeola builds up an insulating layer around Camille and me, getting ready to be struck herself.

"Don't," I whimper, unable to see my best friend hurt.

There must be something I can do! Throw the staff maybe? *Oh, don't be silly.* The thunderina is dancing at least five metres above me. She's glowing, her skin crackling with energy. Soon, she'll strike again.

"Aeola, Camille, down!" I throw myself flat onto the ground, dragging the others down with me.

Lightning strikes and thunder splits the air, and we splash into some kind of pool. Irritated, I look around, only to find myself under the pavement. Somehow, we fell right through the ground into sewage.

"Ew." Camille grabs my arm and pulls me to a stand, then tries to wipe off some of the contaminated water.

"Sorry, glimmers," my favourite preposterous voice says. Alexander stands on the thin ledge at the wall and looks down at me. "If I'd gotten to you sooner, I could've managed a better landing."

Shaking, I look around. The smell is obnoxious, but at least there's no wind down here. And no lightning-mad thunderina. "That's okay. Thanks."

But there are spirits. Lots of them. A snake-like nymph slithers past my hip, stinking worse than any toilet ever did. Salamanders are scaling the walls, staying as far away from the water as they can. Some sylphs hover under the ceiling, and gnomes are huddling on the ledge. All of

Brussels' spirits are hiding down here, away from the storm, and away from the spirit seekers.

"The spirits are hiding here," I whisper.

Camille turns to me. "Huh?"

"The spirits of Brussels. The Gnomian Union has been hiding them throughout the conference, so no spirit seeker would bother them. This is where." I turn to Alexander. "We need to get to Parc Maximilien, near the Senne. The Travellers are staying there."

"Well, hop on, glimmers!" He points towards the ledge.

I relay his message to Camille, and we slug through the water until our fingers find purchase. With Alexander's help, I drag myself and Aeola up onto the narrow ledge. Lying face-down, I try to catch my breath while he helps Camille. But before I can sit up, the rock beneath me moves at high speed.

"Alex!" I shout in terror, as the water splashes past me, whipping me in the face. I barely manage to hold onto my staff, while Aeola has wrapped herself tight around my arm, just as terrified, as we zoom through the sewage. I'm pretty sure I left my stomach somewhere around the corner where I almost slipped from the ledge.

Just as I consider letting myself fall into the sewage to escape this mad ride, we stop.

"I have to lift you through the rock now," Alexander announces. Behind me, Camille throws up into the river.

Shakily, I get to my knees. My fingertips and knuckles are bleeding from where I held onto the side and my staff for dear life. "No, please..."

But there's no time to reconsider. I wanted to go up, so up we go, right through tightly compacted, dark stone into... another small space, closed-off from the world. Only this time, it's wood that surrounds me.

"Oh my, this is a bit tight," Alexander says as he bumps into me. "Excuse me, stepping on toes and roots here. Yes, yes, I'll take that slab with me."

A dryad rustles her leaves and huffs. "I did not invite them in."

"Oh, but you've got the Travellers. And Rika is one of them," Alexander explains.

"Rika?" a familiar voice asks in the darkness.

"Pavel!" Oh, thank god, he's inside this tree. Outside, I hear the storm howl, tearing at the branches, but the dryad holds strong, not allowing her tree to get damaged.

In the darkness, I find Pavel, who folds my hands into his. "You're here. That's good."

"Is everyone safe?" I ask, concentrating hard on the touch of Pavel's hands, so I don't have to think of tight, dark spaces.

"Everyone's safe," he assures me with his deep, gentle voice. "The dryads have given us shelter."

"It was the least we could do," the dryad announces.

And suddenly, there it is. The solution. "I know how to do it!"

"Do what?" Camille asks, her sentiment echoed by the spirits around us.

Slowly, the plan unfurls in my mind. There are no guarantees that it'll work. "I know how to save everyone without going against everything I've just told the world. We've got to go now."

"Go where?" Now it's Pavel who sounds panicked.

My own terror has subsided, excitement and determination pushing the fear aside. "Camille, you stay with the Travellers. Make sure they're safe. Meanwhile, I have a petition to make. Alexander, please bring me to a Gnomian Union statue."

The statue Alexander brings me to is one of several in the Laeken Cemetery. It's a classic statue, featuring a big green man in a thinking pose. Very appropriate for the severity of the situation. Between the headstones and statues, the wind is a little more subdued than in the surrounding trees, and I wonder if that's the gnome influence. If so, it gives me hope.

"So, how do they want their petitions? I don't have anything to write with. Do gnomes write?" I ask Alexander.

"We scratch runes," he replies promptly. Then he grins wildly. "Nah, wouldn't want to mar a beautiful rock. Just put your hand on his and state your business."

That's easier said than done. His closest hand is still higher than my head. Fortunately, all sensible people have run for cover, so nobody sees me climbing the granite slab the statue sits on and grabbing the hand lying on his knee. At first, I feel rather stupid, but then I detect a faint park of life in the rock. Could it truly be?

"Hi. My name is Rika Csorba, and I would like to make a petition to the Gnomian Union," I announce, then check with Aeola what she thinks.

Aeola's still wrapping herself around my other wrist, half coiled around Grune's staff. "What do you want to ask them?"

The statue wants to know that, too. He suddenly lifts his head and peers down at me. The hand under mine moves around, his fingers gripping mine in a tight, almost bone-crushing grip. "State your business, Rika Csorba."

"Uhm…" It's hard to concentrate when my mind would much rather think about never being able to let go of this statue again. "The human inhabitants of Brussels need your assistance. In order to further positive human-spirit relationships, may I suggest that the Gnomian Union includes humans in their protection program by strengthening their houses in this storm, providing shelter, and stabilising monuments and infrastructure?"

Time to hold my breath. I know I'm asking a lot. The spirits have no reason to trust the humans. Quite the opposite.

"Does this petition include the spirit seekers?" the statue asks, and I think his grip just got a little stronger.

"Yes, they are humans, too." Though I'd love nothing more than to throw the entire SSA board out on the streets and into the Erlking's path.

The statue's gaze bores into mine. The pressure around my hand increases even more, and this time I can't help but wince. At last, he says, "The Gnomian Union will discuss your petition. Please wait."

Just as suddenly, he returns to his position, thinking hard. With my hand suddenly free, I tumble backwards, landing hard on my backside. "Ouch."

"I guess the GU system isn't built for humans," Alexander comments dryly. "Don't get your hopes up, glimmer."

Looking at Aeola, I ask, "You think it's useless as well?"

"You want spirits to make the first step when humans are the ones hunting us?" she asks, doubt swirling around her.

"Someone has to." I get up to my feet, steadying myself against the granite block. "What good does it do if everyone waits for the other to make the first move? We'll never get anywhere. An eye for an eye means that this war will go on and on. People will die today, might have already. And it doesn't matter that the SSA released the Erlking. The spirits will get blamed. But we can make a difference. By showing that not all spirits are like him! It's not all spirits! It's not even most of them. Just a loud, violent, little group of spirits. Do you really want them to dictate our human-spirit relationships? How are we ever gonna move on from all this hurt if we don't extend a hand in need?"

Aeola uncurls slowly until she can float right ahead of me. She has grown larger, more powerful. "As you extended a hand when I was in need? You could've died that day."

"And I told you then, this is what we do. We look out for each other. Doesn't matter if you're a spirit or a human." At least, I'll do that until the end of my life. Which might be sooner than I hope if this storm continues to grow.

Suddenly, the rock under my hands shifts. Cracks appear. As I hastily step back, the block splits. Out of the chasm comes Madeline. The statue is still, and I realise it never had a life of its own but was always connected to the gnomes.

"We have reviewed your petition, Rika," she starts in a grave voice that gives no hints of the outcome. "And heard your reasoning."

Blushing, I look down at my fingers. I didn't realise I was transmitting my words through the stone when I was holding onto it for balance.

Slowly, a smile appears on Madeline's knobbly face. "We have decided to heed your petition. The Gnomian Union once again proves to be wiser than that of humans. Our grievances can wait. They have no place in this state of emergency. Gnomes will be distributing their power through the city and help the humans withstand the storm. But there is one thing we ask of you in return."

"Of me?" What could I possibly give them in return for this more than gracious offer?

"The Erlking doesn't belong here. He doesn't belong anywhere in this world. You will have to remove him," Madeline announces.

My heart skips a beat. The scar tissue on my arms itches, and I recall the words he once spoke to me. *I see all, I hear all, and I will kill all.* But Madeline is right. The Erlking can't be allowed to rule. The SSA can't be allowed to bring back his terror into the world. "I'll do my best or die trying." Some things are worth dying for.

"You won't be alone," Madeline promises. "The Erlking directs his storm on top of the Atomium not far from here. We will bring you to the spirit seekers who have approached him."

"Not me," Aeola announces and lets go of me. "This is sylph business, and I have my own battle to fight." She turns to face me. "I pray to the winds we'll meet again, but if we don't, know that you're dearest to me in this world."

My throat is constricting as tears sting my eyes. Aeola's announcement shocks me. I thought we were going to face her father together. As much as it hurts me that it won't be the case, I have to trust her. And one thing is indisputably true. "I love you, too."

Once more, her soft breeze caresses my face, then she's gone, lost in the storm.

Madeline reaches out her hand to me. "Are you ready?"

"Yes. I think I am this time."

Gripping my staff tightly, I follow her into the stone.

23

Madeline drops me off in what looks like a restaurant near the Atomium. Beyond a hedge, I can see the giant metal spheres rising in the air. Lightning crackles around the stainless-steel rods while an almost pitch-black cloud has descended upon it. On our side of the hedge, the whole of Europe has been devastated. Notre Dame has fallen over, and Big Ben has been reduced to splinters. The Széchenyi Baths of Budapest have been flooded, the Berlin Wall toppled over, and Vesuvius reduced to ashes.

"It's a miniature park," Wulf says, barely reacting to the fact that I appeared magically in front of him. He and a handful of the others have made it this far. "Mini Europe."

Well, it looks to me like the future the Erlking has laid out for us. "How are you?"

There are ten spirit seekers in this temporary base, among them Miro and Carina, and a whole bunch of tourists who've been caught out by the storm. Blood is running down Miro's face, which he continuously wipes away as if it were only a bleeding nose. Carina is kneeling on the ground, helping to set the arm of another seeker. With the white of bone showing from the elbow, he won't go any further.

"Exhausted, but glad we made it this far," Wulf says. He matches his words, dark shadows pooling under his eyes, skin scratched and pale, hair matted to his face. "We're having one last rest, then we'll move to the Atomium. You coming?" He's mostly eyeing my staff as he asks.

"I'm coming." I put my hand on his arm and feel him relax slightly. "Listen, I—"

Something big slams into the house. It feels like a truck. Sure enough, the walls are cracking. The ceiling is sagging. Screams cut through the room as dust trickles down on us. Everyone's face is turned up in worry. The storm is howling outside, putting further pressure on the already-compromised structure. The windows are blocked by something large and silver. One of the spheres of the Atomium.

"We need to evacuate," Carina calls.

"No time," Miro shouts. Then he bellows, "Duck and cover!"

Wulf drags me down, pulling me under a table the moment the restaurant begins to shake. I clutch his arms, digging my fingers into his skin as my biggest nightmare comes true: being buried under tons of stone.

The ground jerks. Wulf puts a hand over my head, pressing me to his chest in a last attempt to protect me. And then it stops.

No more howling wind, no creaking walls. In fact, the walls look better than ever, quartz filling the cracks in them. The ceiling has been stabilised, now impervious once more.

Slowly, the people lift their heads again. "What's happening?" someone asks in sheer wonder. We were all sure we were going to die.

And I'm laughing. "The gnomes. The Gnomian Union is protecting us!" I clasp my hand over my mouth to stifle the laughter, but it keeps bubbling up. Never has a closed-off room felt any safer. "It's like a bunker." They truly did it! They used their power over the earth to protect us. And I can only assume they're doing it all over the city.

I look at Wulf, my face aching from the wide grin. "I petitioned the GU, asking them to protect Brussels. All of it. All the humans. They're safe! Spirits are saving them."

Instead of answering, Wulf grabs my face and kisses me. My thoughts are swept away as all his love and gratefulness pour into me. The rain had me drenched and cold, but now I'm feeling warm all over. Too bad it can't stay that way.

"So, are they going to take out the Erlking, too?" a very cranky Carina asks. "Or are we gonna be stuck inside forever?"

"I, for one, am glad, Rika," Miro says. "If the gnomes are protecting my family, I'll never touch a staff again."

"Don't say that!" Wulf and I crawl out from under the table. "They can't defeat the Erlking. So, we need you and your staff."

Miro looks rather glad about that, despite his emotional declaration. Carina, however, sniffs. "Right, so they leave the bad guys to us."

"You know there wouldn't be a bad guy if your parents and the rest of the board hadn't released him back into the world?" I've never seen Wulf this angry. Now that saving people isn't an immediate concern, it seems he can allow these emotions to surface. "My team fought and trapped the Erlking. Now, the SSA's bastardised Piero's research to make the Erlking even more vicious, and used him to induce terror!"

It becomes clear this is the first time Miro's heard of it. "They did what?"

"The polluted spirits—they're SSA-crafted!"

"That's not true!" Carina protests. "They're all lies! Her lies!" Her voice breaks at the end. With a distorted face, she points to Wulf. "And you're going along with it!" Judging by the pain in her voice, that's the worst of it.

I get it. Her brother is dead, her parents and uncle are criminals—no, worse! They're terrorists! And her brother... or rather ex-lover is washing his hands clean from all that mess. But it's not my mess. I didn't make these decisions. This is on her family. "We've got proof."

"I don't care if you have proof! The SSA aren't a bunch of terrorists! And I'll show you!" Her eyes are almost popping out of her head. "We're spirit seekers. We defeat spirits. And I'm going to defeat that storm sprite! Single-handedly, if I have to."

With that, she grabs her staff and runs out the door, the gnome protecting it quickly giving way to her.

"Carina!" Naturally, Wulf runs after her.

Miro looks at me apologetically. "Sorry, she's always been like this. Proud and full of drama." He's eyeing me up. "So, is it true? Has that spirit been modified and released by the board?"

"He has. Just like the spirits in Budapest and Dublin. And in Berlin. Or the one in Rue des Bouchers a few days ago."

I have to say, Miro takes it better than Wulf ever did. He curses colourfully in Russian and then snaps back from it. "Right. A problem for another day. What now, Spirit Girl?"

"Now, we take down the Erlking." Not that I have any idea how to do that.

"You heard Rika," Miro bellows to the other spirit seekers who've been watching us. "Anyone who's not hurt or too tired to keep going comes with us."

There are only six of us who brave the storm. Protected by the gnomes, we were able to forget about nature's force for a bit, but as soon as we step outside, we're strongly reminded. Mini Europe has been flattened by a metal sphere from the Atomium. I see the Eiffel Tower hanging in a tree while the other monuments are nearly unrecognisable. Miro does his best to find us a way through the debris, keeping close to the metal wall of the giant atom. Still, we get hit by tiny towers and figurines.

Then a whole array of sylphs takes notice of us. Howling, they storm against us. "Staffs up. Frontal attack!" Miro bellows.

The wind pushes me against the steel. Rain falls horizontally into our faces, practically blinding us. Soon, it doesn't matter whom among us has a high NAV and who doesn't. Forward is the only way to go. I push my staff up, trying to wield it in all directions. The wind grabs hold of my hair, pulling at it. Something bangs into the atom, causing the whole metal sphere to vibrate. A spirit seeker cries out further down the line. Sylphs screech.

Someone grabs my arm and pushes me along. "Go! Go! Go!"

Miro is herding us towards the hedge. The storm has ripped out huge sections, leaving several holes for us to cross the train tracks behind it. I hope no dryad has ever put claim to it. Once again, the Erlking shows he doesn't care for anything or anyone. Human or spirit.

It's nearly impossible to get through the hedge. Despite using my staff, the wind is so strong I'm pushed back several times. "Duck!" Miro yells and gives me a push.

Together, we make it through the hole. Once out in the open, I crouch down as close to the ground as I can to avoid being pushed back into the hedge. Another spirit seeker isn't as lucky, screaming as she gets skewered and scratched by the branches. Miro pulls her out, bleeding, but she stumbles forward, quickly losing consciousness. Just then, a train sign hits Miro over the head, and he goes down.

As the sign skitters away, I crawl over to him. Thank the spirits. He's still conscious. His breathing is shallow, though, and the bleeding has started again. As I cradle his face, his pupils dilate. "Stop him..." he mutters. "Manya..."

"Your beautiful daughters and Manya will be fine!" I cry. "And you will be, too." Panicked, I look around until I find another spirit seeker pulling himself through the hole. "You stay with them!" I tell him. "Get them back to the restaurant!"

This must be one of the lower-level spirit seekers, because he immediately heeds my command and ropes in another guy on the other side of the hedge.

I grasp Miro's face once more, forcing him to look into my eyes. "You stay alive for your family. I'm gonna get him."

After I lower his head, I cross the tracks, climb the fence on the other side, and make a beeline for the Atomium, which looks scarily out of balance, with one sphere missing and the connecting rods dangling in the air.

I narrowly escape a car toppled over by the wind. My staff rips apart another sylph screaming obscenities at me. The Atomium isn't far, but crossing the street is as much going backwards and sideways as it is making progress. The storm doesn't want me to reach its centre.

At last, I notice two figures fighting back-to-back against a cloud of sylphs. Wulf and Carina have only managed to get a little further than me, still too far from the Atomium to use its entrance for cover. "Wulf!"

He doesn't hear me against the howl of the storm, his staff tearing through two sylphs. Carina is equally efficient with a second ancient staff. This is what her parents want. Wulf and Carina, the power couple who'll save Brussels from the Erlking. But they've underestimated their creation.

While I'm still making my way over to them, using my staff as a windbreaker, a terrible creak splits the air. One of the outside stairs is dangling from its railing. For a moment, it looks like the metal is bending but staying attached. Then the wind rips off the railing and several stairs and sends them crashing down, straight at Wulf and Carina.

"No, no, no!" Enough energy fills me to push through the storm.

In an instant, I'm at the foot of the Atomium. The sight of splintered dryad wood brings me to my knees. "Wulf!"

Carina is there. Somehow, she's escaped unscathed, but her staff lies uselessly on the ground, rolling away in the next gust. She's on her knees, tears streaming down her face as she cradles Wulf's head in her lap. And then I see it. His lower body is buried under the broken stairs, blood pooling around him.

"Wulf!" I cry once more, falling to my knees next to him.

"Rika?" Carina looks up at me, as if she's seeing me for the first time.

Just then, the wind picks up again. Three sylphs fly at us, screeching. Above them, a thunderina charges herself for a strike. Before any of them can reach us, the earth moves and huge slabs of pavement guard us on three sides. Lightning flashes, its electricity rippling less than an arm-length from us over the rock. The sylphs howl and whistle, but they can't do much to us down here.

"Oh my, that was close," Alexander announces. Then he looks down at Wulf, whose eyelids are fluttering as he struggles to keep conscious. "Your friend is leaking."

Carina stares at him, completely out of her wits. I, however, won't see Wulf bleed out. "He needs to get to the hospital."

"How?" Carina asks, almost sighing the word.

"Alexander, can you bring them there? As fast as you can? Please." Wulf can't die. I just won't allow it.

The gnome shrugs. "One gravel train coming right up. Won't be harder than moving all the others."

I have no idea what he's talking about, but I almost cry from relief. Time is of the essence, so I quickly put my hand on Wulf's cheek, ignoring how clammy it is. "Don't die, okay? I'm going to stop him."

He winces, his breath coming in sharp bursts. "Ri-ka."

"You have to go with him," I tell Carina.

"But…"

I put my hand on hers. "Trust Alexander! Keep Wulf alive for me. Please."

Maybe it's how my voice breaks on that last word or that this accident has finally broken her, but Carina's shoulders and chin slump. "Trust the gnome." She looks up at Alexander. "Please make it quick. He doesn't have much time."

And just like that, they're gone, and I'm left alone with Wulf's blood all around me.

Breathe, Rika. Breathe. Wulf would fight on to the end. If he can't, I'll have to do it for him. Whether he lives or dies doesn't matter right now. I did all I could for him. Still, it breaks my heart every time I look at his blood. How can I do this all alone?

It doesn't matter. I have to try, anyway.

With shaky, shallow breaths, I squeeze myself and my staff through the gaps in the slabs, then run over to the entrance doors. Somehow, I make it, narrowly escaping another lightning strike. At the door, the sylphs behind me blow it shut. No matter how much I pull, the storm is too strong.

Angrily, I turn around, waving my staff in their faces. "The Erlking is expecting me! Let me through!"

I must've surprised them, because for an instant, the pressure on the door lessens enough for me to rip it open and fall through. It slams shut right behind me, the glass shattering as it does so. Glaring at the sylphs, I walk backwards, taking my first real breath since Wulf was hurt.

"Rika!"

Surprised, I turn around. I know this voice. Sure enough, there's Camille. But she's not the only one. In the centre of the entrance, a group of spirit seekers and Travellers have assembled, staying as far away from the doors as they can. There are Leon and Lukas, and good old

Pavel. Even Miriam has come. And there are more. Rory, Eoghan, and Henny are there, and so are my friends from Budapest. All of them have proper dryad wood staffs with them.

Camille comes running up to me, grabbing my hand. "Are you okay?"

"I... Wulf..." I'm so surprised I forget to guard myself against the despair I've pushed aside to get here. And suddenly I'm sobbing in Camille's swift embrace. "He got hit. And... he might die."

"What?" Camille squeezes me even tighter. "Is he—"

"Carina's taking him to the hospital." I let myself have another moment, but then it's time to pull myself back together again. "What are you all doing here?"

"Camille and Pavel asked who'd be willing to assist you," Rory explains. "We're the ones who said yes."

"Yeah, are we gonna kick that Erlking's airy ass, or what?" Lukas shouts loudly, raising his staff in the air.

It's so him, a sad little giggle escapes my throat. I nod. "Of course we are. Where did you get the staffs?"

"Courtesy of the dryads," Camille explains. "Your grandfather or, well, Pavel convinced them to give them to us."

"They don't want this storm any more than we do," he says with a soft smile.

Oh, Pavel. He's the best. "Thanks."

"So, what's the plan?" Iván asks. "The elevator's still running."

I take a few moments to breathe in deeply and sort my thoughts. We need to get up as high as we can. Right now, the elevator's our best chance. "Then let's take it."

24

The elevator ride is the longest of my life, despite being only a few seconds long. Since it can't hold all of us, I've convinced Pavel and the other Travellers to stay at ground level with Miriam and defend our exit, taking only trained spirit seekers with me.

On the way up, I regret my decision a dozen time over. How are we going to defeat the Erlking a second time, now that he's been filled with the remnants of so many other spirits? We don't even have a trap to capture him. Not that any could hold him.

"We'll have to weaken him," I say. Spirits may regenerate, but if we can weaken him enough that his storm dies down to a natural level, it'll be a win. "Any ideas?" We don't exactly know what awaits us.

"Bounce him," Lukas says. "We spread out and bounce him between the best fighters. The others take care of his entourage."

The Varga brothers nod in unison. "That could work," Iván says. "Who are the best?"

"You two, Lukas, Eoghan, and Camille," I suggest. With half a year of partial training, I can't hold a candle to them.

The elevator stops. Lukas nods. "Alright, everyone on their marks. Stay low to the ground!"

I'm not ready for the doors to open, but they do so anyway. The sight is eerily like the Television Tower. We're in a restaurant. Fortunately, it's not one with a rotating floor. There are a couple of sylphs laying waste to the platform, but they're no match for the dryad wood staffs. The spirit seekers spread out and break the spirits down until they're no more than wisps in the air. I try not to feel too bad for them. Since no one's captured them, they'll regenerate in time. And probably grow up to hate us even more. It's high time we broke out of that vicious cycle.

"He's not here," József tells me, and I realise that despite Lukas' instructions, they're still looking at me as their leader.

"There's another floor!" Rebeka calls over, standing near a staircase. Iván hurries to her side, staff ready for attack.

My stomach feels like it's filled with stones, but I manage the command just fine. "We go as far up as we can."

We're in the eye of the storm, thus climbing the stairs is deceivingly easy. We're just about to reach the upper level when I notice the tension in the air. The entire upper level is charged!

"Iván, down!"

But it's too late. A flash of lightning blinds us all. The stairs shake under the impact as thunder splits the air. I trip and crash against the wall. As I fall onto the steps, the sickening smell of burning flesh fills my nostrils.

Slowly, the brightness recedes. Dark specks dance in front of my eyes as they regain their sight. Something's flickering nearby. Iván's staff. It's been charred almost completely, the rest of it burning across the stairs. I don't want to look, but my eyes have a mind of their own. Without mercy, they drag my gaze to the smoking husk of the Budapester commander.

His brother József is sitting next to him, looking dazed as he cradles his severely burnt arm. He must've tried to drag Iván down before the explosion. Further down, Rebeka cries out, pushing through the spirit seekers who've stumbled like me. She can't even touch him without harming herself. Instead, József takes her hand and squeezes it, tears burning in his eyes.

"Is it safe to go up?" Lukas asks in the stunned silence.

I want to yell at him about how he can even think about that when we've just lost Iván, but he's right. We can't afford the time to grieve. My throat grows tight as I try to push breath through it and reach out with my senses. It's so hard.

"No charge," I finally manage. It's all unloaded into Iván. The one who's always first in line, no matter the danger. There's another like that. I grab Lukas' hand, jerking him back. "Be careful." He's only just recovered from his last major injury.

When he just nods instead of giving me a snarky response, I realise he's just as shaken. He uses my grip to haul me back up on my feet. "I will."

Together, we creep past the scene of tragedy, keeping our staffs and heads down until we can peer over the edge. Behind us, I hear Rory giving Iván an Irish blessing. A small comfort.

"Holy shit!" Lukas whispers.

I agree. The top floor is not what I expected. It occurs to me now that we didn't truly have a plan on how to get to the Erlking if he's on top of the sphere and we're inside. But fortunately, that's no longer an issue. The storm has torn away the huge steel panels, exposing the floor to the dark sky above. The clouds are so thick, height is no longer an issue. We can't even see the next sphere of the Atomium.

"What are we dealing with?" Lukas asks, his voice uncharacteristically breathless.

"He's built himself a throne in the centre." I don't know what it is. Some human garbage by the looks of it, bent steel rods, and what looks like slimy black water plants.

On it looms the Erlking, larger than he ever was before. His long, haggard face, which used to be full of wrinkles, is unnaturally smooth. His long hair is black, glistening like oil, the crown of thorns made of steel. He's beautiful now, no longer old, but new and improved. Hate burns in his eyes as always, now fuelled by the fire of some poor salamander. The air bristles around him as his eyes meet mine. "Hello, Rika. I have awaited you." His lips don't even move, the words blooming in my head.

A sharp pain in my side reminds me of the others. Lukas pulls back his elbow, glaring at me. "Anything else?"

Quickly, I describe the floor to him and the others, avoiding the Erlking's gaze as I do so. For some reason, he seems content to wait until I'm finished. Probably because he knows we won't even get close to him. "He's got them all," I say, "fire, steel, water... All spirit matter is in his control."

"Don't care," Lukas announces. "Still going to take him down."

"Lukas," Camille says, having joined us. "We'll try our best, but no stunts. That goes for you, too, Rika."

"Me?" When have I ever pulled a stunt?

Camille gives me a long stare, reminiscent of the seeker she once was. "Sacrificing yourself because he called to you?"

The Erlking's no longer calling me. He knows I'm coming. "Fine. Let's spread out. His focus will still be on me, so try to get behind him while I keep my head down."

Rory speaks a quick prayer to the Aos Sí. I'd appreciate some spirit help, but in the Erlking's realm, all the air spirits are hostile.

"Finally." The Erlking's voice crawls over my skin, vibrating through my nerves as I walk towards him, staff ready. "I see you made friends with Grune. He's a weak one, allowing the humans to take from his forest."

"At least he still knows compassion." Why am I talking back to this monster? Doesn't he hate me enough already?

His response is immediate. A gust hits me in the face, bringing with it toxic smoke. Coughing, I drop to the ground, shielding my face. The smoke burns in my throat, etching away the mucosa until it feels like my entire throat is dissolving.

"Compassion for those who poison the skies?" The Erlking chuckles.

Around me, I hear the others cough and splutter. Too bad none of us had any gas masks ready.

"How do you like my poison?"

If I stay here, I'm going to die. Centimetre by centimetre, I claw myself across the ground, trying to breathe as little as possible and keep my face down. Winds try to pick me up, but they can't get a good grip.

"What of the acid rain you love so much?" the Erlking asks.

Immediately, large drops fall from the skies. Where they splash on my naked skin, pain erupts. It eats itself into my flesh like his words once did. I curl into a ball, screaming for the pain to stop. I can only hope it's less harmful to those who are less attuned to nature. But there are several cries from Rory, Henny, and József.

With an eerie scream that reverberates in my bones, the rain stops. The Erlking's attention is elsewhere.

Quickly, I look up to see Henny, Rory, and Eoghan on the ground as well. The others, however, got lucky and escaped the Erlking's more vile attacks. Rebeka has made it to the disgusting throne and thrust her staff into it. Black liquid pools from the wound, spreading a foul stench.

The Erlking turns to her, but by then, Camille is attacking his other side. Eoghan gets to his feet and runs at the Erlking, vaulting himself off a chair and driving his staff straight through his Erlking's beautiful face. Part of the Erlking is repelling him, but as Eoghan falls, he gets partially stuck in the throne. A steel vine coils itself around his upper body and starts squeezing.

"Eoghan!" Henny is up on their feet, too, digging their fingers under the coil in an effort to rip it from their friend.

Bones crack, and Eoghan screams. At the same time, a whirlwind grabs the others and throws them against the remaining walls as if they were nothing more than the figurines in Mini Europe. Camille crashes into a pile of stored chairs, causing the entire tower to topple down on her. Leon and Lukas slam into the opposite wall, narrowly missing a gap in the panels that would've sent them tumbling from the Atomium. Rebeka hits the ground hard, her body tossed around like a rag doll until it lies still near the stairs we came from.

I only escape the brunt force of the storm because Rory is suddenly in front of me, whirling his staff around so fast it breaks the wind. "We have to push on!" he bellows, extending his hand to me.

Holding on to him, we press closer to the Erlking. The attacks have cost him, but you wouldn't know it by the calm expression on his face. Eoghan's hit him in the face, but the skin there has smoothed over almost instantly, giving it a grisly white shine.

Eoghan screams again as another rib cracks under the pressure. The whirlwind has picked Henny up and thrown them across the room. Their short-lived flight ends with one of their legs skewered by a snapped steel rod. Just like with Wulf, blood pools around them.

Oh, why did I have to think of him? He can't help us. I'm not sure anyone can. All we can do is attack the Erlking again and again until his storm lessens enough for the people of Brussels to survive.

"Go, help your brother!" I shout at Rory when we reach the throne.

From the corner of my eye, I see Rory bringing his staff down on the steel rods, fighting spirit essence with spirit essence. Meanwhile, I catch the Erlking's eye. I know it's insane, but I need to try and buy the others time. No stunts, Camille said. Well, that's not how it works in Rika world. "Let the others go!" I tell the Erlking with every ounce of confidence I can muster. "You want me, not them."

The Erlking's laughter crawls across my arms like a thousand insects. "You? You're nothing."

And with that, he grabs me and hurtles me through the air. A violent gust picks me up and slams me against the sharp edge of an outside panel. For a moment, all I see are the roiling clouds around the dull silver sphere. Then my legs are swiped up from under me and I'm thrown over the edge completely.

Steel digs painfully into my palms. Somehow, I've managed to hold on to the edge. If I let go, no cloud will hold me. I'll drop to the ground. My entire body knows it won't survive that.

Everything hurts. My skin, my bones, my muscles. I'm holding on for dear life, but the rain has made the metal slippery. Already, my fingers are ready to give up.

Just then, Leon grabs my arm. "I've got you!"

But he doesn't really. He has no purchase on his side of the sphere. He'll hold me for a little while longer, but without help, he won't be able to haul me back in. And right now, the storm is picking up again, dragging on my legs.

"Don't let go!" Leon begs, doing his best to pull me up. Slowly, my body rises along the smooth surface. Then a gust hits him from behind and I drop again.

Leon's fingers slip until they catch my wrist. With a jerk, my body stops sliding. But now I have nothing to hold onto anymore. It's hopeless. Leon's face is distorted by pain. He can't do this much longer, either.

We've weakened the Erlking. That must be enough. There are others who will continue our work. I've kept my word. I've tried my best until the end.

A warm breeze comforts my skin. At least I'll die under the open sky.

"It's okay to let go." The words ring true, and suddenly I feel at peace. Half a year ago, only Fez would've shared a thought for me if I died. Now, there'll be many more people who'll remember me. I guess it *is* okay to leave this fight to someone else now.

"Let me go!" I say, my voice merely more than a whisper. My arm hurts from the strain Leon's desperate hold puts on it.

"No, Rika, I—"

"It's okay." I'll be fine.

Though he doesn't want to, Leon can't hold on any longer. With a sharp gasp, I slip through his fingers, sliding across the steel sphere until I'm free falling. Above me, the storm clouds are easing. There's a speck of blue shining through. A warm breeze brushes my face once more, and I find myself smiling.

This storm won't last forever. Summer is coming.

25

One moment, I'm tumbling through the air. Next, I land soft as a feather on the cold body of a well-known tempest.

"Flitzer!" I can't believe they're here.

The beautiful horse neighs as they sprint around the central pole of the Atomium. Their mane crackles with lightning, but the tiny sparks of electricity are welcome. They would never hurt me.

"Hold on!" Flitzer says.

As we're racing back into the sky, I see how close I came to the ground. Only a few more seconds, and there would be no more Rika. My mind's still trying to wrap itself around what's happening. "You're here!" I exclaim, holding on tight to their neck.

"We all are," Flitzer announces.

And truly, there are their twin babies. They've grown but are as playful as ever. And they're not the only spirits Flitzer meant. Countless sylphs and storm sprites, and even the occasional thunderina, have appeared in the sky.

For a moment, I'm reminded of the Erlking's original storm, a dark turmoil of spirits bent to his will. Then, a familiar face appears in front of me. "Aeola!"

"I'm sorry if we're a little late. It was a long way from Berlin." She's more beautiful than ever, sunlight dancing through her hair.

That's right. Sunlight. The skies are clearing around us, pushing away the Erlking's dark storm. I can actually see Brussels sprawling out in front of me. "You came back."

From the coils of her body, she produces my staff. It must've fallen to the ground when the Erlking swept me over the edge. Tentatively, I take the wood from her. "Together?"

"Together," Aeola confirms. "As it should be."

The cloud of air spirits rises above the highest sphere, giving me a bird's eye view of the carnage the Erlking has wrought. Anxiously, I scan the floor, looking for my friends. József has pulled himself together and is attacking the Erlking, although he only has one good arm to do so. Behind the storm king, I see Lukas climbing onto an overarching steel beam, ready to launch himself at the foe. Blood's running down his face, making him look even more menacing.

Rory has managed to free Eoghan, or the Erlking has let him go, but they're both hiding under a make-shift shelter, taking care of Henny's bleeding leg. Leon's sitting against the outside panel, grabbing his side, his face still distorted by pain. I look around for Camille and am amazed to find her climbing the beam behind Lukas. They both nod at each other, then take the jump together, staffs ready to pierce the Erlking.

But of course, he won't let them get that far. Another burst of wind swipes everyone off their feet. Lukas and Camille get blown through the gap in the panels, their bodies hurtling through the air.

"No!" I shout, but then the storm picks them up and throws them right back into the sphere. Several sylphs pin them down, keeping them safe from the Erlking.

That finally gets his attention. He stops focusing on the humans and turns his gaze upon the spirits in the air. "Have you come to join me at last?" His voice oozes power. It ripples through the crowd, bending them to his will.

"We don't want to join you," a small voice pipes up.

My heart goes out to the little tempest brave enough to stand up to the storm king. Her brother does the same. "We follow a queen now."

The Erlking roars. The clouds around him draw together, getting darker by the second. Lightning crackles around him. "You belong to me!" a voice like thunder booms. Fear takes hold of the sylphs. Any moment, they'll bow to him.

"No." It's Aeola whose voice cuts through the turmoil like a fresh breath of air. "We denounce you, Father. We want no part in your war."

"Then go!" he flings the words at them and follows them up with lightning and fire.

But the thunderinas in the crowd diffuse the lightning, and the sylphs blow out the fires.

Aeola turns her back on her father, as if he's no longer of importance to her. "Let's make an end of him, Rika."

She coils her body tightly around my staff, infusing her life force into the wood until I feel like I've just had an intravenous shot of caffeine. The rest is on me. Well, and Flitzer. "Get us close, Flitzer!"

It's good that they're so fast because the Erlking throws everything he has at us: thunder and lightning, thorns and steel, even a splash of boiling water. Flitzer escapes all of it, changing direction like a hare. It's hard not to get dizzy, but Aeola's intent guides me. Just as we're above the Erlking, I drop from Flitzer's back onto his, ramming my staff straight into his heart, the same spot I hit so many months ago.

Then it wasn't enough, but this time, Aeola is onto it. The staff lets her tear into her father, releasing her own storm from within. The smell of flowers and summer rain, heat-baked pine cones, and sweet berries explode inside the Erlking, ripping him into a million fragments.

I fall to the ground, looking up in wonder as the spirits descend, each of them picking up a piece of their fallen king and flinging it into the wind. The summer storm spreads them fast across the world. If the Erlking ever regenerates, he'll never be whole.

Rain is falling down on us, but it's the soothing spray of summer, warm and refreshing. It eases the wounds on my skin and the pain in my throat. It smells like life. Nature's life.

"We did it." I laugh when Aeola descends, looking more complete than ever. Her hair shimmers in the rain. Her beautiful long face shines down on me. "It's you. You're the new queen."

"Someone had to replace him, eventually." She smirks. Under all that elegance, she's still my Aeola.

I drop my staff and embrace her, not caring that part of me grabs nothing but thin air. Warm air envelops me, infusing me with joy. When I let go of her, I bow my head. "All hail the Erlqueen."

The words are picked up by the wind and tossed between the spirits as they repeat them. Aeola did it. She united them all behind her, leading them with compassion and care, not hate and fear. I hope her reign will be long and peaceful. For both our people.

As the air spirits disperse, the skies open up. The winds carry the clouds away. The raindrops stop falling. Blue replaces grey, and the brightest of days follows.

26

It's not all smiles and sunshine. Iván is dead. People got hurt. I'm in a whole lot of pain. The Atomium has been trashed and won't have visitors any time soon.

"Camille!" Miriam's running up the stairs, looking around wildly. When she sees Camille dragging herself up from the ground, Miriam throws her arms around her girlfriend's neck and showers her with kissing.

"I could use some of that," Lukas comments, dabbing at the blood welling up from a cut on his cheekbone.

Leon boxes his shoulder. "Try being nicer, and someone might like you enough." His grin becomes a gentle smile when his gaze meets mine. "You did it, Rika."

"Aeola did most of it."

Lukas snorts. "Can't believe I owe my life to a bunch of spirits."

"What are you saying?" Leon asks. "They've saved you countless times, or have you forgotten how you jumped down from Central Station and barely got a scratch?"

"Or when the dryads in Dublin saved you from drowning," I add, joining in their banter.

"Fine, fine, they're not all bad." A small gust of wind makes him reconsider his words. "Most of them are alright. Even if I can't see them properly."

I exchange a glance with Aeola. "I assume that's as good as it gets with him."

She nods sagely. "Yeah, I guess that makes him alright."

Our laughter's cut short when I see Rory and Eoghan helping Henny to get up. The steel rod is still in their leg, but Rory has wrapped it tight, so it doesn't move. Eoghan winces pitifully with each step.

"Wait, we can help." We run to them.

Leon and Lukas steady Henny, half carrying them down the stairs, while Rory and I help Eoghan. "I'm fine," the younger brother says.

"Yeah, sure," Rory mutters. "Half your ribs are broken, but you're fine."

"I'm alive, am I not?" Eoghan replies, but his face looks awfully white.

His words make me search out Rebeka and József. Now that the fight is over, she's kneeling on the floor, crying her eyes out, while József has his good arm wrapped around her. On our way down, we have to go past Iván, who's stopped smoking. Still, I can't bring myself to look at him. The smell alone is enough to bring tears to my eyes.

"The SSA will pay for that." Rory says grimly.

"Will they?" A deep tiredness is settling in my bones. I've just defeated the Erlking after he was enhanced with all kinds of poisons. But what'll stop them from throwing the next spirit at us? How many did they even bring? "They've got money. Lots and lots of money."

"Not enough to pay their way out of this," Rory promises.

Between us, Eoghan snorts. His breathing gets shallower, his head dropping as he struggles to keep conscious.

The rest of the way down, we all keep quiet, mulling over our own thoughts. I remember Humberto's spiel, turning my moral dilemma into a weapon. Or what Dante said about his sister: how she builds you up high, so the fall will break your neck. It almost did that today, and I don't know if I have the energy to go up against them straight away.

The elevator brings us down into the lobby, and for the first time, I stagger. Cars are arriving. A few of them ambulances, but many more carry journalists and TV crews. The moment they detect us, they cram at the doors. I hear Lukas bellow, "Out of the way!" but that doesn't stop people from pushing a microphone or camera into our faces.

"Can you tell us what happened up there?"

"Is Brussels safe again?"

"Did you catch the spirit?"

"Is it true the SSA set this spirit free?"

"What can you tell us about the Gnomian Union?"

So many questions. Thankfully, the emergency workers assert themselves and come up to us with gurneys. They take Eoghan, asking a lot of questions, which Rory answers. Henny's also being seen, and I'm glad to see Lukas and Leon herded towards the ambulances as well. There, Inga is waiting, ready to fuss over Leon's injuries.

"We need more help upstairs," I tell someone who looks like she's in charge. "There's a casualty," I add belatedly. A casualty. It's Iván who died at the Erlking's hand.

The rescue worker nods at me and directs her team towards the elevator. Then it's just me and the journalists.

"Are you Rika Csorba?" someone asks. "The spirit expert of the SSA?"

Okay, I have to set that one right. This is my victory, not the SSA's. "I'm Marika Csorba, yes, but I don't work for the SSA. In fact, I'm going to sue them on a bunch of charges, including manslaughter, fraud, and acts of terrorism." Okay, I have no idea, whether I can actually do that, but let the SSA wriggle out of that public opinion fiasco.

"So, it's true? The SSA is responsible for this storm?" someone else asks.

Well, now that I've started, I might as well keep going. "That's what it looks like. Please don't ask any more questions. We've submitted all evidence to the police, and they'll take care of the investigation. The spirit in question was the Erlking, a powerful storm sprite from Berlin, previously captured in March. He was more powerful this time thanks to human modification. Almost too powerful, but an alliance between spirits and true spirit seekers has won the day. The Erlking has been defeated, and there will be no storms for a while." That should be enough to satisfy them, shouldn't it?

Of course it isn't. From my statement, a hundred new questions spawn, asking about the spirits, my own role, and the SSA. Before I can answer even a tenth of them, the police arrive and are pushing the masses of reporters away. A woman comes to me. I recognise her as the EU delegate who wanted me to work with them on spirit relationships. Carole Dubois.

"Come, Ms Csorba. We've got much to discuss. There'll be a press conference later." She puts an arm around my shoulders and guides me away.

Oh, dear. This won't ever stop, will it?

On the side of the road where the park begins, Pavel and a couple of Travellers are standing and watching me. When he smiles at me, I wish I could run over and bury my face against his shoulder. But it'll have to wait.

"What happened to working with Humberto Vallesco?" I ask.

"Oh, he and his wife were arrested," Mrs Dubois informs me. For a quick moment, her mouth is a thin line. "Along with the rest of the board. It's quite appalling. It'll take the police months to sift through the evidence. It's quite obvious now the SSA needs to be completely remodelled or disbanded." She smiles at me. "And that's where you come in. You were right. Working with the spirits is the only way forward. I don't know how many casualties we'd have to mourn if it weren't for the protection of the Gnomian Union. It's bad enough as it is. And do I understand correctly that sylphs helped you defeat that monster that was controlling the storm?"

All this information is making me quite heady. The game is over. The Vallescos, my father, and the rest of them are under investigation. Thanks to Dante's files, they might actually be convicted. And Europe will move forward with positive human-spirit relationships.

"Yes, that was right. An army of sylphs led by the Erlqueen Aeola helped us take down the storm king. The local dryads also helped, providing us with the necessary weapons to stand a chance." I smile. "It seems like you owe the spirits of this city a lot."

Fortunately, she chuckles. "It seems like it. And I want you to tell us what we can do to repay them. What do the spirits want that's in our control?"

I almost answer "a lot". The European Union has the actual power to tackle some of the major issues regarding spirits. But before I can say anything, we're interrupted again. Someone puts a hand on my shoulder and says with a distinct Russian accent. "I'm sorry, but we booked her first."

"Miro!" I throw my arms around him, happy to see him on his own two feet. He's got a bandage around his head. Unfortunately, seeing him reminds me of someone else. "Have you heard from Wulf?"

So much has been going on I'd almost forgotten about him. Now, all the memories are back. I see the blood, see his ashen face on Carina's lap, the splinters of his staff lying everywhere.

Miro catches me when my knees give way. My heart is aching, and it feels like my throat has got worse again. "Please say he's alive. Please."

Miro's face darkens. "Cari wrote he's in surgery. I don't know any more. But you should head to the hospital, just in case. And also because you look like you've been knocked about quite a bit." He looks at the crowd of reporters still yelling out questions. "I'll take care of everything here."

"You can take my car," Mrs Dubois offers, and Miro gently ushers me towards the black limousine.

I'm almost inside when I remember something. "Miro!" He turns around. "Did you get hold of your family?"

A smile softens his face. "They were on Grand Place, buildings toppling around them, but your gnome friends erected a dome, protecting everyone. They're safe."

Relief washes over me. "Thank the spirits."

He winks at me. "I will."

When I arrive at the hospital, there's no news. Wulf's still in surgery. I don't want to, but the nurses insist on seeing me as well. Turns out I cracked my hip bone and got some poisoning that'll have to be monitored closely. Since most of my ailments are spirit injuries, though, they should vanish with time. None of that truly matters until I hear something about Wulf.

When he's finally wheeled out of surgery, attached to more wires than I can stomach, I'm sitting in the recovery room with Carina. The entire time, her eyes are unfocused.

"I'm sorry about your parents," I find myself saying after several minutes of silence.

Carina stares at me. It's the same kind of broken look she had on the street. Her lips move, but the words only come out on her second try. "Are you?"

Be nice, Rika. She might have a difficult personality, but she wasn't complicit in her parents' crimes. "Well, I can imagine how hard it is for you. I... It hurt when I found out my mother never came looking for me," I suddenly admit. Yeah, maybe I can commiserate.

Carina fiddles with her phone, not really looking at the messages. "But that was never her choice, was it? She was kidnapped, like you."

So, she's finally admitting it. "It still hurt."

She takes a deep breath, her eyes gazing somewhere at the ceiling. "I saw the news. They showed the Atomium." With a shrug, a little of her cockiness returns to her voice. "Most of them didn't see what was going on of course, but it was quite a sight. You did surprisingly well. Then again, it runs in the family."

I wince. Family isn't exactly my favourite topic. "If you say so."

At last, Carina returns her gaze to me. "I'm sorry, Rika. I know it doesn't mean much to you, but I truly wish we were introduced differently. Properly. To me, you're my cousin. My annoying little boyfriend-stealing cousin, but my cousin, nonetheless."

"I didn't steal him."

"I know." Carina rubs Wulf's hand. "I messed that up before you ever came on the scene."

For a moment, I wonder how it could've been. If instead of running away, my mother had stayed in Rome and given birth to Marika Antonelli. Life would've been a whole lot easier for me, but I would've never known the wild. Never known freedom. Never befriended a spirit.

And let's not forget that I would've been born into a manipulative dynasty who would've used me for their own gains until I became just like them. Yeah, things are better the way they are.

"What are you gonna do now?" I ask Carina. She probably hasn't even had time to think about it yet.

But Carina has an answer, nonetheless. Her face hardens. "I'll go home and clean up this mess. I'll do everything in my power to cleanse the SSA, and if that means uprooting everything and upsetting a few people, then... well, they'll just have to deal with it."

I'm not quite sure, but it sounds like she's on my side now.

"We'll make it great again," Wulf says groggily between us. "But right this time. As a defence force, not an attack force."

"Wulf!" Neither of us really cares what he just said. I'd hug him tight, but I don't want to hurt him any more. Instead, I grab his other hand and squeeze it as tight as I dare. "You're awake."

"I'm not sure about that," Wulf replies. "I see you and Carina together in a room, after all."

"You're lucky you're already hurt or I'd beat you up!" Carina huffs. "While you were knocked out, Rika saved the day."

His finger gently taps my hand. "I had no doubt of that."

"Yeah?" I look at his dreamy smile. "I think you're delirious."

"Most definitely high," Carina agrees, sharing a flash of a grin with me.

When I chuckle, Wulf looks sceptically from me to Carina and back again. "Yeah, you might have a point. This does seem like a hallucination."

It's nice to joke around a little and forget about the condition in which I sent him here. Unfortunately, it isn't long until the doctor arrives and it's truth time. He rattles off a number of injuries Wulf has sustained and which they've repaired. He'll have a second surgery once he's recovered from this one, and there'll be a permanent plate and rods in his leg. "Since you're very fit, there's a very good chance you'll regain the ability to walk with physical therapy. Maybe even run one day, but

I'm afraid we won't get you back to a hundred per cent. Eighty, if you're lucky."

"Thank you, doctor," Wulf says, back to his stoic self. I rub his arm, feeling more defeated by the news than he seems to be.

"We'll move you to your room soon. Who can I ask a couple of administrative questions?" The doctor looks at us, prompting Carina to jump up.

"I'll do it. I'm his sister." She squeezes Wulf's fingers one last time, takes a deep breath, and follows the doctor outside.

I'm left alone with Wulf, whose face muscles are twitching as he processes the news. "At least you're alive," I whisper. For a very long time, I didn't know if he would be. "You're gonna excel at physical therapy and bounce back."

"Not completely," Wulf says, breathing in sharply. He closes his eyes, allowing himself a short moment. When he opens his eyes, desperation has crept in. His fingers search for mine. Once I hold them in my hand, he breathes out in relief. "Guess my fighting days are over," he quips half-heartedly.

I squeeze his hand and run my other one through his hair. "There are more important tasks ahead of you now. And me. We'll change the world together, remember?"

The ghost of a smile appears on his face. "I love you so much."

Yeah, definitely delirious. Bending down, I whisper, "I love you, too." Then I kiss him on the forehead. "We're gonna be fine. I promise."

27

Things are changing at the citadel. It used to be this big, quiet place, totally cut off from the world around it. Now it's bursting with life. The courtyard provides a safe space for Travellers and spirits to come together. Their interaction is important to teach the young students, who are filling up the remodelled rooms of the citadel as they train to become true spirit seekers under Wulf's tutelage.

Not all former academy students are making the move to Berlin, just as not all spirit seekers continue serving the new Spirit Defence Force, which is part of Interpol, rather than its own thing. Tiago was happy changing the direction of his studies and opting out of battle training. His sister has stayed on course, returning to class with Eoghan and Henny.

While the NAV is still in use, it's less of a competence marker and more of a measure of progress. Lukas has to learn that the hard way when Wulf asks him to lead the Berlin defence team.

"But I can't even see spirits," he protests. Despite all efforts, he's never been comfortable enough around spirits to raise his NAV above the threshold.

Wulf shrugs. "You'll have someone on your team who can. I need good leaders, not just someone with an arbitrary value."

"Oh." Lukas is actually speechless for once. "Okay."

It will be a completely new team. Leon has taken over the new chair of trapping, having found his true vocation in teaching. Sometimes, spirits still have to be trapped. But now they're actually being released or rehabilitated with the help of our spirit friends.

Speaking of traps, after successfully defending her PhD, Miriam has relocated to Rome. It would've cost too much to move the entire SSA lab, so spirit research will still be conducted there. Her first project is processing the thousands of spirits trapped down there and preparing them for release.

Camille has joined her, of course, after completing a proper run of rehab and continuing with therapy. She's no longer an active spirit seeker, concentrating on her health first and planning to join me eventually on my new venture.

My new venture. I've sat down with the EU for countless of meetings. In the end, I left Rory to head up the new programme. He's much better with policy, and I trust him more than anyone to do right by the spirits. Besides, the Gnomian Union has adopted him as the human ambassador, so now he has to split his time between Brussels and Dublin, so Liffey doesn't get too jealous.

I, however, will travel the world, starting with Russia. I'm now an EU-certified expert in spirit communication, and with Inga's help, I've set up my own kind of agency, with which I'll help communities build meaningful relationships with the spirits in their area. I'll be working closely with climate change experts since a lot of my work addresses those issues. My first, well-paid contract will be sorting the problem with the tundra spirits in Russia, and I can't wait to make their acquaintance.

Before I leave, though, there's one more visitor to receive. Or two, actually. My mother's coming up with Carina, and I couldn't be more nervous.

"Relax," Wulf says for the tenth time, or thereabouts.

We're sitting under the branches of Grune's oak, enjoying the surprisingly warm sunshine of a mid-October day. The leaves above us have turned yellow and the ground is littered with acorns. Nearby, Lukas trains a group of students with training staffs. Once they graduate, they'll ask the dryads for a true staff. Until then, they're using normal non-dryad wood. In my lap, Glut purrs, emitting an extra layer of heat. Vesuvius has been very pleased with my progress.

"What if she doesn't want to speak to me?" It's not like my mother jumped on the next plane after the battle in Brussels.

Wulf wraps his fingers around mine. "She's coming up only to see you. Give her time. It's not easy to shed a bunch of lies and deception."

Now, it's my time to comfort him. But just for a short time, because the gate opens, and I recognise Carina's familiar figure striding into the courtyard. "They're here." Glut raises his sleepy head and skitters away when he sees Carina. I can't say I blame him, though I try not to harbour any ill towards her.

Getting Wulf to his feet isn't the easiest task, but he demands to be treated normally. Despite all physical therapy, his left leg has remained stiff, and I can tell from his tense face that it still hurts him. I hand him the walking stick that's replaced the familiar sight of the ancient staff.

By then, Carina has found us, kissing first Wulf than me on the cheeks. "There you are. It took us ages to get here. Ugh." Her gaze get stuck on the walking stick for a moment, but she snaps her gaze up again. "How are you? You won't believe the enormous amount of shit I have to wade through. Sometimes I catch myself thinking it's good that our parents are in prison, because I could strangle them."

Carina has made good on her promise and cooperated with Interpol in their investigation of the old SSA. Her parents and my father, as well as the rest of the board, are still being held in custody as the terrorists they are. I probably won't have to go to court any time soon since there's so much evidence for the police to go through. They'll most likely be sentenced to several decades of prison, though.

"Now, Rome," Carina says. "You're still keeping me on as commander, right?"

Wulf sighs. "Yes, Carina. I told you before. You're capable. You deserve a command. Come on, let's go to my office and let Rika have some time with her mum. Mrs Csorba." He nods to the second woman, who's standing several metres away.

Traitor! When did I ask to be left alone with her?

"Hi." I give the most pitiful wave.

My mother smiles warmly. She has once again assumed a style closer to her travelling roots, just like I did. It makes her look more like the woman I remember. Slowly, she comes closer, spreading her arms ever so slightly. "Can I hug you?"

"I guess." In fact, I'd like her to hug me very much.

My resolve to be distanced and careful with my feelings melts away the moment we touch each other. Suddenly, I'm back in her arms, clutching her back, and melting into her embrace.

"Oh, Rika, look at you!" My mum holds me at arm's length, running her gaze all over me. "I'm so proud of you. Everything you've done. You've succeeded where your father and I failed."

"Yeah, Dante is a very low bar," I say, only to snort after. It actually does mean a lot to me. "Thank you."

She strokes my hair. "I wish I could've been there for you through all this."

To dwell on the reasons why she couldn't makes me sad, so I take her hand and pull her towards Grune instead. "May I introduce you to my spirit mentor, Grune?"

"Of the forest?" my mother asks, sounding positively surprised.

The large tree moves in a greeting. "It's an honour to meet you, Mother of Rika."

My mother laughs. "Oh, call me Magda. Thank you for taking care of my little girl."

"She has taken more care of me and my dryads, but she'll always find shelter between my roots," he says in that wonderful deep voice of his.

I put my hand on his bark, smiling up at him. "You'll be my home. As long as I live." Then I look at my mother. "What will you do? Teach at Wulf's academy?"

My mum shakes her head. "No. I've had enough of the sedentary life. I might do a few guest lectures, but then I want to travel. I want to taste the salt of the sea on my lips, feel the wind in my hair, visit friends and family I had to leave behind." She steps forward to take my hand. "But we'll keep in touch, and perhaps we'll travel together again, one day."

Part of me wants to ask her to come with me to Russia. It's the part that still remembers the Spring Cleaning, the part that's always followed in my mother's footsteps. But I'm old enough to tread my own path, and have been for nine years. "I'd love to do that."

"Magdaléna?" Pavel has approached, and it's pure pleasure to watch the two reunite. He might not be my real grandfather, but he certainly takes that role in our little family.

"You two catch up. I'll find you later and introduce you to Aeola and Glut. They can't wait to meet you." A huge smile graces my lips as I watch Pavel show my mother around the Traveller camp.

I know that one of the reasons it took her so long to come was she was in therapy for what the SSA and Dante did to her. It'll take her much longer to heal from it, but fresh air and the ground under her feet will do a lot for her. And perhaps one day, our interactions will be normal again.

"Is it already time?" Wulf asks groggily, stretching his body as he tries to wake up. A flash of pain washes over his face. His legs are still bothering him.

I'm already dressed and ready to go, my backpack lying next to the door. "It's morning." I crawl onto the bed and lean down to kiss him.

Suddenly, Wulf grabs my face and rolls himself on top of me. After the initial grunt, he grins. "And you thought you could just sneak out?"

"What are the students supposed to think?" I tease him.

Wulf kisses my neck up to the ear before saying bluntly. "They know."

Laughing, I put my arms around him and pull him close, sinking into a delicious kiss. It might be the last one for a while, so I'd better make it count.

Way too soon, Wulf pushes himself up again and sits up. "Let me get dressed, so I can bring you to the gate at least."

"You don't have to do that." I know how much the stairs torture him.

He looks over his shoulder, casting me a long glance. "Yeah, I do."

"Fine." In truth, I enjoy it when he cares for me.

The citadel is still asleep as we make our way to the courtyard. I love this time the most, when it's only me and the spirits. Wulf's walking stick echoes through the courtyard, but not loud enough to wake anyone. I already said my goodbyes the night before, not wanting to make too much of a fuss about it. After all, I'll be back.

Outside the walls, the sun has started rising over the Havel. Mist maidens are dancing on the water's surface. The air is crisp but not too cold yet.

"I don't want you to go," Wulf says, sighing deeply.

I lean into him, snatching a kiss from his lips. "Yes, you do. You want me to do great things. Go out there and change the world."

He laughs and nods at last. "That's true. Tell Miro that I *will* be coming. I just need to get a couple more things going here." He wraps an arm around my waist. "Maybe in a month?"

"I'll believe it when I see it." For a couple more moments, I enjoy the warmth of his body. "I have to go."

With another sigh, Wulf kisses my neck. "Well, I won't attempt to hold a Traveller. Just know that you've always got a home here, with me."

Turning around, I give him another long kiss. "And I'll be back, probably more often than you want me to."

Wulf laughs, shaking his head. He finally lets go of me. "Safe travels."

"See you in a month."

At long last, I turn my back on the Citadel of Spandau. The sun is slowly warming the air, promising a fine day for travelling. At the end of the bridge, a soft breeze envelops me, and Aeola appears. Instead of the old thorny crown, the dryads have made her a flower crown, befitting of a summer queen.

However, it's not the Erlqueen who greets me today, but my friend. "I can't wait to see the tundra."

"Me neither. We might even catch some northern lights." That's certainly one of the many things I've yet to experience in this world.

"Do you think they're spirits?" Aeola asks, curious as ever.

I laugh at her as we skip down the path. "Let's find out, shall we?"

NATURAL DISASTER

Want to read more?

Find out what Wulf has been up to in the free Spirit Seeker Prequel "Natural Selection" by signing up to my Story Seeker newsletter

www.janna-ruth.com/newsletter

Please review

If you enjoyed this book, please consider reviewing it on your favourite platform. Reviews help other readers decide whether this book might be for them.

Want to connect with other readers?

Join my Story Seeker group for sneak peeks, games, events, and book discussions:

https://www.facebook.com/groups/storyseekers

Nature has declared war on us, and we're here to answer that call.

Wulf might be the greatest spirit seeker the agency who leads the war against nature has to offer. A new mission calls him and other elite spirit seekers to Italy where they face off against an active volcano. Two thousand years ago, Vesuvius obliterated the city of Pompeii. Now the fire spirit has set his eyes on Naples.

Leading the spirit seekers into the volcano, Wulf begins to realise that his biggest challenge might not be the spirits but keeping this group of big egos in check. Tensions rise as the heat is turned up and one false move could spell out their death.

Join the Spirit Seekers in this prequel to meet the greatest of them all in action!

Get this book for free by signing up to my mailing list
www.janna-ruth.com/newsletter

Free to read!

Discover Wulf's story!

Magic, Demons and High School Drama

Urban Fantasy with French Flair

About Janna Ruth

Once upon a time, Janna Ruth studied the plate boundaries of this world. Now, she's creating her own worlds. Born in Berlin, Germany, Janna lives in Wellington, New Zealand, writing both English and German books.

Janna's writing career kicked off when she won a writing competition for German publisher Ueberreuter. Her first self-published novel "Im Bann der zertanzten Schuhe" (Melody of Curse, coming in June 2022) went on to win the 2018 SERAPH for "Best Independent Title". She debuted in English with her witchy novella "Witching with Dolphins" in 2020 and has since published urban fantasy, YA sci-fi, and contemporary coming-of-age novels and series.

When Janna isn't writing, she has a plethora of hobbies, such as aerial acrobatics, cake decorating, drawing, reading, and anything crafty you can throw her way.

Find out more about Janna and her books here:

Website: www.janna-ruth.com
BookBub: www.bookbub.com/authors/janna-ruth
Facebook: www.facebook.com/authorjannaruth
Reader Group: www.facebook.com/groups/storyseeker
Goodreads:
www.goodreads.com/author/show/16513923.Janna_Ruth
BlueSky: https://bsky.app/profile/janna-ruth.bsky.social
Instagram: www.instagram.com/janna_ruth
TikTok: www.tiktok.com/@jannaruthwrites
Pinterest: www.pinterest.com/jannaruthwrites